TALL AGAIN

About the Author

Zoe Caswell lives in Sacramento, California with her marvelous wife, Cat, and three cats: Jack Jack, Penelope, and Pop Rocks. When she is not busy writing, she is either outside looking at birds or in her dark office playing video games. Zoe's dream is to be surprised with a mariachi band way before she turns sixty-five years old.

First Edition - 2025

Editor: Heather Flournoy
Cover Designer: Kayla Mancuso

ISBN: 978-1-64247-629-3

PUBLISHER'S NOTE

TALL AGAIN

ZOE CASWELL

BELLA
BOOKS

Acknowledgments

There is no way I could have finished this book without the support of the people below:

There aren't enough words in the world to pay back my beautiful and intelligent wife, who not only supported me wholeheartedly throughout this process but also taught me so many grammar lessons that I promptly forgot after resolving them. My eternal muse, biggest fan, and strongest critic. I love you so much!

To my betas, Dana, Leah, and Whitney, I am indebted to you. You all jumped at the challenge with pure joy and dedication. Thank you!

To all my beloved friends, especially Waffles, Kirstin, Reina, and Maizie, who heard about my plans to write a book and cheered me on. I cannot thank you all enough for believing in me.

To my family members, found and related, who knew about the book and made sure they would be there if I needed anything at all. I am so thankful. Special shout out to Travis, Rainer, and Arie. I'll make sure that I do my best to live up to your expectations.

And finally, to my cats: Jack Jack, Penelope, and Pop Rocks. You don't know what a book is, but you kept my legs warm throughout the process.

Dedication

I dedicate this book to Archibald, the purest cat that ever lived. I miss you more and more every day.

Content Warning

This story explores themes that some people may find triggering, including suicidal ideation, severe depression, death of a spouse, childhood neglect, and emotional abuse. Please read with care.

CHAPTER ONE

"The house, Mo? Of all the decisions you'd make on your own, selling the house—really?"

Mo, cradling her phone between her ear and shoulder, pushed her lanky frame through a crowded hotel elevator before responding, "It's a seller's market, Bud. Stop freaking out."

"A seller's market?"

"We live in Palo Alto, California. It never stops being a seller's market. I'm just glad we decided to get all of those renovations done back in 2015. Everything from setting up the sale to closing went smoothly. Not a single person was scammed. So relax, dude."

"That isn't my issue, and you know it," Bud Pepperidge practically yelled in her ear, causing her to fumble with her phone. "This isn't like you had an unused beach house or were finally getting your act together and selling your sailboat. That pile of sticks and stucco was y'alls—I mean, your home. Where are you gonna live?"

This was not the conversation Mo wanted to have on her way to another lonely hotel room. If she had even a semblance of control over the universe, she would have avoided telling her old friend at all. But selling a home she had owned for over a decade was a huge step. Mo knew the new homeowners would not know what to do if a giant teddy bear of a man like Bud showed up, confused and shouting, on their doorstep. Even if it would have bought her the precious alone time she had been yearning for.

"Mo?" Bud interrupted her thoughts just as she reached the last door at the end of the long hallway. "Are you even fucking listening to me?"

Mo shuffled her bags in an attempt to free up a hand, her work laptop dropping from underneath her arm onto the floor with a crack. "Shit. I'm sorry, I'm a bit preoccupied. I have a one-on-one with my supervisor in…" Mo checked her watch, the long hand sitting firmly on the three. "Fifteen minutes ago."

"Jesus Christ, man."

Mo ignored him, tapping her card against the reader while simultaneously snatching her poor laptop off the grubby carpet. The door popped open with a few familiar electronic clicks, and her eyes adjusted to take in the less-than-inviting decor, indicative of any run-of-the-mill beige hotel room. She moved her bags just inside the entryway before reaching back to lock herself inside. Mo's laptop must have remembered the Wi-Fi to this particular hotel, as the Slack video call jingle made her jump forward.

"God, I hate that sound," Bud droned in her ear. "Nothing productive comes from it. So…are you, like, in trouble?"

"Eh, I don't know and I don't care," Mo responded lackadaisically, placing her laptop on the hotel desk before popping in one of her wireless headphones. "I'll even let you listen in."

With a press of her fingerprint to the small unlock scanner, her home screen popped up, bright and familiar. Too familiar. An ache spread across her chest. Even after all this time, Mo had failed to change her computer's background photo. Her right hand quickly danced across the touchpad to answer the Slack call before maximizing the window to fill her screen.

"Are you really having a meeting with me still on the phone?"

"Good afternoon, Mrs. Reeves." Her boss's voice, stern and plain, crackled electronically through her computer's less-than-stellar speakers. "You're late."

"Neal," Mo sighed, her arms reflexively crossing over her chest. "Sorry, the move took a tad longer than I thought."

"What move?" Neal questioned as Mo watched the older, paler man fingerstyle his thinning salt-and-pepper hair to better cover his balding head. "Forget it. I don't have time to be playing games with you. Do you remember that discussion we had about a year ago…with Victoria?"

Mo closed her eyes, already tired of this conversation. "Victoria Goodman from billing or Victoria Taylor from HR?"

Neal's annoyed sigh was emotive enough for Bud to mumble, "Oh, you're like actually fucked."

"Winchester Bank Financial prides itself in being the leading financial institution for Americans, whenever and wherever they are." Neal adjusted himself in his seat, pride beaming from his crooked lips. "An integral part to every Winchester client experience is our state-of-the-art fraud protection, making sure that their money stays safe and accessible."

"I've seen the commercials."

"You, Mo Reeves, used to be one of the best fraud investigators on our team. Even fresh out of college, the data you could collect and analyze—breathtaking. You were a three-man team wrapped up in a one-woman show."

"Thanks."

"Used to be." His voice was now seething. "Your productivity over the past four years has declined. It's so bad that I've had to take some of your client load and distribute it amongst other investigators, some of which don't even have the luxury for remote work. A reward which you have squandered. When you, Victoria, and I sat down a year ago, you made a promise to be more present and productive at work, and frankly, that has not been the case."

"Okay," Mo replied dully, her fingers already hovering the cursor over the end call button. She knew she had become a terrible employee, and she didn't need Neal getting any more satisfaction out of firing her then he already would be.

"I have spoken with Victoria, and I am annoyed that she wants to give you another chance. Even after you have proved, time and time again, to not have pulled yourself out of your… funk."

"Funk?" Bud questioned protectively in her ear.

Neal blew air through his nose before leaning closer to the camera. "Victoria thinks you need more bereavement. But I…I talked to upper management. My condolences for Annie's suffering, but the dead wife shtick isn't going to cut it anymore."

"I'm gonna kill him," Bud bristled. "Who does he think he is—"

But Mo's own heart was too numb to care about Neal's snide comment, so she stayed silent, hoping he would hurry up and get to the point.

"I'm sorry, but Winchester Bank Financial has decided to part ways with you. We will be sending a severance check, along with your last paycheck, for your…unfortunate circumstances."

Mo could hear Bud's continued yelling in her ear, but her mind refused to translate it into anything beyond white noise. Neal, whose lips she could see were moving, was probably also adding some sort of half-assed thank-you or maybe even another insensitive jab. Anger would be instinctive, but instead she felt nothing but relief. Another responsibility lifted from her heavy shoulders.

So instead of fighting it, Mo just gave another simple, "Okay," before ending the call.

The window minimized, leaving behind the previously ignored background. The brightness of the photo made her eyes strain, but she kept staring. She was suddenly entranced, feasting on every detail like it was water and her eyes hadn't drunk in weeks. The only thing she wanted to do was stand up and climb inside, just to relive the moment the photo had captured. But Bud's annoyed jabbering was still rattling around in her ear, while a tiny voice in the back of her head was reminding her that photos were just memories.

"I'll call you later."

"Wait a second—" Bud tried to reason, but Mo ended the call.

Now alone, Mo leaned back, fully taking in the details. It was her favorite wedding photo of her and Annie, blissfully happy on the bow of Mo's sailboat. Mo recognized the unadulterated glee that was evident across Annie's attractive features. Lightly olive skin, strong cheekbones, soft lips, and blue eyes one could drown in for hours. Annie's straight, dirty-blond hair was styled in an intricately braided bun, fallen wisps lightly touching her athletic shoulders. Mo smiled as she remembered how beautifully the bone-white mermaid wedding dress hugged Annie's body, the feeling of silk chiffon as she held on to her. The memories continued to flow in, and she briefly closed her eyes, remembering each moment like it was happening all over again.

The feeling was unfortunately short-lived and Mo's eyes opened, straying to her own face. The boyish butch grin was accented by her hazel eyes focused fully on Annie in a dopey but loving gaze. A wind-worn blush stained her pale complexion, highlighting the large number of freckles she had scattered across her lean cheeks and nose. She kept her light, almost blond, brown hair short. Well known for allowing it to lie styled in a lazy fluff on top of her head, she kept the sides cut in close. Mo had always been extremely lanky, her five-foot, ten-inch frame barely filling out the tailored black tux she was sporting. After a while of studying the photo, it was apparent that Annie's focus was on the photographer, but Mo's was on Annie.

Annie had always been the center of Mo's world.

Abruptly, Mo reached forward and slammed the monitor down hard, pushing away from the desk. She stood, tumultuous emotions rapidly welling up in her sinuses. But she didn't feel like thinking about Annie right now. Instead, Mo turned toward the window, pulling back both sets of shades to reveal a view of downtown San Jose. The city was pretty unremarkable compared to Palo Alto, but this hotel had a view that was far more sentimental. Besides, a good amount of space between her and Bud was ideal too. All Mo wanted was to be alone.

With a quick turn she grabbed a pillow from the bed, tossing it onto the armchair that sat in the corner of the room. Then she pulled the chair right up to the window before sliding over and down the arm, plopping onto the cushion with a crinkling sound. Mo propped the pillow behind her head and looked down at the afternoon rush, her position giving her just enough of an angle that she could see the other side of the main street. The hustle and bustle brought her a meager helping of calm, as the people down below had no inkling of her existence.

They didn't know why she picked this hotel.

They didn't know why she sold her house.

They didn't know why she lost her job.

They didn't know Annie.

"Shit," she breathed, closing her eyes altogether.

Mo needed to go down and grab her valuables out of her Subaru Outback, unpack her things into the dresser, maybe even venture out for food and drinks for the mini fridge. But her usual exhaustion had set in, so she stayed where she was. Her brain slowly pulled her to sleep, even as she tried to avoid her mind's eye's unyielding focus on Annie's passionate gaze.

* * *

A loud knock shot Mo forward in her chair, her eyes quickly adjusting to the dim lighting of the hotel room. She had slept past sunset, the only light illuminating the room the neons from the street outside. Blinking rapidly, she sat up fully, rubbing her face before letting out a long yawn. Another even louder knock came from the other side of the door.

"What?" Mo groaned loudly, still trying to pull herself up into a comfortable position.

"Imogen Laurel Reeves," Bud's thick Appalachian accent bellowed through the door. "Unlock this door and let us in!"

"How in the—" Mo whined, untangling her lanky limbs from the chair to cross to the door. With a few clicks, she pulled it open and was met by the worried faces of her friends.

"Come in, I guess?"

Mo opened the door wide and Bud trudged through, flipping on the light before his wide frame waddled quickly down the hallway. Another woman followed him in, and Mo smiled down at her with apology, knowing she was probably way more disappointed in Mo than Bud was.

"Hi, Opal."

"Hello, stranger," Opal lamented before turning to close the door behind them all. After it locked, she slid into Mo's arms for a deep hug. "You smell like sleep."

"That means you smell like shit," Bud commented from her desk chair.

Mo turned to her old friend. His usually short, well-kept, dark-brown curly hair and matching Gandalf-style beard were disheveled. It seemed like he had been running his fingers through them nonstop, ruining any style he would normally wear. Bud was at least two shades paler than his normal pasty white. And his face, usually rounded and friendly, was pulled taut into almost horizontal lines. Even his work shirt, a deep-blue Dickie's style button-up, was buttoned incorrectly, highlighting his mandolin-shaped belt buckle and extremely stained, worn jeans.

"Don't listen to him," Opal said, her voice lighter now. "He's grumpy."

"I have every right to be grumpy."

"Yes, you do, babe."

"Damn right."

"Such a Taurus." Opal chuckled lightly, finally pulling away from the hug.

Mo looked down at her friend, seeing nary a change. Opal always seemed to be in a Zen-like calm. Her brown skin, warm with red-orange undertones, was accentuated perfectly by her bright brown eyes and sharp features. Opal's midnight-black hair was colored with an aqua ombre, styled beautifully into box braids that were pulled up into three separate buns on the crest of her head. Normally, Mo would be able to see the various tattoos that adorned Opal's collarbone and arms, but she was wearing one of her long-sleeved logo tees, *Hecate Tattoo* displayed across her chest. Opal rarely wore pants, so she had matched her top with a pair of butt-enhancing black jean short shorts, the pockets hanging below the jean fabric decorated with constellations. An interweaving ivy tattoo led down Opal's right leg, disappearing beneath her white, shin-high Doc Martens.

"I'm sorry he dragged you all the way out here." Mo sighed, meeting Opal's eyes. "I'm fine, I promise."

"I doubt that." Opal smiled softly.

She glided farther into the room, immediately grabbing the chair Mo had just been sleeping in, turning it to face the side of bed. Bud inch-wormed the desk chair along the ground until his knees met the end of the bed. Once his task was complete, he patted a space between them for Mo.

"Get over here, Beanstalk. We are having us an intervention."

"Wait, how did y'all find me?" Mo asked before finally kicking off her sneakers. Then she crossed over the spot he requested, choosing to sit against the headboard instead. "I definitely did not tell you where I was staying."

"I installed parental tracking software on your phone." Bud grinned deviously.

Mo turned to Opal, who laughed slightly before adding, "You love a good Marriott. Besides…" Opal tilted her head toward the window. "This is where we always stayed when you and Annie played at Whose Boots."

Mo's eyes reflexively closed. Whose Boots was the best country-western bar in the Bay Area. Mo and Annie had played together in multiple country and folk cover bands over the past decade, and Whose Boots was Mo's favorite venue. "I'm far too sentimental, huh?"

"Yeah, you've always been a big ol' sap. Also, I smooth-talked the guy downstairs. That security risk of an employee gave me your room number. You've obviously been compromised. Sounds like you should probably just leave."

Mo let out a guttural groan. There was no way she was going back to Palo Alto tonight. Or ever again, for that matter.

"I want you to come home with us. I set up a spare place near the living room with dividers, and I took some extra time to make it all pretty and shit. I even put a TV in there so you can watch *The L Word*, *Wynonna Earp*, and, uh…whatever other lesbian shows they got streaming." Bud put his hands out in a welcoming motion, and Mo glanced at him to see the first sign of hope in his eyes.

"No."

"Oh, come on, we'd love to have you stay," Bud whined, his eyebrows tilting in aggravation. "It'll be like old times."

"I definitely don't mind," Opal added softly. "As long as you are cool with me coming in and out at odd hours to work with clients downstairs."

Bud and Opal lived above Hecate Tattoo, Opal's all-female, Black-owned-and-operated tattoo parlor right in the heart of the college part of Palo Alto. Their loft-style place was on the small side, but it had tall industrial ceilings and an entirely open concept. After nights of bar hopping, Mo and Annie had crashed there numerous times. But no matter how comfortable she felt in their home, it was still located in Palo Alto. And Mo just couldn't bear Palo Alto anymore.

"I can't."

"The hell you won't," Bud half yelled, half begged. "You just got fired from your job, dude."

"Yeah," Mo agreed, punctuating it with another sigh. "And I fired my therapist."

"What?"

"Bud," Opal cooed softly, reaching out for her husband's hand. "You're going to have an aneurysm."

"Good, then we can hire Mo to take care of me—in Palo Alto—at home."

"I sold Annie's Prius too," Mo added, ignoring Bud's outburst. "Oh, and, like, all the furniture. All I have left is down in the Outback or in the suitcases over there."

"What about *Like Clockwork*?" Opal questioned softly, her well-chosen words actually reaching Mo. "You've not been to the boat in a while."

"I'm gonna sell it too. I called the harbor master, he's gonna ask around to see if anyone is interested."

"But you bought that thing for like a hundred dollars and a bottle of twenty-one-year-old scotch," Bud said. "That's such a good story."

"The story won't go away just because I sell her," Mo reminded him, her hands coming up to rub at her eyes again.

"But you sailed it down to Big Sur for—"

"It's okay. Change is good." Opal cut him off, obviously trying to play mediator.

"We looked inside the Outback before coming up here," Bud said with a new burst of conviction. "Opal pointed out Annie's backpacking equipment. You're too much like me and never wanted to hike. Did you sell all of your things but keep hers?"

This comment hit a nerve. "My steel guitar is out there too."

"So is Annie's acoustic," Bud added, his eyes laser focused on her. "Good thing the parking is validated, I'd hate to see you lose it all."

"I was gonna bring it in, I just—" Mo stopped midsentence. Her need for her friends to leave so she could be alone again was growing inside her chest.

"We could just leave and go back—"

"No," Mo yelled, a lot louder than she intended.

Bud jumped a little, his face falling as he studied her. Finally, he let out a big sigh, "Alrighty then, have it your way. We'll go get it all."

The room went mostly silent, the only noise the shuffling sounds created by Bud and Opal as they took a few trips to the car and back. Once finished, Mo watched as Bud opened her suitcases carefully. He began folding her clothes, putting each piece away in a drawer, pointedly skipping anything Mo packed that was Annie's. After a few more moments, Bud found Annie's jean jacket tucked protectively at the bottom of her main suitcase. His fingers lightly glided over the patches across the back before he found the one he was looking for. It was a band patch, Annie and the Strings, from back when Bud was the drummer in their cover band. Bud studied it a bit longer, finally bringing it to his lips to kiss it lightly. Mo couldn't help but smile, even as her chest tightened painfully.

"I don't want to hurt your feelings." Bud sighed, his eyes still on the patch. "It's just..."

"Well, that's ominous."

"I just—" Bud cleared his throat, putting the jacket lightly on the bed. "I think it's time."

Opal, who had just been quietly observing Mo, turned all her attention on her husband. This made Mo sit up in the bed, even as her brain screamed at her to ask them to leave.

"It's time...for me to move in?" Mo asked, her eyes darting between her friends. "Because I thought I said—"

"Kinda. I think it's time to move on."

"From California?" A lump formed in Mo's throat as she continued to search their faces for answers. "I'm confused..."

"No." Bud sucked air past his teeth. "Annie."

The lump blocked her throat completely, and her left thumb came up to rub at the spot as her vision blurred. How could Bud ask that of her? She scoffed and cleared her throat, almost incredulous that he would even suggest such a notion. She wanted to find words, to release all her feelings in a rage-filled scream. To let him know how disrespectful that was. But instead, she stayed silent, diverting her eyes down to the bed.

"Annie and you, well, y'all were definitely made for each other. Hell, you took care of Annie all the way through to the end. There wasn't a moment where you faltered. And honestly, you've done nothing but torture yourself every day since she died. I think it's time to put yourself first. God, Mo, you just have lost so much time."

Blinking hard, Mo bit her lip to keep hold of the energy building behind her eyes. She didn't want to break down, especially not now, cornered and defenseless. After a few more tense moments, he started folding again, and Mo moved her focus to her hands, hoping he would just drop the subject altogether. But that was too much to ask from someone like Bud.

"What ya think?"

"I—" Mo blew a raspberry before putting her hands in the air. "What do you want from me?"

The drawer shut suddenly, a concerned Bud now lumbering toward her. But Opal put out a hand to stop him, choosing to take control of the intense moment and crawl up next to Mo on the bed. With a gentle touch of her hand on the side of Mo's knee, Opal offered, "I mean, I have an idea."

Bud put each of his large hands on either hip, his face softening at her words. "What's that, babe?"

"Maybe," Opal started, her voice hesitant. "You should go on a trip?"

"A trip?" Mo whined slightly, the whiplash of this conversation getting to her.

"Sure. Maybe somewhere more..." Opal looked out the window, pursing her lips in thought. "More adventurous than an old country-western bar."

"Okay..."

"I know you never really had interest in backpacking with Annie and I, but she absolutely loved Redwoods National Park. There is a creek there, Redwood Creek, it runs vertically through the park."

"Can she even do that?" Bud questioned. "I think her coming to the loft—"

"The water levels drop as summer goes along," Opal cut him off, squeezing Mo's knee. "May was challenging enough for her without being unsafe for the two of us."

"You want me to go to a national park?" Mo met Opal's gaze, hoping her facial expression was sending home how ridiculous that request was.

"Could be one of them grand gestures," Bud added. "Kinda like they do for people to find closure in the movies?"

"You don't have to backpack it, but you could maybe make a trek up there. Pitch a tent, check out the redwood groves, find your peace along the creek side." Opal squeezed her knee again. "It's just an idea."

"I—"

"I think you should go for it!" Bud exclaimed, clambering up onto the bed and into Mo's space. "Annie woulda loved for you to become one with the trees. She always said the closest you got to nature was what splashed up on you from the bow of your boat."

"Annie loved it out there," Opal said, her wistful smile pulling at the strands of Mo's heart. "She loved you more, though."

Before Mo could respond, Opal leaned back slightly, sliding her hand into the pocket of her shorts. She then pulled out a small, cylindrical object that was foreign to Mo. She watched as Opal twisted it slowly in her palm, almost reverently, before offering it to Mo. "This was Annie's. I found it mixed in with some of my gear and I—I think she'd prefer you have it. Especially if you are going up there."

Mo took the cold object from her friend, studying it delicately. It was mostly cylindrical, with another smaller circle attached along the side in a lip-like parallel, about an inch in diameter and at least three inches long. The casing was sealed wood, an almost medium ash, with steel edging. Intricate leaves were engraved in the steel, dancing around the outside in a random pattern. The partially circular bottom had a single indented line, and the top sported a small, grip-edged dial over the circle that jutted out from the main body of the piece. Mo had no idea what it was, but before she could ask Opal, her eyes spotted the engraved *AR* along the top edging, nestled amongst the engraved leaves.

"What do you think?"

"I think…" Mo pulled away. "I want to be alone."

"We could pack the Subaru for you—" Bud started, his body leaning toward Mo's.

"No," Opal interrupted him, standing from the bed before pulling lightly at his elbow. "Let's go."

She led Bud from the room, and Mo didn't move until the door clicked shut. With an exasperated groan, she fell back on the bed. Too tired to turn off the light, she ignored the deep pain of hunger from her stomach. Bud and Opal's visit had only deepened her melancholy. There was no way she was going to move in with the pair, especially after seeing Bud's true perception of who she had become. But the thought of a road trip north was not as rewarding as Opal was making it sound.

The redwoods had sort of haunted her for a few years now because she knew how much they had meant to Annie. Going there didn't sound like a beginning—it sounded more like the end.

Maybe that is what it would be. A poetic end to what Mo's life had become. Her eyes slowly moved around the room, taking in how empty and sterile it felt. It was all too similar to the feeling their home had given her when Annie wasn't there to fill it. This wasn't the type of place she wanted to die in. Cold, alone, and without any decent memories of Annie to help comfort her.

But as she considered her friends' offer, all those post-backpacking talks where Annie had explained every minute detail of Redwood Creek filled her mind. The enormous trees, lush greenery, clear water, wide skies. The descriptors enveloped her soul while a memory of an excited Annie, dirty and tired, sat firmly in front of her. The overwhelming feelings cascaded over her, pulling her center in one direction. Her wife's lifelong passion could be her savior.

A more selfish part of her was hoping it could be her executioner instead.

Mo cleared her throat then, with a lurch, she reached for her cell phone and quickly dialed Opal. Barely one ring in and Opal's confused voice answered, "Mo?"

"I think you two are right."

"I'm sorry? What do you mean?"

Mo cleared her throat, willing her voice to sound more hopeful than tragic. "I don't know if you knew, but I regret not going on a backpacking trip with Annie. I remember her endlessly describing the redwoods and how much she loved it there. And every time she asked, I promised her that I would go next year. Next year. Next year. I think I'll do it. I think I'll go."

"Awesome." Opal's voice calmed rapidly. "Do you want me to accompany you?"

"No, too last minute. And besides, you have a shop to run and clients to please. I'll be fine by myself."

"How long will you stay?"

Mo pondered for a moment, choosing her words carefully. "At least a few weeks. Maybe a month. I want to take my time with it."

"Okay, sounds good. I will let Bud know." Opal paused for a few moments. "And if you need me, or Bud, we are just a phone call away."

"I know, and I will call if I need anything," Mo lied. "Thanks, bye."

"Bye."

Mo tossed her phone off the side of the bed, not caring where it landed. She instead held Annie's little mystery cylinder up above her head, returning her focus to the engraved letters, letting them bounce painfully around in her head.

CHAPTER TWO

Tires spun loudly, spitting gravel in all directions, as Aspen Anderson flung her Honda Fit into a lonely parking spot. Some top-forty pop song bopped loudly from the speakers while she hummed along. After shifting the car into park, she flung down her visor, popping open the mirror to check her appearance. Aspen's shoulder-length chocolate-brown hair was gator clipped out of her face, with golden highlights scattered throughout. The bags under her warm brown eyes weren't as bad today, so she tilted her head in approval before reaching across the middle console for her small makeup bag.

Shuffling through it, Aspen pulled out a fair- to medium-colored concealer and began applying it to her lightly tanned—but usually pale—skin using her middle finger. Eyeliner was next, and she added a minimal cat eye to both of her lids, foregoing eyeshadow altogether. Light rose blush and a pop of red lip stain rounded out the simple look, and she quickly threw the bag back onto the passenger seat. With one last look, she closed her visor, turned off her car, and exited out onto the gravel.

Once outside, she checked her usual work attire for anything that might have been out of place. Aspen always wore a pair of matte black kitten heels, tight high-waisted dark-blue jeans that hugged her thick thighs and curvaceous butt, and a heather-gray Dry Creek Bar & Grill T-shirt that she tied low in front to show off a thin line of her midriff.

"Oops, my cardigan," she mumbled to herself before turning to open her door, grabbing the well-worn black sweater thrown over the back of the driver's seat. Aspen flung it on quickly, noting how even an afternoon in late May was still kind of brisk.

"That'll do, pig." Aspen nodded to herself. "That'll do."

A click and her car was locked before she turned to face what she lovingly referred to as "The Strip." It was a group of five businesses, conjoined but inaccessible to each other. The building as a whole was very midseventies California ranch style, with a chipping beige exterior and a rusting aluminum roof. Closest to Aspen was the meager post office, next to it was a few vacant spaces, then the Orick Family Market. Past the far end of The Strip was a much larger, separate building that sported a large pole sign that read *Dry Creek Bar & Grill.*

Aspen looked at the sign before glancing down at her wristwatch to check the time. She was a little more than ten minutes early, so she decided to make her way toward the post office instead.

"Good afternoon," Aspen singsonged brightly, greeting the man behind the counter. "It's another beautiful day in Orick, Paul."

Paul chuckled good-naturedly, his eyes not leaving the mail he was in the middle of sorting. He was a lean but strong-looking man, midseventies, wrinkled, with leathery deep-brown skin. His bald head shone under the fluorescent tube lighting, only his wrinkles and bushy white eyebrows showing the depth of his years. The classic blue postal uniform he sported was well-kept, free of any blemishes or wrinkles.

"How is Charlotte?" Aspen smiled, hopping up onto the counter with a quick jump.

"The grandbaby is fine."

"Wonderful." She leaned forward to look at the mail in his hands. "Anything for me?"

"It's in your box already," Paul replied, finally looking up to give her a small smile. "Grab Dry Creek's while you're at it. Salvador's memory is about as good as a dull knife in the woods."

"He does seem to forget a lot, huh?" Aspen giggled, sliding off the counter to stroll over to the PO boxes along the wall. She fished her keys from her jeans pocket and opened the box labeled *202*. Only one lonely credit card offer greeted her, and she grumbled before pulling it out to rip it in half.

"I don't want this crap."

"I know, but by law I gotta give you that crap."

Aspen shut her box before moving to a larger one, labeled *6*, that was closer to the main counter. Inside were a few bills for the bar and a very large manila envelope. She took a closer look at the larger envelope's label, recognizing it to be invitational signage to promote the Redwood National Park summer season. Elbowing the box closed, Aspen locked it back before sliding the mail underneath her arm.

"Another off season gone," Paul mused.

"Not looking forward to the tourists?" Aspen asked, watching as Paul flung a box full of mail onto a workbench behind him.

"They drive like idiots," he stated grimly before flashing her knowing grin. "But so do you, Ms. Anderson."

Aspen feigned a gasp, grabbing theatrically at her chest. "Rude!"

"Ain't rude if it's true. Now, I've got some packages to sort, so I'll see you tomorrow," Paul finished, giving Aspen a parting wink before he ambled toward the back room.

"Sounds like a plan," she called after him. "Make sure you bring me some updated photos of Charlotte. I am very invested in that child's growth. Babies always get cuter with age!"

Aspen didn't receive a response, so she just smiled and shrugged, turning for the door. On her way out, Aspen ran into a redheaded woman decked out in a park ranger uniform, campaign hat and all. She steadied herself on the woman's arm before letting out a hearty laugh. "Sorry, Caroline, I didn't see you there."

"No worries, Aspen. I wasn't paying attention. I feel like I have been all over the place today—I missed my morning coffee," Caroline responded apologetically, nudging open the post office door.

"No, it was one hundred percent my fault. I'm a notorious klutz."

"No harm done." Caroline smiled wide.

"Well, I won't keep you, but please do stop by the bar sometime soon. I wanna catch up with you about your winter in Lake Tahoe."

"Totally."

Aspen checked her watch—only a few minutes to spare before she needed to be at the bar to prepare for the dinner shift. She trotted past the large windows of the market, meeting the gaze of the owner inside. Stopping quickly, Aspen waved enthusiastically at him, but he did not wave back. The man instead made a point to look down at his cash register like it needed his immediate attention.

"Mr. Pearson is a grumpy old fart," a familiar voice remarked behind Aspen.

She turned to meet the soft, trusting black eyes of one of her bosses, Salvador Díaz. His five-foot, three-inch frame was a bit shorter than her own five foot seven, but Salvador's sixty-four-year-old body was lean in comparison to her fuller one. He sported a full head of shaggy black hair, matching bristle-brush mustache, and skin that was a deep reddish tan, but he wasn't as wrinkled as one would expect for a man his age. Tequila was his secret, and he would spend the whole day touting it if you let him.

"Oh, hey, Salvador." Aspen smiled, reaching forward to give him a quick hug. "Mr. Pearson, uh—"

"He still don't like you?"

She looked back through the window. Mr. Pearson was now counting his money very slowly. Aspen turned to Salvador and shrugged. "I guess."

"Did you tell him his tomatillos were mushy?" Salvador asked, his signature grin barely peeking out from under his mustache. "Or that the clothes he sells are itchy?"

"Did you buy those in there?" Aspen pointed at his paint-covered red-and-blue flannel, wide black chef's pants, and neon-green clogs from at least three seasons ago.

"No, of course not. His shit would melt after one drop of grease."

Aspen laughed fully, allowing herself a little amusement at Mr. Pearson's expense. "Well, his TV dinners are always frozen."

"Stop eating that shit," Salvador scolded. "You know I will make you anything you want, all you gotta do is ask."

"Thank you, Dad," Aspen responded sarcastically, rolling her eyes. Looking back at Mr. Pearson, she pondered out loud, "No, he just plain doesn't like me. Maybe I annoy him? Either way, I decided a long time ago that I would continue to kill him with kindness. That way, he might keep selling my favorite flavors of Hungry Man."

"Probably your best bet." Salvador nodded before tapping Aspen lightly on her arm. "You headed to the bar?"

"Yep."

"Cool, let Ginny know I am off to Eureka to go to Ace Hardware. The men's urinal is clogged again."

"Virginia hates it when you go to Eureka," Aspen responded, her hands naturally going to her hips.

Salvador grinned again, backing away from her slowly. "That's why I am asking her favorite employee to break the news to her."

"You are a scoundrel," Aspen teased. "But I will let her know. Oh! Also—I picked up the bar's mail. The National Park Service sent over the summer season signage. I'll get it all hung up for you."

"And that is why you are the best, Aspen. Tell Ginny I love her," Salvador shouted a little too loudly while throwing dramatic air kisses, already off the sidewalk and on the beat-up pavement of the parking lot.

"She's gonna be pissed," Aspen remarked to herself, waving one last time before turning toward the bar.

Dry Creek Bar & Grill was in far better shape than the rest of the buildings in The Strip. Wide white wood panels, deep red trim accents, and a well-maintained shingle roof showed off the care her bosses placed in their establishment. Beer advertisements adorned the windows, while two heavy-duty wooden doors led inside. Aspen pushed one open with her hip, and her eyes slowly adjusted to the dim lighting. She was met with familiar wall-to-wall deep-brown oak paneling, polished concrete floors, and a huge wood-and-wrought-iron wraparound bar.

The bar took up most of the right side of the building. The space behind it was lined with liquor bottles, random knickknacks, and suspended flat-screen TVs. It also protected the entrance to the kitchen, which led back to the walk-in coolers and management office. A few booths lined the far left wall, a smattering of random sized antique wood tables and chairs littered the center of the space, and the rear wall sported two old pool tables set up under antique stained glass lampshades that advertised popular beers. A hallway in the back led to the bathrooms and maintenance closet, Salvador's usual hiding spot away from Virginia. The bar was clean, well maintained, and far more comfortable to Aspen than her own one-room cabin a few miles away.

Before she could get behind the bar to start her usual prerush rituals, a short gray-haired woman limped from the bathroom hallway, a wicked frown splayed across her face. Aspen couldn't help but smirk.

"Looking for Sal, Virginia?" Aspen asked while moving behind the bar, shoving the mail next to Virginia's coffee cup.

"That good-for-nothing man has done disappeared on me again," Virginia whined, steading her wobbly, pear-shaped frame against a pool table.

Aspen noted the pain in her sixty-eight-year-old boss's eyes, her wrinkled pale face showing how much she had frowned in her life. Virginia Stubbs was a proud woman, pulling her long gray hair into a low ponytail. She dressed in wide, high-waisted tan pants and a country-western-style button-up. The limp was a new development over the winter season, and Virginia was far less mobile now then she used to be.

"He went to Eureka for some stuff, but he'll be back to close the bar."

"That little weasel—I don't know why I stay with him."

"Well," Aspen started merrily, making her way to the sink to wash her hands. "It probably has something to do with his dashing good looks. Or maybe his commitment to not marrying you. Both things I know you highly cherish in a man."

"I don't know." Virginia scowled in response, her movements haggard as she joined Aspen behind the bar. "That review of his looks don't mean too much to me. Your taste is tall, dark, and female."

"True," Aspen agreed, reaching under the bar for a knife and cutting board.

"Oh…and unavailable," Virginia added, her eyes keenly focused on Aspen's face. "So what happened with Cindy—no, Carrie—oh wait, was it Karen?"

"Cathy," Aspen corrected quietly, grabbing bins of whole washed lemons and limes from the bar fridge. "She was just a bit of fun. I'm sure she's already in Portland by now."

"Route 101 giveth, Route 101 taketh away."

The comment, while funny, stung. Aspen feigned being taken aback. "When did you get hip?"

"Honey." Virginia pulled up a high-backed chair that she kept behind the bar just for herself and slowly hauled herself into it. "You send me more TikToks than my own grandkids."

"My bad," Aspen said, hoping Virginia would drop Cathy altogether.

For a few minutes the only sounds in the empty bar were Aspen's knife slicing fruit and the light classic rock playing from the speakers. Just as Aspen began to forget the older woman's jabs, Virginia cleared her throat to announce, "Your birthday is coming up."

Now Aspen was annoyed. She had been avoiding calendars in all shapes and sizes, trying desperately to not think about the looming anniversary.

"You're gonna be…what? Thirty-three?"

Aspen bit her lip. "Thirty-five."

"Wow, your ass looks great for thirty-five."

"Thanks." Aspen blinked, her focus solely on filling the bar stock with cut limes. "I guess?"

"You should be more confident. I'd kill to have my body curve like yours. All my weight sits on my stomach, like someone installed a tire behind my belly button."

Aspen turned to meet Virginia's eyes. "Hey, now, I love my body. Big bellies, boobs, thighs, and even asses are things of beauty. I've never not loved how I look."

"Uh-huh."

"I'm just not used to you complimenting my butt."

"Maybe I wanna be a lesbian now."

"I will take 'Doubt' for two hundred, Alex." Aspen laughed, walking by Virginia to wash her hands in the sink, idling awkwardly.

"True. Unfortunately Salvador does something for me no woman ever could." Virginia sighed before looking at Aspen again. "Is something bothering you?"

"No, I just—" She let her hands drop to the bottom of the sink. "I feel like when you say these things that there is some kind of expectation behind them."

"What kind of expectation?"

"Like—like you think I'm not happy with how things are." Aspen sighed, flipping off the faucet before turning around to lean against the edge. "I love how my life is now. This town, my job, being this close to the redwoods. You know how it was five years ago. I just—I want you to know that I really do enjoy where I'm at in life. I'm happy."

"So you like sleeping with random tourists?"

"Better than sleeping next to Kyle," Aspen responded, trying her best to keep her voice light and playful. "Anyway, I got Cathy's WhatsApp. I'll text her or whatever. Who knows, love may bloom. Then you and Salvador can get off my case."

"Hmm…" Virginia murmured, her eyes still sizing Aspen up. "Most anything is better than Kyle."

"Besides, if I meet somebody, aren't you worried I'm gonna quit? Who would tell you Salvador is skirting his responsibilities then?"

Virginia carefully began wiggling herself off the barstool and Aspen instinctively stepped forward to help her. Just as the older woman righted herself, the large bar door creaked open, and Aspen turned to see Caroline stepping into the bar. With a quick flick of her wrist, the ranger removed her campaign hat and slid it neatly under her arm.

"I'd say marry her, but I think she's flirting with a Pearson boy."

Aspen slapped Virginia softly on the arm but laughed all the same. Caroline's eyes were confused as she walked to a barstool, making herself comfortable. Aspen moved in front of her, placing down a paper napkin coaster.

"Howdy again! Can I get you something cold to drink?"

"Hey," Caroline replied, but her eyes were on Virginia. "I very badly want a Bud Light, but I'm actually here on National Park business. I need to talk to Ms. Stubbs, if you don't mind."

"Not at all." Aspen breathed a full sigh of relief. "I was just trying to get her off my case."

Virginia, seemingly ignoring her, hobbled around the bar to sit next to Caroline. The two began talking, finally giving Aspen the excuse to check the beer levels in the cooler. She made her way by the two cooks, who were in a heated discussion about oil temperature, to the walk-in. Aspen pulled open the heavy insulated door and quickly closed herself inside. Once it was just her and a bunch of chilling kegs, Aspen let out a long, exasperated groan. Virginia had struck a nerve she had been trying to protect for the past few weeks. Her birthday was coming soon. Too soon. And Aspen had stupidly thought she could mask all of her vulnerabilities surrounding it.

"It was going fine until Virginia stuck her nose in it," she grumbled out loud, reaching out to tilt kegs to see which brew was close to being finished.

It was probably not as bad as Aspen was making it out to be, but everything in her personal life was best kept under lock and key. Happiness didn't come from vulnerability, it came from making other people happy. It was why Aspen had moved from Eureka to Orick in the first place. There wasn't a better place than amongst tall redwood trees where she could ignore the disappointment of how her life had turned out. Or at least, that's what Aspen had convinced herself.

But before she could ponder it any more, the door flung open and one of the cooks popped in his head. "Virginia is yelling for ya."

"Thanks, Ben," Aspen responded sweetly, instantly masking any of her discontent before making her way back out to the bar.

Virginia was still next to Caroline, but there were now two short glasses of what she assumed was Bud Light in front of them. Aspen smiled wide, almost skipping to the bar before leaning over it toward the pair. "You rang?"

"You planning on leaving me this summer?" Virginia asked, her gruff voice lined with a bit of amusement.

"Now wait a second, Virginia…" Caroline began, her face paler than before. "We are not trying to steal Aspen from you."

"Then how would Betty put it?"

"Well, as you both know, Betty pretty much runs our summers. At this point, she kind of runs the entire Redwoods Park Service. And, well, she is looking to bolster the programs offered by the visitor center for the coming season."

"How so?" Aspen asked.

"By stealing my best bartender for backpacking trips."

Excitement suddenly shot through Aspen, her head quickly spinning to Caroline for confirmation.

"Not steal, more like share? If you want to, of course."

"I'm listening," Aspen replied, already over the moon at the idea of getting more time outdoors.

Virginia cleared her throat. "Good help seems hard to find these days."

"For the most part, yeah. Aspen is one of the few experienced backpackers who isn't on the Park Service staff, so we were hoping you might be flexible with hours if the interest is high."

"And I was telling Caroline here that Betty can't be demanding my best bartender go gallivanting around in the forest for weeks on end," Virginia gruffed, subtly winking at Aspen. "It's one thing to put up posters and signs in here for those events at the visitor center, but it's a whole other thing to poach my employees! This town only has a population of three hundred something, and most of 'em live and work at the park."

"Let's take a few steps back here, I don't want to upset you. That's why she sent me to ask. The park ranger team would never want to break a good relationship—"

"Oh, honey." Aspen couldn't hold back from laughing anymore. Caroline's distress was getting to her. "She's just messing with you."

"What?"

Virginia gave Caroline's arm a quick squeeze, her own laughter now matching Aspen's. "Of course you can take Aspen. I was just giving you some shit because I get bored sitting here all day. I work her like a dog all winter long so she can play in the creek when it's nice and low. Besides, I hire a few seasonal people to fill glasses during the summer anyway."

"Oh good, I thought I was going to go back to Betty empty-handed." Caroline breathed, obviously relieved.

Aspen thought about Betty for a few moments before reaching across the bar to grab Caroline's wrist. "Virginia is cruel, but not that cruel."

"Yeah, tell that beast of a woman she can have her favorite Girl Scout. Besides, if I didn't let Aspen go, we'd have an influx of dead tourists who'd probably drown in the creek. I much rather they drown here in the bar."

"Thank you so much!" Caroline grinned, sipping rapidly from her beer. "This tastes so much better now."

"Now about the signage." Virginia changed the subject quickly. "I'm thinking that one Smokey the Bear poster will look much better in the bathroom."

Aspen tuned Caroline's response out, her eyes closing momentarily as she thought about a summer filled with backpacking. It was her favorite thing to do in the whole world, and Virginia had needed her a lot the past few summers. Now it looked like her boss had taken notice, deciding to give her free rein. But maybe she too had seen that Aspen needed a break, a distraction from all the things that had not panned out in her life. At some point these feelings had to give way, and what better place to accept her fate but along Redwood Creek, beneath the towering trees?

At least, that is what Aspen told herself.

CHAPTER THREE

Mo drove along Route 101 in complete silence, her brain entirely focused on the road and nothing else. She had already wound through wine country, passed Lake Mendocino, and traversed into the Northern Coastal Mountain Range. Mo's addled brain had missed her first glimpses of massive redwood trees and beautiful pine thickets, but as she passed a large brown sign denoting *Humboldt Lagoons State Park Visitor's Center – 1/4 mile*, she suddenly clicked out of autopilot. A beautiful fog was rolling down the hills on her right, floating out over a wide lagoon to her left. Mo flicked her eyes to check the clock, finally realizing she had been driving for over five hours straight.

"Well, that's a win, I guess," Mo mumbled to herself.

She craned her neck to look at the view as she drove along, noticing how beautiful the thick, unruly, green Sitka spruces looked in contrast with the dark gray-blue water. The road wound its way between the lagoon, different types of coastal trees, and rolling green and brown fields. The Pacific Ocean was suddenly closer, and she barely caught a glimpse of waves lapping on dark-tan sand. Hills that were probably sand dunes, thick with tangled brush and seawater-worn Douglas firs, quickly obscured her view. She turned to look at her GPS, which showed her blue dot running along a thin line of land between the ocean and a lagoon.

"Neat." Mo's childlike interest slightly waned as her eyes met with a large, worn, basic wooden sign. She lifted her foot off the gas, reading the white lettering out loud to herself. "Redwood National and State Parks."

Mo's chest tightened significantly. She cleared her throat in an attempt to ease some of her anxiety. Here Mo was enjoying tall trees and picturesque bodies of water, knowing full well that it was precious scenery she could have shared with Annie years ago. The guilt hit her like a wave, and she suddenly pulled the Outback to the side of the road, sliding into a well-worn divot that was probably used by tourists to take pictures with the sign. Mo didn't want a picture. She wanted Annie back in the passenger seat beside her.

If she were alive, Annie would most definitely have grabbed Mo's arm in glee, squealing before rolling the window down so she could peer up at the enormous trees. She would have dragged Mo, with pure exuberance, next to the sign for a cute selfie. Nothing could have stopped her joy at watching her wife's face. How Annie's voice would have sounded. How it would have made her feel. Mo even considered the annoying stuff Annie would have pulled, like dropping trail mix between the seats or putting her bare feet up on the dashboard. Oh, what Mo would give to nag at Annie for that.

Even a crumb of interaction would revitalize Mo now.

Mo silently rubbed her billowing tears back into her eyes. She had hoped to make it to her rented cabin relatively unscathed, but Mo had no idea how powerfully a bleached-out wooden sign could affect her. Instinctively she reached into her front right pocket, fingering the cold item that Opal had given her. She still had no idea what it was, so she had taken to calling it "Annie's treasure," allowing the many textures of the object to center her. After a few long moments of composing herself, Mo looked back at the GPS to see how far away her cabin was.

"Orick, Orick, Orick," she chanted to herself, using her fingers to zoom out the map.

Orick, California was the next town after this land bridge and not more than ten minutes away. Mo took one more deep breath in before checking her mirrors to safely merge back onto the road. Time flowed a lot slower now, and she wished she could concentrate better on the task at hand. This, even though she had advertised it as much, was not a pleasure trip. Mo felt like it was the end for her.

Mo desperately wanted it to be the end.

More minutes passed by before the tree-lined road broadened into an open, flat, grassy field that was surrounded by tree-covered hills. A few random dilapidated houses and a tiny run-down gas station clued Mo in that she had found Orick. Most businesses that lined the main road seemed closed for the season—or forever, for that matter. But as she drove slowly through, Mo noticed more than one burl shop, the huge redwood carvings out front doing far more for advertising then the faded signs she couldn't read.

"How is more than one carving shop surviving out here?" Mo mumbled to herself, her head swiveling as she took in both sides of the tiny town.

Mo followed the directions down the road a bit farther, finally turning right before a bridge that ran over a rock-filled creek. The houses she saw all seemed old, but only a few seemed like they weren't in livable condition. Because of that, everyone seemed to have their own space, and that gave a promise of privacy Mo hadn't experienced since she was young.

As Mo passed a sign that read *Orick Horse Trailhead – 3 miles*, the GPS chimed in to tell her she had arrived at her destination. Tucked back beneath a smattering of pine trees, Mo saw a small, box-shaped, reddish-brown building sporting a green tin roof. It wasn't a charming cabin you would find outside Lake Tahoe or in downtown Mammoth, but it wasn't as beat up as most of Orick seemed. She maneuvered the Outback down the driveway, backing it in close to where a deep-green door was covered by a log post awning. Turning off the car, Mo pulled out her phone to check her email for directions about the rental.

She had found the place on Airbnb but had done a bit of sneaky research to contact the renter separately. After a few moments of trying to read the instructions, the words started to blur, so she decided to just give the owner a call.

"Hello?"

"Hi, is this Odessa Pearson?" Mo asked, popping open her door to stretch out her achingly long legs.

"Yes, it is," an elderly woman's curt voice replied. "How can I help you?"

"Hi, this is Imogen Reeves. I talked to you earlier this morning about renting one of your lovely cabins."

Odessa's voice immediately perked up. "Ah yes, Ms. Reeves. You rented out the small one near the horse trail, correct?"

"Mrs. Reeves," Mo corrected, grimacing at the habit she had yet to shake. "I sent you the first week's payment through PayPal like you requested. I think I will take you up on your stellar price for the full month, though, so I will send that over once I get myself situated inside. Where are the keys?"

"My apologies for the mistake, Mrs. Reeves. But I am overjoyed that you are staying longer. You'll find the keys, a cabin know-how booklet, and plenty of wood all inside the overhang behind the cabin. There is electricity, running water, and a wood stove inside. Everything you need to know will be inside that booklet."

"Thank you so much—" Mo tried to finish, but she was cut off by Odessa.

"There is also a lovely coupon inside the booklet for my husband and I's store, the Orick Family Market. Please come down and grab some groceries for you and your husband. I hope you both enjoy your stay." Odessa's voice was so strong and sure, she almost had Mo believing she had a husband. "If you need anything at all, just give me a ring or come on down to the store. We are located right across the bridge on 101, next to the post office."

"Thank you, Mrs. Pearson, but just so you know it's just me staying here. Also, I've never had a husband."

"Oh."

"I hope to see you around, goodbye."

"Bu—" was the only syllable Odessa could get out before Mo hung up on her.

She pulled herself out of the car, ignoring the deep-seated pain of hunger she felt in her stomach. The cabin was really small, but Mo wasn't here for luxury. Crossing around the side, she finally saw the overhang Odessa was talking about. It was made with weathered four-by-four posts, tall redwood picket fence panels on three sides, and a matching green tin roof. To the common eye, it looked more like a sturdy chicken coop, minus the chicken wire, than a shed for wood storage. Mo ducked to walk inside, admiring the large amount of dry, cut wood for her to choose from. At the highest point of the pile was a set of two keys sat atop a ratty, neon green, plastic three-ring binder, and Mo reached for it and two pieces of wood.

Back at the door, Mo deposited the wood on top of a few more pieces set by the threshold and used the keys to let herself inside. If Mo Googled "one-room cabin," she was mighty sure a picture of this place would show up. The floors were large plank oak stained a deep golden color and accented with a beautifully ornate, large, traditionally styled rug. The walls were a mix of the same oak planks and white painted drywall, leading up to a vaulted oak-lined ceiling. To the left was a small kitchenette framing the window that looked toward the road. It sported a microwave, small sink, and a toaster. The wood stove was next to it, its black piping leading all the way up into the roof. Straight across was the doorway to the small bathroom, with bare essentials inside. Finally, to the right was a double bed scooched into the far corner. There was a love seat placed against the footboard, a skinny but tall bookcase filled with books and old VHS tapes, and the front wall sported a tiny wood dresser with an old tube-style TV sitting on top of it. The entire place was dated for sure, but it was clean and felt far more comfortable than a hotel room would.

"Alrighty then," Mo said out loud to no one, turning back toward her car to start bringing stuff in.

Once her things were just inside the door, Mo turned to shut and lock it behind herself. Stepping over her pile, she pulled the long-sleeved shirt she was wearing up and over her head in a fluid movement, flinging it onto the love seat. She adjusted the tank top she was wearing underneath before kicking her boots to the side, undoing her belt and chinos, then dropping them to the floor. With an agile maneuver, she jumped up onto the counter to close the blinds on the singular kitchen window and made a beeline for the bed. Launching herself into the middle, Mo groaned in satisfaction at finally being able to lay horizontal.

Of course she knew she needed to unpack her things, get acquainted with the space, and maybe even take that coupon Odessa mentioned down to the local market for food. But lying on this unfamiliar bedding, undeniably hungry, with a heart that yearned to meticulously go through the VHS collection with Annie, was what Mo believed she deserved.

So she didn't move, allowing her eyes to slowly creep closed instead.

* * *

The melodic ring of Mo's cell phone stirred her from a deep, heavy slumber. Blinking rapidly, she groaned as she noticed a terrible headache that was radiating outward from between her eyes. There was light filtering in around the shades, and Mo had somehow ended up tangled in cotton sheets beneath the comforter she remembered falling asleep on.

"What the fuck?" Mo groaned, her voice deep and crackly, as she tried to kick out of her bed prison.

Dazed, she rolled to the edge and stretched out her long arms to grab her chinos and drag them closer to her. Just as she pulled her cell phone from her pocket, it stopped ringing, so she checked her notifications instead.

(3) Missed Calls

(12) Text Messages

(982) Emails

Mo had been ignoring her emails for a really long time, so she swiped that notification right off the screen. Then she clicked on missed calls—all three were from Bud. If Mo had to guess, the twelve texts were probably also from Bud, as he had a penchant for overcommunication. But before she could check her messages, Mo noticed that she had been sleeping for a little over twenty-four hours and it was now the next afternoon. For a normal functioning person, that would be cause for alarm, but for Mo, that was the most sleep she had gotten in months.

She wiggled her way back to the headboard, propping herself against the cold, bare wood as she checked her messages. They were indeed all from her old friend, and she moaned loudly at his lack of tact as she scrolled up to the oldest one.

Hey beanstalk, did you get to the park?
MO
IMOGEN
You better not be dead you little shit
Opal said its like only 5 hours so where the fuck are you?
Are you ignoring me?
I don't want to annoy you and shit, being as you are a grown ass adult
But I will come up there and I will tan your hide so red you'll look the Kool-Aid man kissed your ass
It's the next morning
Please respond
This is ridiculous, Mo. I will remember you doing this to me
Pepperidge Farms always remembers

Mo couldn't help but laugh at the joke made at the expense of his last name, even as she felt a twinge of guilt for ignoring him. So Mo typed out a noncommittal apology, figuring something was better than nothing.

Sorry dude, I fell asleep right after I got here.
Please forgive me. Also, service is spotty as fuck.
Don't expect me to check in daily.

I hate you
But also, glad you're alive
And you better fucking check in with me hourly!!!

Mo rolled her eyes at his response, closing her phone with a click before tossing it onto the pillow next to her. It was then she pondered just going back to bed. It was comfortable, warm, and expectations were always at their lowest under the covers. But Mo had ignored her stomach for too long, and she knew her general weak disposition was because she hadn't eaten since before the drive.

A few steps from the bed, Mo took off the rest of her clothes for a hot shower, utilizing the little shampoo bottles she found already inside. Never a long shower kind of gal, Mo finished the basics before hopping out, dripping wet, moving to the mirror to get a good look at herself. She was having difficulty recognizing her now exceptionally gaunt features. She was almost painful to look at, so she focused on using a towel to style her hair so that it could dry in a semipresentable way.

Mo opened her suitcase by the door, pulling out each piece of clothing without much care for where it landed. She dressed herself slowly, thinking about what she would wear on her jaunt to the market. Odessa Pearson had sounded like a casual sort of woman, so she figured her family's market was probably like most rural places and needed very little in the way of fanfare. Annie had loved her masculine style, so she finally decided on her favorite green, yellow, and cream long-sleeved flannel shirt. Then she pulled on a pair of chinos, unfortunately deeply wrinkled, and rolled up the bottom cuffs. Mo had always made sure to roll the bottoms of her pants in order to highlight her many nice pairs of boots. But in the wake of losing Annie, she was left with only one brown pair. She had given the rest to her favorite cobbler at the Downtown Palo Alto Farmers' Market. It felt wrong to keep them when Annie wasn't around to enjoy them.

Tightening her belt one more hole than usual, Mo leaned over to grab her boots and slip them on. Part of her wanted to take everything right back off and climb back into bed. But if she was gonna make the redwoods her last stop, there was no way she was gonna go out asleep in a random cabin nearby. No, Mo wanted to see Annie's favorite creek, and in order to do that, she needed to eat. She didn't check herself in the mirror before grabbing her keys, wallet, and Annie's treasure from her dirty pair of pants. After she was satisfied that she was ready to go, Mo expertly stepped over all her things in the doorway and made her way out onto the porch.

Once in the car, Mo didn't mess with any of the GPS settings before pulling out of the driveway. She let her brain go into autopilot, retracing her path back to the 101. Mo looked both ways before making a right, going over the bridge she had passed earlier. She took it slowly, glancing to her left and right frequently to take in the flowing clear water and multitude of large gray rocks that littered the creek bed. At the end of the bridge and off to the right was a huge—at least twelve feet in diameter—circular slice of a redwood tree mounted unceremoniously on rather weak-looking sawhorses. To the left was a boarded-up old cinema, the faded red letters above the marquee reading *Orick*. The marquee itself displayed *Star Wars: A New Hope*, with the H barely hanging on by a thread. Mo snorted, wondering if that was the last movie that played there.

She turned her head again and noticed the Orick Family Market sign. She checked her mirrors before swinging into the gravel lot, instantly noticing how badly maintained it was. She parked her Outback next to a baby-blue Honda Fit, using it as a guide because she couldn't figure out how the spaces were marked. Mo's eyes stayed on the redwood disk as she unceremoniously climbed out of her car, locking it behind her.

She wanted to move toward it. To reach out and touch the hundreds of rings. To see if the texture was soft or scratchy. How had the tree fallen? Did humans intervene for their own personal gains, or did someone stumble upon it, fallen and broken on the ground? A certain kinship to that idea bubbled up inside of her, urging her to walk toward it. To wonder if a similar fate could befall her in the forest.

But instead, Mo just turned away, deciding to walk toward the sidewalk near what looked like a small post office. She strolled on by, her focus on getting the bare essentials and retreating back to her cabin. But as she arrived at the front of the market, a strong savory scent hit her nostrils, making her mouth water. The smell reminded her of burgers and wings, transporting her to a sports bar in the middle of the 49ers playoff season. It was heavenly, drawing Mo past the market to finally notice the large sign for Dry Creek Bar & Grill.

A bar was not really where Mo preferred to spend her time. People frequented bars, and she had kind of given up on people as a whole. But nothing hit like a warm meal, so Mo crossed to the double doors, pushing her way inside. The place was dim, eclectically decorated, and reminded her immediately of every dive country-western bar she had performed in with Annie and the band. But instead of being purposefully decorated that way, this was definitely styled to fit someone's personal tastes, making it all the more comfortable to her. There was a decent crowd for late afternoon, mostly elderly couples or groups of middle-aged men watching repeats of popular sports games on one of the many TVs hanging throughout. Mo moved purposefully to the farthest edge of the bar, hopping into a barstool that was intentionally far away from any of the other patrons. She squinted her eyes toward the beer taps, trying her best to recognize the brands on the handles just as the kitchen door popped open.

Mo forgot about the beer.

The woman, dressed in normal bartender fare but with her own charming style choices, was unconventionally gorgeous in a way that felt illegal. She was carrying two large plates of what looked like chicken-fried steaks with one hand and a pitcher of iced tea in the other. Mo watched as she made unadulterated eye contact with a man sitting by himself at a table, her eyes mesmerizing as she flashed a quirky smile at him while refilling his iced tea. She laughed a genuinely full laugh before walking away, almost skipping to a corner booth where she delivered the plates of food. Mo could hear notes of her singsong voice across the bar. She sounded undeniably pleasant and attentive. At this point Mo was twisted on her stool, her heart skipping a beat as she watched how sensuously the adorably curvy woman leaned over the table.

While her eyes were locked on the woman's shapely butt, Mo didn't notice that another, older woman had placed a glass of water and a menu behind her.

"Aspen will be with you soon."

Mo shot around, almost knocking over the water, her face showing all the signs of someone who had been caught staring for too long. "Uh…"

This woman, much older and much grumpier looking, definitely knew what Mo had been doing. Before Mo could come up with a suitable excuse, the woman slyly winked at her before repeating herself, "Aspen…" She was now nodding toward the woman Mo had been staring at. "Will be with you soon."

"Okay," was all Mo could mutter before the older woman hobbled off and she was left blinking down at a menu, heat radiating off her ears in embarrassment.

So the undeniably hot woman's name was Aspen. Mo felt her mind wobble back and forth, thinking about what she could possibly do with that information. Before she could decide, a flash of movement appeared in her peripheral vision and she was suddenly back to looking at Aspen, who was now at the taps, expertly pouring a beer. This was not what Mo had planned to do with her evening, so even as she studied Aspen's soft features, Mo was considering just running for the door. As her left leg began to spin her body off the stool, Aspen's brown eyes caught her hazel ones, and Mo forgot about anything else. They couldn't have held the gaze for more than a few seconds, but Mo definitely saw light dance across Aspen's features. Aspen placed the beer down in front of a man farther down the bar before quickly making her way toward Mo.

Just as she got within ten feet of her, a much older, rather stern-looking man came out of nowhere and leaned across the bar top toward Aspen. Mo saw the woman's face fall a tad as she finally broke her gaze to give the man her attention.

"Mr. Pearson," Aspen greeted. "Do you need a refill?"

"No. Can you just tell Virginia I forgot my wallet at home? I promise I ain't walking out, I just need to go pick up my grandkids, go home, then I'll grab it and come back before close."

Aspen leaned away from him, but her voice stayed bubbly. "I don't think all of that is necessary, Mr. Pearson. Your store is right next to the bar, you can come in tomorrow and pay up your tab."

"This isn't your establishment," Mr. Pearson responded, obvious annoyance in his voice.

"No, but this has happened before with Odessa." Mo watched as Aspen smiled wide. "I promise Virginia won't ban you from your nightly BLTs."

"Just go tell her," he grumbled before turning quickly, ambling out of the bar without another word.

"Good night, Mr. Pearson. See you tomorrow!" Aspen yelled after him before turning to finally stand in front of Mo, all of that precious attention solely placed on her. "Hi, newcomer. I haven't seen you here before."

Mo felt herself blush deeply, suddenly very aware that she had been ogling Aspen for far longer than was appropriate. She turned down to focus on the menu instead of Aspen's face, hoping it would allow her to string together a sentence properly. "Yeah, I've uh…never been here before."

"I know," Aspen responded deliberately. "I definitely would have remembered you."

CHAPTER FOUR

Aspen leaned against the bar as far as her body would allow, pulling her lower lip between her teeth as she took in a better view of her new customer. Even seated she could tell the woman was tall, her soft-looking short hair messily styled in a way that taunted Aspen to run her fingers through it. Aspen also noticed she was lean, barely filling out the flannel shirt she was wearing. Her gaunt face was gorgeous, soft, and handsome all at the same time. But it was easy to tell the woman hadn't had much sleep, the bags under her eyes slightly puffy and dark. She could barely pay attention to all that, though, finding herself easily lost in the woman's hazel eyes, the deep green pulling her in toward the golden flecks of brown. They were the saddest eyes she had ever seen.

"What brings you to Orick?"

"I uh—" The woman fumbled, her eyes flipping between the menu and Aspen's. "Do you have a drink menu?"

"I am the walking drink menu. What's your poison?" Aspen asked, her voice coming out far more sultry than she meant.

"You seem like a sour kind of gal. Definitely something tastier than a Bud Light, but not overly hoppy like a bitter IPA. Also, I'd love to know your name…"

"Huh?"

"For the order." Aspen winked.

"I've not ordered." She laughed, finally giving up on the menu. "Do you have cider on tap?"

"For you, of course. Short or tall?"

The flirting fell easily from her mouth, a practice she had honed on tourists since moving to Orick. But unlike the many women she had made subtle playful banter with before, this one twinged differently in her chest. There was something about this woman that intrigued Aspen more than her attractive butch exterior and adorable awkward vibes. Aspen was compelled to learn as much about her as she could.

"Tall," the woman said, finally seeming to relax a tad. "Mo."

"Mo?"

"My name. For the order."

"Ah yes." Aspen grinned. "Nice to meet you, Mo. My name is Aspen. Is Mo short for something? Like Morticia? Or Morgan? Ooh, is it Montana?"

"It's short for Imogen." A small smile curved the edges of Mo's lips. "Why did you think of Morticia before Morgan?"

"*The Addams Family* is my third-favorite movie," Aspen explained, picking up the menu. "What's your favorite movie? Oh, and did you wanna order food as well?"

"I've not thought about movies in a long time." Mo chuckled, her face lighting up in a way that was infectious for Aspen. "And yeah, I'm really hungry, actually. You seem a whole lot more put together than I am, what do you recommend?"

"When I am famished, I get a cheeseburger. All the toppings. With fries. You can never go wrong with a classic," Aspen replied gleefully, her eyebrows lifting as she waited for Mo's reply.

Aspen watched Mo look around, taking in the rather slow weekday evening crowd. Nervous energy seemed to come off her in waves, like she was constantly swinging between being comfortable and uncomfortable. Aspen desperately wanted to know why.

"I'll try it," Mo finally agreed.

"Ten-four." Aspen resisted the urge to wink at her again as she backed away slowly, clutching the menu to her chest. "And while I am gone, you can think of that favorite movie of yours."

"Okay."

Aspen couldn't hide her excitement as she skipped through the doors to the kitchen window, happily writing down Mo's order. Virginia was behind her before she could register it properly.

"Fresh meat?"

Aspen jumped, replying as uninterested as she could make her voice sound. "I have no idea what you are talking about."

"I'll finish up the floor tables," Virginia said, ignoring Aspen's denial and reaching around her to grab a handful of napkins from the server station. "I think you can handle the now one bar patron on your own, just make sure you get this one's number before she leaves your bed tomorrow morning."

"Oh my God, stop," Aspen whined, putting the order onto the slider. "Order in, Ben!"

"Never," Virginia teased, ambling back through the doors.

"Oh, by the way, Mr. Pearson forgot his wallet. He'll pay tomorrow," Aspen yelled in her direction, following her out to grab a tall glass. "He was very insistent that I tell you. So don't let him convince you I didn't do my job properly."

Aspen poured the cider, her eyes back on Mo, who was fiddling with the paper coaster in front of her. She wondered why the woman glossed over her reason for being in town. Orick obviously wasn't a popular Northern California destination like Monterrey or Lake Tahoe. Its sole purpose was being a pass-through on the way to the Redwood National Park, and most people were either camping there, staying in Eureka, or driving up to Crescent City afterward. Aspen wondered if there even was a reason Mo was here, walking the cider back to where Mo was now ripping the paper coaster into tiny strips.

"Hey, stop that, silly. Those are fifty cents a pop," Aspen joked, pulling out a new coaster and placing it over the shreds before plopping the cider down on top. "One Humboldt Cider Company Drysdale for Mo."

Mo looked up, her face a tad sheepish. "Thank you."

"You are very, very welcome."

"I didn't figure a small-town bar would have cider," Mo remarked, sipping. "Ooh yeah, nice and dry."

"My boss likes having a variety. She always says that the people eating and drinking here aren't hardcore backpackers and they need something that tastes like home. Did you think of that movie?" Aspen leaned over, placing her chin in her hands as she locked eyes with Mo. "If it helps, my favorite movie is *The Parent Trap*—of the Lindsay Lohan variety."

"That…" Mo closed her eyes, her face pulled in amusement. "Makes a ton of sense, actually."

"How so?"

"I feel like the high jinks of Hallie and Ann—" Mo stopped short, clearing her throat instead of finishing her sentence. Aspen watched curiously as she reached for the glass of cider instead, pulling a long sip before looking back in Aspen's general direction but not directly into her eyes. "Twin high jinks seem down your alley for sure."

Aspen felt the atmosphere around them shift, watching as Mo used the glass to block the view of her face. Rarely at a loss for words, Aspen pressed on. "It's the perfect romantic comedy. I would watch it on repeat as a kid, quoting it religiously, desperately wanting to discover if I had a long-lost twin. I think I also just wanted Dennis Quaid to be my cool ranch-owning dad who actually gave a crap about me."

"I had a crush on Chessy," Mo replied, her eyes still on her drink.

"Mmm, good taste."

"Thanks," Mo remarked, her voice low and sad.

Aspen watched as Mo covered her glass with both hands, slowly bringing it to her lips. Her shoulders were tilted inward, and Aspen considered giving the woman some space as something was obviously bothering her. Just as she was about to make an excuse to walk off, Aspen noticed a small glint on Mo's left hand. It was a wide but very simple silver wedding band, resting gently on her ring finger. Aspen's heart sank.

"I think I like *Speed* the best."

"Huh?" Aspen blinked, pulling her gaze away.

"My favorite movie." Mo finally met her eyes. "It's called *Speed*. It's got everything you could want. Edge-of-campy action, interesting twists, and a cute romance subplot. I mean, who doesn't like a good explosion or five?"

"I don't think I've seen it…" Aspen crossed her arms, racking her brain. "What's it about?"

"Your order is up, Aspen!" an older male voice yelled across the bar, reminding Aspen where she was.

"Oops, I forgot I was at work. I bet your food is ready." Aspen beamed. She reached forward to squeeze Mo's hand instinctively, the cold of the ring very obvious on her palm. "Be right back."

Aspen strode off, hipping her way into the bright kitchen. "Sorry, Ben."

"You good?" Ben queried, his concerned eyes staring at her between the counter and heat lamp.

"Totally, just got lost in the sauce. What needs running?"

Ben didn't respond, instead pushing a plate with a delicious-looking cheeseburger and fries toward her.

"You're the best." Aspen grabbed the plate and a bottle of ketchup before walking back out to the bar. She slid expertly by Virginia, reaching Mo quickly with her meal. "One cheeseburger all the way with fries. Ketchup?"

Mo drained her glass silently, nodding.

"Another cider?"

"Please."

Aspen switched the ketchup bottle for Mo's empty glass, striding away to go and fill a new one. The easy conversation between them had obviously lulled, and she couldn't help but feel disappointed. She looked around, noticing that Virginia was making her way back toward the bar. Aspen waved her over with her head, her confidence a tad shot.

"Are those wedding bells I hear?" Virginia demanded in her usual gruff way, depositing bar glasses into the sink. "You been smiling like a dumbass since you seen her sitting over there."

"No go on this one, Virginia," Aspen responded, trying to stay cool about it. If she could convince Virginia it was a bad idea, then she'd probably make less of a fool of herself in front of Mo later. "She's married."

"Do what? That woman is manlier than Sal."

"Gay marriage is legal in all fifty states, grandma."

Virginia backhanded her on the arm, spilling a bit of cider. "I ain't your grandma. Anyway, what's a little marriage if you're between the sheets?"

"Oh my God," Aspen replied with shock, making her way back toward Mo. "I can't believe you."

"Tell her that her clothes would look better on your cabin floor!" Virginia shouted, starting yet another eye roll.

Aspen ignored her boss, placing the cider down with a bit of force. "How's the burger?"

"It's divine." Mo groaned, obviously enjoying the meal. "I forget how much I love food until I've forgotten to eat it."

"I'm glad! I also tend to forget to eat sometimes, so I understand how you're feeling," Aspen said, mentally trying to come up with more to say to her. "So…"

"Mm-hmm?" Mo murmured after taking another bite, her face unreadable.

"What are you and your"—Aspen nodded toward her ring—"partner doing in the redwoods?"

Mo's eyes followed her motion, and she let out a little, "Oh."

"Everything okay?"

"Yeah, I just expected you to ask something different." Mo set her burger down on the plate.

"Like what?" Aspen leaned forward inquisitively.

"Like if my clothes would look better on your floor?" Mo smirked slightly, not meeting Aspen's gaze. Aspen watched her instead grab a fry and dip it in ketchup on the edge of the burger, moving it to her mouth for a slow chew. "Or some other similar pickup line."

Aspen laughed, not embarrassed in the slightest. "As much as I want to be mad at Virginia for not being subtle with that, she ain't wrong. That would be my usual go-to for sure. But I saw the ring and figured I would be respectful."

Mo was quiet for a long moment, and Aspen watched as she fiddled with the ring on her hand before lifting her head to meet Aspen's gaze. "I was married. My wife, um…she died about four years back. I've just not taken it off, is all."

Aspen felt warmth spread throughout her body and she immediately turned to walk away.

"Wait," Mo said suddenly, but Aspen was already under the bar gate near the taps and making her way back toward Mo on her side of the counter.

Aspen jumped up into the stool next to Mo and placed her hands softly onto Mo's left forearm. "That's a great way to remember her."

"I thought—" Mo half laughed, half choked out. "I thought I had scared you off."

"Sorry." Aspen laughed with her, squeezing her forearm. "I just didn't think it was proper to show respect for her from across a bar, is all."

"Thanks, but it's, uh…no big deal."

"I bet she was a big deal," Aspen said earnestly. "What was her name?"

"Uh…" Mo pulled her arm away.

"You don't have to tell me anything you don't want to. I'm sorry I made it awkward. I am well known for being too much, too quick," Aspen added, watching as Mo twisted in her seat uncomfortably. "Now, enjoy the rest of your meal, and I'll come back over and see if you need anything in a bit, okay?"

"All right."

"Good. Now eat before your fries get too cold." Aspen smiled, jumping down from the seat and making her way back behind the bar.

A few more locals wandered in, and Aspen made quick work of their orders. Working the bar was something Aspen could do with her eyes closed, but she did find herself a bit distracted tonight looking over toward Mo just to check and make sure she was still there. She felt a bit of regret for bringing up the ring, but Mo's general disposition made a lot more sense with the new context. And in a way, Aspen now felt closer to Mo even though they had only just met. As she considered this new feeling, her peripheral vision caught Salvador sneaking toward the kitchen, letting her know it was probably just about six. Checking the time proved her theory correct.

"Like clockwork," Aspen mused, her eyes then darting to Mo.

Mo's head was down, her hands playing with something in her lap. Aspen made her way over and she was happy to see an empty glass and clean plate. "Someone hated dinner."

"It was terrible," Mo agreed cheekily, quickly pocketing whatever she was playing with below the bar. "And the server just would not leave me alone."

"You should definitely make sure to put that in the Yelp review." Aspen played along, moving the dishes out of Mo's way. "Can I possibly bother you some more?"

"Depends."

"Can I maybe tempt you with—"

Mo cut her off. "I thought you already did that."

Aspen felt her cheeks warm at that comment. "I meant dessert, but I do get off around ten."

Mo smiled the smallest of smiles. "I don't think so, but I appreciate the offer."

"No worries. Let me grab your check." Aspen tried to keep her voice happy and even, but she did feel the slightest bit of disappointment as she sauntered off to grab the check and deposit the dishes.

On her way back, she noticed Mo was now standing, her hands awkwardly stuffed in her pockets. Aspen's heart couldn't help but melt, so she just placed the check down and said, "Here ya are."

Mo pulled a wad of cash from her pocket and dropped three twenties on the bar. "Keep the change."

"Wow, thank you. You didn't need to do that."

"No, I did. I'm not the easiest to hang out with, and you made my dinner more than bearable, so..." Mo shrugged.

"Well, thank you. And don't act like it's a goodbye, I will see you here tomorrow before noon for breakfast," Aspen said enthusiastically, watching as Mo's face twisted in confusion. "I'll be here around nine, so make sure you get up and at 'em, all right?"

"I mean, I don't know if I—" Mo began to argue.

"I do." Aspen winked. "See you then."

CHAPTER FIVE

Unfortunately, Mo had woken up before dawn this morning. She had allowed herself to rot in bed, spending what felt like hours disassociating. Watching as the ceiling fan slowly turned, counting every time the one slightly bent blade turned past her head. Decent at math, she had estimated the motor on the fan was broken because the rotations per minute were sitting around one hundred and sixteen, give or take a rotation. Which in her despondent mind seemed slow.

"How many rotations does a ceiling fan normally do in a minute?" Mo wondered out loud to herself, finally finding the strength to kick off the blanket and turn toward the tiny nightstand to grab her phone. "Save me, Google."

As she clicked open the phone, Mo noticed it was 8:32 in the morning, and she couldn't help but think about Aspen and her offer of breakfast. She groaned in guilt, rolling back over onto her back and letting the phone drop unceremoniously to her chest. Mo was a tad infatuated with Aspen, and that kind of feeling hadn't happened to her in a really long time. Aspen was not only gorgeous, she was a twister of adorable questions and unyielding confidence. If she hadn't been in this sorry state for the past forever, Mo probably would have taken her up on her offer of sex.

"Would I have, though?"

The indecision of whether to go or not was eating at her. Especially after Aspen's reaction once she found out about Annie. Her forearm instinctively came up to cover her eyes as she groaned, "God, she was so sweet to me."

The words felt like they hung in the air, reminding Mo of not only her loneliness but also her general state of being. It was a terrible feeling, so she flipped over on her stomach, debating whether sleep was possible. But the thoughts of Aspen wouldn't yield, compounding with her hungry stomach and achy neck from lying in the bed for so long.

"Ah, fuck it." Mo finally decided, rolling out of the bed and onto the hardwood floor.

She looked toward the bathroom, not interested in the slightest in expending energy on a shower. But if she was going to go see Aspen, she should at least smell good. Once Mo finished, she got dressed and made sure Annie's treasure was safely deposited in her pocket. Her eyes trailed across her still-packed bags and strewn clothes, the guilt of leaving them messily piled burning a hole in her stomach.

"I'll deal with you later," she tried to convince herself, nodding respectfully at the pile before clambering over it and out the door, locking her cabin behind her.

Just as she got in the driver's seat of her Subaru, Mo decided she needed more fresh air, so she hopped out and made her way toward town on foot. If she was going to backpack the creek, then she needed to get her body used to walking again, even if she had no idea how to plan that excursion. Mo shook that responsibility from her mind, instead focusing on the dark yellow of the fields contrasting with the emerald green of the trees. It looked a lot like the farmland of the Sierra Nevadas near Lake Tahoe, a place Mo and Annie frequented together on weekend getaways. Mo turned in a slow three-sixty, taking in the flat, slow fields and how they rolled into more hilly forests, full of redwoods and pines. It was not only beautiful but also comforting. Mo's pace slowed to a stop as her eyes zoned in on a natural opening of the trees where a path wound from the golden fields in between two large pines. She immediately saw a beaming Annie, hiking poles in hand, her blaze-orange rain jacket slightly blinding Mo's mind's eye, just standing inside the opening to the woods.

She could just follow her inside. No supplies, no water, no direction. Just a bunch of tall trees and Annie's memory. Why plan for a journey that didn't require survival? Mo's heart burned at the thought, so she turned her focus away from the trees and headed toward town.

The walk was rather quick, even though her pace was barely more than a stroll. Once she arrived at the bridge, Mo noticed an ample cloud of fog drifting over the creek in the direction of the ocean. She slowed to a stop halfway across, moving to lean on the railing and look down at the creek. The creek was extremely clear, even through the mist. The water flowed quickly over beige and gray stones of all sizes, making slow splashing sounds. It was the exact kind of sound she would expect in a meditation app or from a therapist's white noise machine. Just as Mo was beginning to get restless, she heard a quick double horn and turned to find the baby-blue Honda Fit she had seen the previous night.

The car's window rolled down with a quick squeak, and Mo leaned over to see Aspen grinning wildly at her. "Hi. I knew you were going to come to breakfast. Hop in!"

"Uh…" Mo hesitated, looking toward the bar like she wasn't on her way there anyway.

"Periwinkle doesn't bite," Aspen declared. "She is a perfectly fine car and very clean, I might add."

Mo watched as Aspen leaned over to grab a plastic bag from the passenger seat and toss it quickly into the back. Her indecision with this woman was comical at this point, so Mo just got inside the car.

"Hell yeah," Aspen squealed before checking her mirrors. "The bar is only right there, but I figured you could ride with me."

The car smelled heavenly, a light mixture of lavender and cedar wood filling Mo's senses. She turned to look at Aspen, whose hair was thrown up into a messy bun, bottom lip pulled between her teeth as she turned into the parking lot. She passed the post office rather hastily, coming to a rough stop in a spot right in front of the bar. Aspen turned to her and gave her a huge smile, her shoulders and eyebrows shooting up with it. Mo couldn't help but grin back.

"Do you like my air freshener?"

Mo looked up, finding a Camp Walden air freshener swaying slowly from her mirror. "You really like *The Parent Trap*."

"Guilty." Aspen threw her hands in the air before turning the car off and unsnapping her seat belt. "Come on, we've got breakfast to eat."

"Okay," was all Mo could muster, her brain flipping and flopping between being grumpy and enjoying the easy company Aspen was offering. Mo got out and looked around, shutting her door with a thump. "The parking lot is empty. Is this place open for breakfast?"

Aspen slammed her own door, using her key fob to lock the car before trotting up to the door and pulling a set of keys from her pocket. "It is for me. I asked Salvador last night."

Mo watched as the shorter woman expertly unlocked the door and used her hip to make her way inside. She followed, her eyes adjusting as Aspen flipped on each light from behind a curtain near the door.

"I figured you were staying somewhere around here and didn't really have the means or ingredients for a hearty breakfast, especially after the way you scarfed down that burger last night."

"I did not 'scarf,'" Mo complained, attempting to fight down another grin. "But you are kinda right. I don't have any groceries."

"See," Aspen shot back playfully, walking briskly behind the bar toward the kitchen. She stopped abruptly at the door, pushing it open before turning her head toward Mo. "Come on back. I ain't making breakfast alone."

"What do you mean?" Mo asked, following her into a very clean, well-lit industrial kitchen.

"I can't cook worth a shit," Aspen explained, pulling open a large commercial refrigeration door and leaning inside. "Do you like eggs and bacon?"

"Yeah, actually," Mo replied, looking around at the well-kept kitchen. "Though I've not had bacon in years."

Mo walked toward the large griddle, holding her hand out over the top to see if it was on. The cold radiating off told her it wasn't, but she was happy to see it scraped clean from the previous night.

"Vegetarian?" Aspen asked, appearing back beside Mo with a carton of eggs and pack of bacon. "Wait, you had a burger last night, duh. My brain doesn't compute sometimes, ya know?"

"I do." Mo snickered, looking at the multitude of knobs and switches.

"The griddle can be turned on with that black switch near your hand."

Mo shrugged, flicking the switch on. "Do I need to adjust the temperature?"

"No, kitchen staff has all that locked and loaded. These things take no time to heat up. Are you down for some toast?"

"Sure."

"White, rye, or burger bun?"

"White," Mo decided.

"I'll have a burger bun, I think," Aspen said, pulling bags of both down from a wire rack. She then knowingly walked to a different area of the kitchen, pulling down a covered dish before coming back over to the prep counter Mo was now leaning against.

"Burger bun?"

"I love bread," Aspen explained like it should make perfect sense, uncovering the dish of what Mo figured was butter. She then grabbed an oversized kitchen knife off the magnetic holder and began buttering the bread with it. Mo was beyond amused, watching as Aspen focused so hard on her task that her tongue was now slightly outside of her mouth, her forehead scrunched in concentration.

Aspen was beyond adorable, and it took everything in Mo not to tell her that.

"Interesting choice of knife."

"A knife is a knife is a knife," Aspen said joyfully, her focus turning to look at the griddle. "Is it hot yet?"

"No idea," Mo responded, leaning forward to hover her hand over it again. There was definitely heat now, but she was unsure if it was fully up to cooking temp. "Is there a way to test it?"

"I don't know, I've not cooked more than a bowl of cereal or a bag of popcorn."

"Yet you're cooking me breakfast?"

"No," Aspen blurted out, turning to give Mo a sly wink. "I was hoping you would know how to cook."

"What makes you think I know how to cook?" Mo asked incredulously, amused at Aspen's confidence.

Aspen looked her up and down slowly, which caused a slight knot to form inside of Mo's stomach. After she was done, Aspen used the knife to grab another pad of butter to spread on a piece of white bread. "You look like a domestic goddess to me."

Mo couldn't help but burst out in laughter. "You might need your eyes checked."

Aspen looked back, meeting her gaze. "No, I think my eyes work fine."

Mo was dumbfounded, so she turned away from the woman to hover her hand over the griddle for a third time. She didn't know how Aspen flirted so effortlessly, but it was totally working on her. Mo racked her brain, remembering an old thing Annie used to do to test if the frying pan was ready.

"Was it water?" Mo mumbled to herself, looking around until she saw the closest sink. With a few long strides, Mo made it to the sink and ran her hand under the water for a few seconds. Dripping wet, she walked back to the griddle and flicked the water on top, watching as the drops sizzled and formed tiny balls of water along the surface before evaporating away. "I think that means it's ready?"

"How do you know?"

Mo popped open the egg carton and grabbed two eggs, returning to the griddle where she cracked them on the edge before opening them next to each other on the black top. The sizzle was instant, and Mo felt pride in herself.

"Annie used to flick water on a frying pan like that. I think she said that if it formed little sizzly balls of water, that means the temperature is just right." Mo grabbed a spatula from the magnetic holder over the oven. "And for the eggs, if I remember correctly, she always used to tell me to be patient and wait for the edges to look perfect before I flipped 'em."

"So you like sunny side up?" Aspen asked, moving next to Mo to watch her cook. "Want me to put the bacon next to the eggs?"

"No, Annie doesn't like—" Mo bit her tongue, grimacing at her slip. "Shit."

"It's all right." Aspen's voice was soft and consoling, and Mo heard her shuffling around behind her. "I fuck with just eggs and toast. Sometimes bacon can be a bit heavy."

The smaller woman tossed the buns and toast straight onto the griddle, and the sound of the butter hitting the heat filled up the space between them. Mo had said too much, and her anxiety was slowly ramping up as she tried to stay focused on the eggs. But the memories of Annie were here now, and her brain was refusing to fight them even as Mo tried.

"Did Annie cover them?" Aspen asked, touching Mo's arm. "Or flip them?"

Mo couldn't help but jerk away, her fight-or-flight response kicking in as she felt a burning behind her eyes. Annie always flipped them. Mo remembered how she preferred to poke the eggs to make the yolk run all over the plate before using her toast to sop it up.

And God, did Annie hate bacon. The smell. The look. The taste of it on Mo's lips.

"No worries, you can do whatever your heart desires. I am not at all picky," Aspen said softly, but Mo continued to back away, her mind in overdrive. "Are you okay?"

"I'm not hungry," was all Mo could choke out as she continued to back toward the door. "Honestly, I gotta go."

And with that she turned and bolted, making her way back outside. Once her face hit the cool morning air, Mo increased her pace and was across the bridge before she even broke her stride.

* * *

Another day passed, and Mo slugged around her cabin in a deep depression. She hadn't eaten a real meal since the burger, instead subsisting on a few old backpacking trail bars Annie had stashed away in her pack. The water from the sink tasted better than Palo Alto city water, so any time she felt thirsty she just dunked her head under the faucet and turned on the spigot. Groceries were becoming a true necessity, but Mo feared running into Aspen and having to explain her quick getaway during breakfast.

So Mo waited until evening time, when she figured Aspen would be working, before venturing out in her Subaru to look for a grocery store that wasn't plumb next to Dry Creek. This plan was fruitless, unfortunately, as neither Mo's GPS nor her own eyes could find anything other than the Orick Family Market. Once that realization hit, Mo drove right up in front of the market and parked the car, hoping if she was quick that she could get in and out without being seen by anyone.

With three large strides, Mo made it inside the small market, noticing how it was more like a New York City bodega than a rural market in a food desert. There was a small beat-up counter kitty-corner to the door and just lines and lines of vertical shelving units stocked full of food. It definitely wasn't the cleanest market Mo had ever seen, but it had food that wasn't attached to Aspen. Mo noticed Mr. Pearson, who she had seen being rather grumpy in the bar the first night, and another shorter, older man with a thick black mustache standing near the counter in conversation. She nodded courteously in their direction before grabbing a hand basket and making her way down an aisle.

The food wasn't cheap but it wasn't expensive either, even though Mo knew it probably cost an arm and a leg to get it all shipped over the mountains to Orick. Choosing stuff was rather difficult, so Mo kept grabbing simple things like bread, instant mashed potatoes, milk, butter, cheese, and frozen meals. There wasn't much in the way of good fresh vegetables or fruit, so Mo figured eating frozen was probably her best bet. After grabbing a week or two's worth of food, she made her way closer to the front counter, finally picking up on the conversation the two men were having.

"A little birdie told me that you are gonna retire at the end of the season. Is that right?" Mr. Pearson's voice was very gruff, causing Mo to stop and act like she was looking at the meager clothing options the owner had on shelves near the front. "I just can't believe you would give this up. The bar is booming. Orick is booming. My son usually works the store's later shift, and he swears all the good business comes from people grabbing post-drinking snacks and alcohol."

"I don't know what you've been smoking, but Orick hasn't boomed in decades. If ever. Plus, Ginny and I ain't ever been about the money, Owen," the shorter man replied, his voice edged with amusement. "We are just getting too old to be slinging beer and wings to backpackers, you know?"

"I do not. I think you two are in your prime."

"Horseshit."

"Oh come on, Salvador, you're being unreasonable," Mr. Pearson implored. "We all gotta be in this together."

"Naw. You got to know when to hold 'em and know when to fold 'em. We're ready to live the slow life. Besides, Aspen is extremely capable of taking over the bar. She'll do a fine job at keeping business local," Salvador said confidently, slapping the counter for emphasis.

Mo's attention perked up at Aspen's name and she moved closer, still acting like she was interested in a dusty sweatshirt that had the market's plain logo haphazardly printed on the front.

"Aspen?" Mr. Pearson asked incredulously. "Air-headed, messy Aspen Anderson?"

"Oh, come on."

"No, you come on. She ain't nearly clever enough to remember my beer order let alone run an entire bar. She'll probably plaster the walls pink and make her uniform shirt a few sizes smaller," Mr. Pearson barked. "No one wants to see that."

"That's extremely judgmental don't you think?" Mo cut in loudly, the words out of her mouth before she could stop herself.

"I'm sorry?" Mr. Pearson said, his attention now on Mo.

Confidently, she strolled up and placed her basket on the counter, looking Mr. Pearson in the eyes. "I may have only met her the other night, but you are being entirely unfair."

Salvador snickered but didn't add anything, instead looking toward Mr. Pearson for his answer.

"She isn't the worst person in town, but she…" Mr. Pearson fumbled, his gaze flicking between Mo and Salvador. "She is always in everybody's business. It's uncouth."

"So is talking negatively about a woman's body."

"This lady has you there, Owen," Salvador pointed out, grinning broadly at Mo. "You know how much I adore Aspen."

"It still doesn't change the fact she ain't up to snuff," Mr. Pearson grumbled as he scanned each of Mo's items into the register, obviously digging his heels in deeper. "She doesn't understand community."

"I watched her be quite community focused when she let you leave without paying." Mo glared at him, her wallet now in her hand, pulling out some cash to pay for her groceries.

"That wasn't—"

"That was exactly the way to play it. Aspen showed you the kind of trust any regular should receive from a small-town business like that. Plus, she let her boss know so your tab would be placed to the side without prejudice. Seems Aspen is very capable to me."

"Oh, I like you." Salvador chuckled, slapping the counter again. "You from around here?"

"No, sir."

Mr. Pearson's lips twitched slightly as he packed her groceries into one large brown paper bag. "Seventy-two fifty."

"Thought so," Mo finished, handing him four twenties. "Keep the change."

And with that, Mo grabbed her bag, nodded to Salvador, and made her way out to the rear of her Subaru. After she deposited her groceries inside the trunk, her eyes strayed toward the front door of the bar. The urge to go in was strong. She could almost see Aspen's face when she told her about the market owner's comments and how she put him in his place. But Mo closed her trunk, deciding to go home alone instead.

CHAPTER SIX

Aspen tapped her fingers rhythmically on the steering wheel, staring through her windshield at the Thomas H. Kuchel Visitor Center with uncertainty. It was her day off. And on every beautiful day off, Aspen's usual routine was to park at the visitor center and walk a chair down to the beach to read. But instead of enjoying the sea air, she hadn't moved a muscle since turning off her car. Mo, just another tourist, had disrupted her world, and she was unsure how to bring it back into alignment.

Aspen glanced over into the passenger seat, her eyes falling to an apology card that had sat untouched since she'd bought it, which was right after Mo had run off. Aspen had felt terrible for pushing Mo about Annie. The guilt had nagged at her, and she desperately wanted a chance to fix it, but that hinged on her ability to find Mo.

An actual stranger.

Just as she was about to give up, an idea popped into Aspen's head. She reached for her cell phone, sliding her thumb across the face to scroll through her contacts. After finding the first prospect, she placed her phone to her ear and listened patiently to the ringing.

"Hello?"

"Hi, Candy. It's Aspen. I had a question if you've got a quick second?"

"Totally, hun. What's up?" Candy replied, her Midwest accent sounding slow and sweet.

"I know it's awkward to ask about your cabin renters, but I had a bar patron the other night who left behind something valuable and I wanted to return it," Aspen lied, hoping her nerves weren't obvious to the woman. "All I know is that her name is Mo and that she's alone."

"Hmm, Mo…" Candy mumbled while Aspen heard the telltale sound of clicking keyboard keys in the background. "I don't have any renters by that name, but I do remember a Mo calling a few days ago. I didn't have anything open for an extended stay, so I referred her to Odessa."

"Oh, Mrs. Pearson does rentals?"

"Indeed she does. I would give her a call. I've left my purse at bars one too many times, so I'm sure Mo will want that back," Candy replied kindly.

"It's unfortunately common. Thank you so much, Candy, you are a lifesaver. The next time you drive down from Seattle, hit up Dry Creek. I have a free margarita with your name on it." Aspen beamed, dancing a jig in her seat with excitement.

"Sounds wonderful, Aspen. I will see you later in the summer."

"Will do, buh-bye!" Aspen ended the call, quickly going back to her contacts to call Mrs. Pearson. "Come on, come on—"

"Hello, Ms. Anderson. Looking to place a pickup order?" Mrs. Pearson answered in her usual business voice.

"Not today, but I do appreciate you asking. I had a different question instead?" Aspen's voice lilted a little, and she chastised herself internally.

"What's that?"

"Well, a recent customer, I think her name was Mo, left something valuable behind at the bar and I've not seen her since. I was wondering if you had anyone by that name staying at one of your beautiful cabins?" Aspen asked sweetly, hoping Odessa would be far easier to work with than her husband.

"Ah yes, Imogen Reeves. She's staying at Horsing Around. She's an interesting lady, not the usual happy and outdoorsy kind that I rent to. Very serious, short with words, but I could care less because she paid up front for a full month," Mrs. Pearson offered easily. "I can text you the address, it's super close to the market."

"Could you? This item seems really important."

"Of course. Do you need anything else?"

"No, thank you, this helps so much. Will I see you for pot pie night?" Aspen asked, hoping to end the conversation soon so that Mrs. Pearson wouldn't forget to text.

"You know it and…" Mrs. Pearson paused momentarily. "There. Text is sent. Thank you for being such a sweetheart, Aspen. See you soon."

"No, thank you. Bye." Aspen ended the call before pumping her fist in the air. "Yes!"

Clicking over to the text, Aspen copied the address and put it into her GPS. After studying the map, she felt confident that she knew exactly where Mo was staying, and she turned on her car. She didn't go straight to the cabin, instead turning right onto Route 101 to go toward the little gas station on the edge of town. After buying two coffees and two egg, bacon, and cheese croissants, she drove her car back toward the creek, making sure to hang the first right before the bridge.

The drive wasn't too difficult, and she found the tiny cabin perched back in the woods pretty easily. Without much thought to how Mo would react to Aspen standing on her doorstep at eleven in the morning, she parked next to the Subaru and hurriedly placed her gifts into one arm. A quick jog to the door and Aspen began knocking out a cute tune against the wood, waiting patiently for an answer.

The only reply was a loud but muffled groan of discontent, which made Aspen grin.

"Hello? It's me. Not a stalker or serial killer but instead a very sorry woman with delicious coffee," Aspen yelled before knocking again. "I promise."

"Did you say coffee?"

"Yes!"

Aspen heard another groan, then a shuffle. A few moments passed before the lock was disengaged and a bed-ruffled Mo was standing in front of Aspen, looking downright cute but exhausted. Blinking in surprise, Aspen quickly noticed that Mo was wearing only boxers and a tank top, allowing her a great view of her lean but toned arms. She swallowed, butterflies floating around in her stomach as her eyes moved up to her collarbone then down to her chest, taking extra care to notice how the tight tank top accentuated her small but round breasts. A few silent moments passed before Aspen dragged herself back to the present and put on a big signature smile before passing Mo one coffee cup from the carrier.

"One 'I'm sorry I'm a big doofus' coffee for Mo and"— Aspen reached for a sandwich, putting it into Mo's other hand— "one bacon, egg, and cheese sandwich made not by me, so you know it's good."

Mo cleared her throat, a dazed but not upset look on her face as she studied the breakfast sandwich's wrapping.

"Oh," Aspen added, sliding past Mo into the cabin. She easily stepped over a pile of bags right in front of the door and made her way straight for the counter where she deposited her own coffee and sandwich. "I also got you a card."

"How did you find me?" Mo asked curiously, closing the door behind her before taking a sip. "Ooh, this is actually really good."

"Of course it is. Joe at the gas station made it, and he does not fuck around with his coffee."

"I can tell." Mo pulled in another sip, making a strange gurgling noise as she tasted the coffee. "For a light roast it has a bit of sweet, a bit of acid, and maybe hints of...vegetables? But overall it runs smoothly over the tongue and isn't bitter or overroasted in the slightest," Mo concluded, taking another longer sip. "I needed this."

"You must be a coffee sommelier or something. I grabbed some milk and sugar if you want, but I have a feeling that's not your jam. All good, now let's…" Aspen started, looking around for a table and chairs. Odessa definitely went bare with this cabin, so Aspen pointed to the next best thing, which was the love seat, and continued, "Sit and eat. I have something else to give you."

Mo seemed to freeze for a moment, but as Aspen took her goodies to the loveseat and flopped down, she made her way to sit next to her. Aspen took a quick sip of her coffee, which she had doctored at the gas station with entirely too much sugar, before placing it on the floor next to the arm of the chair. Then she happily unwrapped her sandwich and took a big bite, moaning at how salty and delicious it was.

"I love these things."

Mo took a smaller bite but hummed in agreement. "Yeah, it's pretty good."

Aspen spun in her spot to face Mo, her jean-capri-covered knee now lightly touching Mo's bare thigh. She grabbed the card from under her arm and presented it with a loud, "Ta-da! For you."

Mo smirked, placing her sandwich down in her lap before slowly opening the card.

"I'm sorry I didn't see…" Mo read aloud, opening the card to display an intricate pop-up design of a black cat chasing a string. "How purrfect you really are. I'm sorry for making you uncomfortable. Aspen."

Aspen couldn't help but bite her lower lip as Mo turned to meet her gaze.

"You didn't…" Mo started, blowing air from her mouth as Aspen watched her guilty hazels study her face. "It wasn't you."

Aspen shrugged. "I'm sorry anyway."

Mo closed the card, turning to put it on the foot of her bed.

"So," Aspen said, changing the subject. "You seem to be quite the coffee connoisseur. Is that what you do for a living?"

"Now hold on here." Mo raised her voice with a commanding tone, taking another bite. "You have asked question after question about me, but I have yet to learn anything about you. Well, other than you're a quirky bartender who somehow figured out where I am staying."

"It's a small town," Aspen reasoned, nervousness bubbling up.

"Ah, well, I think I'm gonna need to know more about you to make sure you aren't a stalker. Protocol and all that."

"Protocol? What are you, a cop?"

"You're deflecting," Mo warned, her voice playful. "I know you live and work here in Orick, but did you also grow up here? Are the bar owners your parents?"

Aspen squirmed under Mo's attention, her mind reeling at how best to answer that question. "Uh…no, I'm not from Orick. And are you asking about Virginia and Salvador?"

"Yep, I actually met Salvador at the market a few nights back. I wondered if he was your dad." Mo's voice was even, but her gaze was fixed on Aspen even as she took another sip of coffee. "You seemed pretty close to that older woman at the bar too."

"No," Aspen replied quietly, looking toward the door to avoid Mo's eyes. "Do you like the beach?"

"Don't like talking about yourself?" Mo chuckled.

"No, I just, it's kinda stuffy in here and today is my day off." Aspen brightened. "And I always try to go to the beach on my day off."

"Do we have to?" Mo grumbled, obviously very comfortable in her current digs.

"Yes, get some loose clothes on and some beach-safe shoes. We are going out."

"Okay, but I'll only go if you promise to answer some of my questions with more than just a yes or no," Mo stated, standing with a tired grunt.

"If it gets you out of the cabin, then I agree. I swear, I don't think you've left since I last saw you," Aspen replied, taking another bite. "Now go shower, change, or whatever. I'll hang out here."

"There isn't a door on the bathroom," Mo said. "So only turn around if you're brave."

That comment threw Aspen off guard, and she choked slightly on her sandwich, which earned a small laugh from Mo, as she heard the woman's bare feet pad across the hardwood behind her. Aspen leaned back, making herself comfortable in a bid to act like Mo getting naked for a shower just a few feet away wasn't as tempting as it was. Instead, she focused on finishing her food and sipping her coffee as she looked around the rather dated cabin. Mo was obviously not interested in keeping the cabin tidy—clothes were strewn about and her bags barely made it past the threshold. That worried Aspen a little, but she knew it wasn't really her business anyway. If Mo wanted to talk about why she was depressed in a small cabin away from home, she'd get there in her own time.

Aspen heard the shower turn on and decided to slide over and look at the VHS tapes instead of sitting and imagining a naked Mo, water droplets gliding down over her soft skin. She shook her head, blowing out a bit of air to keep herself grounded as she reviewed the selection on the shelf. Most of the movie cases were pretty beat up, ranging from Disney classics to all the *National Lampoon* movies. Aspen moved to kneel in front, pulling out each case to look at the cover design and remember how much she loved popping in a VHS when she was kid. The sound as the player loaded, the pitch as the reel began to spin, and the crackle of the speakers as the ads would roll. Movies were her best friend on lonely weekend nights in the camper. The perfect distraction from her despair.

It was utterly nostalgic.

Aspen didn't even notice when Mo returned to the room to dress, instead continuing to study each and every tape. But when she happened upon *Speed* in the lineup, she yelped in excitement. "I found your movie Mo!"

"Did you, now?" Mo answered, her voice closer than Aspen expected.

She reeled around to find an almost fully clothed Mo standing right behind her as she fell on her butt. A quick laugh was shared between the two of them as Mo slowly buttoned up a wrinkled maroon, loose-fitting long-sleeved shirt. Aspen gave a nervous wave.

"You are quick."

"I am." Mo nodded, leaning down to offer Aspen a hand, which she took graciously. "Though, I don't really have beach shoes."

Aspen, now standing, rubbed her hands together in embarrassment before taking charge. "What size are your feet?"

"I'm a nine."

"Ooh, me too. I actually have a pair of water shoes in the back of Periwinkle that you can borrow."

"It's settled, then, I guess," Mo said unenthusiastically. "We are off to the beach."

"Yay!" Aspen exclaimed, clapping her hands together before trotting toward the door. "It's not too windy or cold right now, so it should be super fun."

"Am I going barefoot?"

"Yeah, until we get to the beach. You'll be fine. The pine litter won't hurt you," Aspen replied with confidence, pulling open the door and walking briskly to the car. She adjusted her old T-shirt down over her belly and the low rise of her waistband, praying to any gods that could hear her thoughts that her butt crack wasn't showing as she hopped into her car. Mo wasn't far behind, sliding in beside her with her coffee cradled protectively.

"Seat belt!"

"Aye aye, captain," Mo said, snapping closed her belt. "How far is the beach?"

"With my lead foot, less than five," Aspen assured, speeding out of the driveway and onto the road. "Us locals have passes to park at the visitor center near the beach, so I usually go there."

"Cool."

"Do you have a beach where you're from?" Aspen asked, hoping Mo wouldn't put up another fight.

"Do you wanna quid pro quo then?"

"Huh?" Aspen wrinkled her forehead, looking over at Mo once she stopped at the cross for the main road.

"Just a Latin saying that means 'something for something.' I know it from the *Silence of the Lambs*."

Aspen shuddered a bit, turning out onto the 101. "That's a scary movie. I'm not the biggest fan of those."

"I get it, but yeah, it just means if I answer a question, then you answer a question," Mo replied. Aspen was glad she seemed much calmer than the past few times they had talked.

"Deal," Aspen agreed. "So, are there beaches from where you're from?"

"I'm originally from rural Massachusetts, but I've spent all of my adult life in Palo Alto. Near San Fran."

"Oh, that's not that far from here."

"It's six or seven hours on a good day." Mo laughed.

"Still closer than Massachusetts," Aspen sang, a grin plastered to her face.

"Where did you grow up?"

Aspen's face fell a bit before she took in a deep breath, knowing full well it was just an innocent question. She wasn't required to go into all the details, even if she felt the pressure. So she simply replied, "I kinda grew up all over Northern California. But if I had to give you a town…Eureka is where I lived until a few years back. Before I moved to Orick, of course."

"A true Cali girl," Mo said.

Aspen didn't reply, instead swinging her car into a spot close to the deck entrance to the beach.

"Brush-covered sand dunes are so odd," Mo observed, opening her door to step out.

"I've not really thought about it." Aspen followed suit, moving to the rear to open the trunk. She reached in and grabbed the water shoes, tossing them to the ground near Mo, before also snagging her baby-blue pop-up shade tent. "Alrighty, we are ready."

"Let me guess, your favorite color is baby blue?" Mo asked as Aspen shut the trunk, hopping around to get one of the water shoes on fully.

"You skipped my question," Aspen teased, waiting for Mo to finish donning the shoes before walking toward the bridge over the sand dunes. "But yeah, you're right. So, what's your favorite color?"

"What is this, a first date?"

Aspen skipped a step, barely catching herself as she climbed the stairs. "I guess that is kind of a lame question."

"It's purple," Mo said with amusement, following Aspen. "Let's just go with it. What's your astrological sign?"

"Gemini," Aspen replied proudly. "Actually, my birthday is in a couple weeks, so you can count this excursion as an early birthday present."

"I don't know if forcing a grumpy stranger to spend time with you counts as a very good present."

She led Mo out onto the beach, breathing in the slight salty air as she walked toward a patch of sand that wasn't too rocky. Mo had stopped behind her, the woman's gaze firmly on the dark-blue Pacific as it lapped rhythmically on the shore. The sun wasn't too bright, allowing the deep color to contrast well with the white of the sea foam. Aspen let her be, instead choosing to set up the shade tent, staking down the corners with expert precision.

Once completed, Aspen called out to Mo, "Come and have a seat, I think I found a patch of sand that isn't too rocky."

Mo, shaking herself from her trance, nodded slowly before making her way over to the shade and crawling underneath to sit cross-legged. Aspen followed suit, sighing comfortably as she watched the sea tumble around.

"It's gorgeous here," Mo finally said, her voice tinted with the same sadness as the first night Aspen met her.

"Yeah," Aspen agreed, even as she stared only at Mo. "So, I told you my sign...what's yours?"

"Virgo," Mo said quickly, turning to meet Aspen's stare. "All right, let's get a little more personal, what—"

"I'm divorced," Aspen blurted out, cutting Mo off.

Mo laughed deeply, her body seeming to loosen with each passing chuckle. "You have a way with conversation that I have yet to experience, Aspen."

"Hey, that's a deeper thing," Aspen defended, glad Mo took the bait. "It was a man too."

"Ah. I don't mean to assume, but how do you identify?"

"Lesbian," Aspen answered. "It took me a while to figure it out, which is why I married my high school sweetheart."

"Late bloomer. I also identify as a lesbian, but I figured it out much, much earlier. My parents weren't so happy."

"I'm sorry," Aspen said empathetically, reaching over to squeeze Mo's forearm. "I get it."

"Eh, it's water under the bridge."

Aspen felt a twinge of jealousy at that comment, changing the subject. "So, there you go. That's all there really is to know about me."

"Liar. I'm sure you are much more than a bubbly, divorced bartender surrounded by folks as elderly as the redwoods," Mo teased, pushing Aspen slightly with her shoulder.

"Hey!" Aspen pouted, drawing out the word. "There are people here that are my age."

"I severely doubt that."

"Okay then, what more do you think there is?"

Mo's lips turned down in thought before she replied. "You are far too confident to lead a life that simple."

"All right, I'll bite." Aspen drummed up the courage as she turned her body toward Mo. "I heard from one of those elderly people that you are going to be around for a month. I'm, uh… down for a more physical thing, if you're interested."

Mo's eyes widened like a deer in headlights as her jaw went slack.

"What? You're hot, I'm hot. There would be no strings attached. I'm not asking to U-Haul," Aspen assured. "I'm just… very interested in what you have to offer in that department."

Mo's face softened but she stayed silent, instead turning to look out at the sea again. The sounds of the waves lapping the shore filled the space between them. After a long while, the silence became too much, so Aspen tried to backtrack.

"Damn, I'm sorry. I fucked it up again, didn't I?"

"No," Mo instantly replied, her eyes still on the water.

"No, I get carried away sometimes."

Mo sighed. "I'll explain."

"You don't have to."

"I know, but I want to." Mo leaned back on her palms. "You asked me why I was up here and well, I…You know about Annie."

Aspen refused to interrupt, keeping her eyes on a few seagulls that were dive-bombing the shallow water in front of them.

"When she was alive, she—well, we, liked to backpack," Mo explained. "Redwood Creek was Annie's favorite place. She was in love with every rock and tree up here. So after my job fired me for taking too much time away from work, I decided to come and do a solo trip. Like a remembrance thing, or whatever. I just…I'm having a hard time getting my trip started."

Aspen turned to look at Mo, noticing that she was nervously picking at her fingernails. She didn't really take Mo for being a lover of the outdoors, even though she had noticed the muted pink Deuter pack inside of Mo's cabin. She finally decided to be direct and asked, "I don't want to be mean or anything, but you don't really seem the backpacking type."

"I know my way around the woods."

"Oh, okay."

Mo shrugged noncommittally before adding, "It's not the backpacking I'm struggling with. It's the whole remembrance, grand gesture thing."

Aspen tilted her head in thought. "All right, well, I might be able to help with that."

"My friends back home already tried. They're kinda the reason I'm here. They thought this trip might get me back on track or whatever." Mo sighed, her phone going off in her pocket. "Speak of the devil, there's Bud now."

"Let's see." Aspen racked her brain, trying to think of something that would be super meaningful on a backpacking trip. "Cairns are bad for the environment. I think tree etching is tacky as all hell…"

"Bud wants to know if you're real," Mo said, her thumbs tapping away. "I told him you're real but he doesn't believe me."

"Why doesn't he think I'm real?" Aspen asked before quickly jumping to, "Do you think monuments are a lot of work?"

"A monument?" Mo was still tapping away at her phone, her face scrunched up.

"Yeah, did she like something in particular? Was she good at a certain thing?"

"I mean, she was good at everything…" Mo said before groaning, throwing her head back in annoyance. "He wants your phone number to check if you're real. I am not giving him—"

The idea hit Aspen like a Mack truck. "A wind phone!"

"A what?" Mo asked, dropping her phone in response to Aspen's loud outburst.

"A wind phone. I read about one up in Washington." Aspen pulled out her own phone, bringing up Google to tap out her search. Her eyes flew across the screen, quickly taking in the information. "It says here they originated in Japan. It's a disconnected rotary phone set up in nature. It's usually either inside a phone booth or hung up on a tree. They are set up so that people can make a journey to the phone and have a one-way conversation with their dead loved ones."

"Oh." Mo faltered, her eyes back on the sea. "That's a thing?"

"Yeah! The one in Olympia is super popular for day hikers who want to work through their grief." Aspen's mind was already working through the logistics. "We'll need Betty's approval, but I'm sure that will be easy enough. Plus, we'll need a place that isn't too close to the protected groves."

Mo didn't reply, so Aspen just kept brainstorming aloud, the nearby calls between seagulls almost drowning her out.

CHAPTER SEVEN

Mo was struggling to juggle all the stimuli she was currently experiencing. Her own brain was ringing the alarm bells to flee, Bud was pestering her from over three hundred miles away, and an adorable stranger was trying to help her with her problems. It was far too much for her depressed brain to process. Unfortunately, she couldn't avoid it all, so she did her best to assess and then manage. Aspen was thankfully still arguing aloud with her own thoughts, so she instead focused on Bud's words appearing on her phone's screen.

What does she look like?

Are you sure she is real? You ain't gotta create some fake gal to make me happy, you know?

Mo?

You there?

Are you in danger?!!;!

Frustration began to grow exponentially inside of Mo, bubbling up from deep inside her stomach and overflowing down her arms and into her thumbs.

Bud, stop! You are suffocating me.
I will call you later.

Mo growled in frustration, tossing her phone into the corner of the shade tent. "Why is he the way he is?"

"Overbearing friend?" Aspen asked, her voice lilting sweetly. It melted a bit of Mo's frustration. "I'm sorry."

Her eyes closed reflexively at that, and she turned to look at Aspen fully. Her soft features and sympathetic gaze tinged guiltily at Mo's heart. "No, I'm the one who should be sorry."

"Why is that?"

"I've not heard a word you've said," Mo admitted. She expected Aspen's reaction to be annoyance or even discontent, but she only smiled goofily from ear to ear. Mo tilted her head in confusion, wondering if Aspen had actually understood what she said. "Did you hear me correctly, or…"

"I did, silly." Aspen winked. "It's okay. I was mostly working through the logistics out loud."

"The wind phone." Mo nodded, reflexively leaning in toward her. "Can you explain that again?"

Aspen bit her lip before lifting up her phone to show Mo the Wikipedia page for it. "It's a disconnected phone that was first installed in a garden in Japan by a man named Itaru Sasaki. As far as I can tell, he created it as a way for him to deal with the death of his cousin. But after the earthquake and tsunami in 2010, it was opened to the public so people could make a journey to it and speak with their dead loved ones. Many other places have kind of co-opted the idea, including a park in Olympia, Washington. Which, through the backpacking circles I run in, is how I heard about it."

Mo studied the picture in the article, her eyes scanning over a white-and-green phone booth placed neatly in a landscaped garden. She looked to Aspen, who was patiently studying her features. "Are we going to drag a phone booth into the woods?"

"No, silly." Aspen giggled, leaning in closer to Mo. "I have a way better idea, just give me a bit to set it all up and I'll reach out. Sound good?"

Mo didn't know what was good. If she went with her knee-jerk reaction, it would be to tell Aspen to kick rocks. But another part of her, the one that still had hope, wanted to embrace the woman with open arms. And that was frightening. So Mo leaned back and gave a half-hearted nod before turning her attention to the sea yet again.

* * *

"This is a fucking nightmare!"

Mo's hands slid back and forth through her hair as she surveyed the gigantic mess she had made of the cabin the past few hours. The gear covered every inch of her bed and the floor around it. If the excursion with Aspen did anything productive, it was to push her to actually inventory what backpacking items Annie had kept stored in their guest room closet all these years.

She reached forward and grabbed a dark-blue bundle, which was obviously Annie's sleeping bag, and squeezed it to her chest. It was the only object that she was familiar with, otherwise everything else would take hours of Googling to fully understand. Mo felt torn between winging the whole thing, death be damned, or getting a hold of Aspen and actually going through with her wind phone idea. But asking Aspen for help seemed oppositional to her urge to be alone. Besides, Mo was nowhere near understanding what her next step would look like.

It was absolutely infuriating.

Mo growled in frustration, pulling her phone from her pocket and calling Opal without much forethought.

"Hey stranger," Opal answered lovingly.

"What's the twenty on Annie's sleeping bag mean?" Mo asked grumpily, her mood getting the best of her manners.

"Temperature rating for the bag. It will keep you warm in thirty- to thirty-five-degree weather."

"But it says twenty?" Mo tossed the bag against the wall before moving to sit grumpily in front of the piles. "Why say twenty if it's thirty?"

Opal chuckled with endearment. "It's just the way it is."

"How did Annie even stay warm in that? She was constantly trying to steal body heat from me in our bed at home. And we kept the house in the seventies year-round." Mo kicked a heavy green tarp bag under the bed for emphasis. "Ow, fuck!"

"Are you okay?"

"No! I just kicked God knows what, which hurt my fucking foot, and I'm wholly in the dark about what half this shit is. Like what is this?" Mo grabbed the next closest item to her, reading the label to Opal. "Traditions UL Trowel, made in Taiwan. Why did she carry a tiny trowel? Did you two garden in the woods?"

Opal laughed even louder now as Mo dropped the trowel, splaying out on her back.

"What did I say?"

"Sorry," Opal said, though she continued to wheeze in amusement. "That's not for gardening, Imogen. That's for pooping in the woods."

"Goddammit!"

"I'm glad you called," Opal replied sweetly, amusement still lingering.

"Yeah, I need help. I'm supposed to be an expert and I am nowhere near an expert," Mo blabbed, grimacing when she thought about what she just said. "I mean, I'd like to be one so I can go on a little hike, well, a long hike, ya know? I have a plan for this whole trip now."

"A plan?" Opal hummed inquisitively, letting Mo know she was on to her. "Hold on, Bud is here."

Mo almost yelled *no* out loud, instead pulling the phone away from her head as the video call ringtone informed her of Opal's intent. She didn't want to talk to Bud, but she also didn't want to hurt anyone's feelings, so she answered the call. Opal's shy but comforting smile and Bud's all-encompassing existence filled the frame.

"Howdy, Imogen!" Bud yelled happily, waving erratically at the screen. "I just got off work."

"Hey," Mo replied, rolling over onto her stomach to prop the phone against the leg of the bed. "Uh, sorry about…you know."

"No biggie," Bud replied easily, leaning his gigantic head in to fill the top right corner of the screen.

Mo watched as Opal's small hand slinked through the gap in Bud's elbow, wrapping around his forearm. Like magic, Bud responded to her touch, leaning back and allowing for Mo to see both of them seated on one of the Hecate Tattoo couches, Opal's intricate artwork displayed proudly above their heads.

"What's going on? Are you coming back soon?" Bud asked, using his free hand to unbutton the top two buttons of his work shirt.

"No, I was just asking Opal for some backpacking gear advice."

"Good choice. She's the fuckin' best at that stuff."

"Yeah," Mo agreed, resting her chin on her hands.

"Mo has a plan," Opal added quietly, her relaxed energy infectious.

"What's that? You gonna do the PCT?" Bud asked.

"No, that's not even near here. I just thought I could do something…" Mo trailed off, her frustrated brain having difficulty keeping up.

"So you've been there for around a week and just tonight you've got a plan to want to backpack?" Bud's head tilted in thought.

"Well, yeah."

"Did she backpack with y'all?" Bud turned to Opal.

"No."

"Do you even know how to do that?" Bud asked Mo, his voice filled with concerned doubt.

"Fuck," Mo said under her breath, closing her eyes. "I get the concept."

"Yeah, I got the concept too, but Opal still hiked circles around my dumb ass."

"You said you are supposed to be an expert?" Opal asked. "What does that mean?"

"Uh—uh," Mo stuttered.

"Wait, is this about that gal you were apologizing about?" Bud asked, his voice raising in volume as he leaned closer to the camera to study Mo's reaction. "Hot diggity dog, you rascal! She is real. I knew it. Opal, baby, Mo has met someone."

"If you mean 'met' like I met a woman at a bar who has spent the past week forcing me to hang out with her, then sure," Mo said, hoping Bud wouldn't press any more than he already had.

"What's her name? Is she hot? Does she have a job?"

"Bud," Opal warned calmly. "Let her speak."

"Aspen," Mo said as evenly as she could, downplaying her affection to not get Bud's hopes up. "Yes, she's hot. And yes, she was the one who recommended the backpacking trip. But honestly, I kinda wanna do this alone. Even though she has a knack for appearing at every place I go, so I'll probably have to sneak into the woods just to get away from her."

"It doesn't sound like you want to get away from her," Bud teased.

"Is she a backpacker?" Opal added thoughtfully, doing her normal, easy defense of Bud's more tactless conversation style.

"Yeah, I think? Well, she's actually a bartender, but she seems knowledgeable. I told her about Annie and the redwoods at the beach the other day, and she just came up with a whole plan, grand gesture and all. She seemed to know quite a lot about the trails and some of the local park rangers." Mo smiled slightly, thinking about how excited Aspen was explaining it all.

"You two were at the beach?" Bud waggled his eyebrows. "Bikinis?"

"It's May on the California coast," Mo murmured with annoyance. "Clothing was worn."

"Never too cold for bikinis."

"Aspen always goes to the beach on her day off," Mo returned, ignoring Bud's addition.

"So you know her routine?" Opal asked, her voice taking on a knowing lilt.

"Hey now, you are reading too much into this," Mo warned playfully, hoping it would make the conversation move in a different direction.

"All right then, what is the plan?"

"Well, Aspen had done some reading on a thing called a wind phone. It's like a disconnected rotary phone that people mount on trees or in phone booths in desolate places. And when you want to talk to someone who has passed on, you kinda make your way out to the phone and have a conversation with them."

"I think that sounds like it would be very healing for you," Opal replied.

"That's some shrink shit," Bud said, adjusting the way he was seated on the couch. "Just invite her over to your cabin and get to know her."

"It's supposed to be cathartic," Mo defended.

"So, what, you and Aspen are just going to hike somewheres and hang up the phone?" Bud continued. "Like on a post or a tree?"

"Well, I am," Mo corrected. "I'm going to do it alone."

"That sounds dangerous." Bud looked to Opal for support. "Is that dangerous?"

"It can be," Opal confirmed.

Mo groaned, rubbing her eyes deeply with her fingers as she tried to think of the best way to stay firm.

"Though, I think it's a beautiful idea. I would love to visit it."

Mo's chest tightened at the sound of Opal's voice, suddenly feeling terrible for being selfish about Annie's memory. "Well, you'll be able to talk to her after I put the phone up. But—but I am going to need your help with all of Annie's stuff."

"Like us come up there?" Bud asked hopefully, his body beginning to creep up from the couch.

"No," Opal said, touching Bud's shoulder before turning back toward the camera. "Take some pictures of everything you have and send it to me. I will send you an itemized list with brief descriptions."

"Do I really need all of it?"

"Probably not. I will tell you what you can leave behind. Annie might have led a spontaneous and messy life, but she was diligent with her gear. Do you have any clothes and hiking shoes?"

Mo sat up at that question, her eyes turning toward the door where Annie's well-worn hiking boots sat haphazardly. "No clothes, but I do have Annie's shoes."

"I recommend getting your own."

"Sure," Mo lied. "Where do I get the clothes and how many outfits?"

"The store," Bud grumped, obviously still disappointed he couldn't come to Mo's aid.

"You only need a couple outfits. Cleanliness and backpacking are never used in the same sentence," Opal said.

"You got food?" Bud questioned.

"Trail mix count?" Mo asked.

"You have to eat more than trail mix, Mo," Opal warned.

"This seems like a lot of stuff, Opal."

"It could be worse. You could be trying to instruct me on how to sail your boat."

"Or to play the steel guitar," Bud added. "Maybe you can get one of them Backpacking For Dummies books when you go get your clothes?"

"Opal?" Mo was getting overwhelmed. "Can't you just meet me at an REI somewhere?"

"No, but I am sure Aspen could help you with everything."

"I don't know. I can't really call her and ask."

"But you've hung out with her enough to see her in a bikini?" Bud laughed.

"She wasn't wearing a bikini," Mo deflected.

"You look great in a bikini," Bud said to Opal, an affectionate smile apparent between his beard and mustache.

"My schedule is pretty booked up with clients," Opal explained, though she smiled slightly at her husband's remark. "I have a few larger pieces I am working on currently."

"Oh, right. I'm sorry, I am probably taking up way too much of your time," Mo said.

"Never," Opal assured, making Mo feel worse.

"If Aspen is any amount of outdoorsy as her name suggests," Bud said, waggling his eyebrows suggestively, "I'm sure she would be happy to help, if you know what I mean."

"But I really want to do this al—"

"No buts!" Opal cut her off, her voice taking a more commanding tone. "Backpacking can be dangerous, Imogen."

"Yeah, I'm with Opal. I'd feel a lot better about you doing this if you took someone with you."

"I'm not a child—"

"We can't lose you too," Opal quietly cut her off.

Her words hit Mo like a ton of bricks. The silence that came after was just as effective. "Okay."

"Hell yeah," Bud exclaimed, happy with Mo's answer. "Now call up your new lady and get to burning that midnight oil."

"And Mo?" Opal asked hopefully.

"Yeah?"

"Can the phone be really, really ugly?" Opal shifted, her right hand coming up to hug at her torso. "Anytime Annie and I stopped in antique stores on our trips, she always loved the ugliest stuff."

Mo let out a breathy but knowing chuckle before responding. "She really did. But yeah, sure, I can do that. I'll talk at you guys later."

"I love you," Bud said quickly. "We love you."

Opal nodded in agreement. Her lips seemed twisted in pent-up emotion, keeping her from speaking.

"I love you guys too," Mo said, finishing the call.

Opal and Bud's assessment of her plan had lowered her frustration but didn't quite alter the struggle. Mo was stuck between multiple desires. Part of her wanted to go out into the forest and let it take her, allowing her regrets to swallow her whole. Another wanted the solace of a long and lonely hike to install the wind phone, eager to see if when she used it, Annie would reply. The final part, the one she figured was the most selfish, was allowing herself to fully give in to Aspen. Bringing the enigmatic woman on her journey, even if it meant moving on from Annie.

But Mo never wanted to move on from Annie.

She pushed herself to her feet, taking pictures of all the items to send Opal's way. After she finished the task, she slid the stuff on her bed to one side before sliding beneath the covers to rest. Her body felt tight and relaxed all at the same time, and she closed her eyes and imagined what Annie's reaction would be to her fretting like this over all the gear. Annie probably would shrug her frustration off, ignoring Mo's grumpiness, to pack exactly what they would need for this trip. Then she would hype Mo up, giving her one of her signature pep talks that always ended with some random metaphor Annie would think up on the spot. Mo felt warmth at the thought, imagining Annie was in the cabin now, watching as her mind's eye had Annie expertly pack everything away, her gorgeous voice singing some old country song as she worked.

Then she thought about going out into the woods again, her mind wandering to the long, lonely walk to nowhere. But this time, she also imagined Annie's discontent. The way Annie's eyebrows would pull in so tight that they almost touched. Mo opened her eyes and turned to look at the side table. Annie's treasure was sitting there, tempting her to at least try. To see what Annie saw. To see what Annie loved. It was a huge, jumbled mess, so Mo did what she did best and pushed the feelings from her mind, reaching for her phone. She normally would look up some concert footage on YouTube to distract herself, but this time she typed out *Dry Creek Bar & Grill* and hovered her thumb over the phone number link.

While Mo's mind hesitated, her thumb pressed the button, so she slid the phone between her ear and the pillow.

"Dry Creek Bar and Grill," a gruff voice answered.

"Hi, is this, uh—is this Virginia?" Mo asked, not expecting someone other than Aspen to answer.

"Sure was when I looked in the mirror this morning," the woman replied, her voice still gravely. "Can I help you with something?"

"Uh, yeah, I was uh…" Mo stumbled around, her uneasiness apparent. "Looking to um…to see…"

"Well spit it out, kid. I ain't got all night."

"Aspen. I want to talk to Aspen?"

"Oh." Virginia's voice lightened a little. "Is this Tall, Dark, and Butch?"

Mo blinked, flipping her phone to her other ear. "My hair isn't what I would call dark."

"Would you rather me call you Googly Eyes? Because you really got your fill looking at my daughter," Virginia countered, her wit quick as a whip.

"Aspen said you weren't her mother?"

"Not by blood, no, but I might as well be. The other one was just a carrier. Anyway, Aspen ain't here tonight, but she'll be on shift tomorrow if you want to come see her again. I told her to give you her number, but she obviously is up to her usual tricks."

"Tricks? It just hasn't come up," Mo replied. "Can you give her my number instead?"

"Sure," Virginia grunted, and Mo heard some shuffling before the clicking of a pen. "Shoot."

Mo recited out her phone number, then added her full name for emphasis. "Just tell her I have a few questions."

"Is that what kids call it nowadays?"

"Are you always this wily?"

"Only on days that end in a 'y.'"

Mo chuckled at that bad joke before adding, "Also, do you happen to know where the closest outdoor store is?"

"Prolly down in Eureka where my good-for-nothing boyfriend spends most of his free time. I swear, men are about as useful as a screen door on a submarine." Virginia sighed. "You really should ask Aspen about those things. She's the best backpacker in NorCal."

"Noted, thanks."

"No, thank you. Now I gotta get back to pouring Bud Lights. Swing by if you're thirsty."

The older woman hung up before Mo could even say goodbye.

CHAPTER EIGHT

"You can do this, it's not like she's gonna fire you."

Aspen was nervously psyching herself up as she pushed her way inside of Dry Creek, her eyes firmly on the ground in front of her. Asking for time off from Virginia, even before the busy season was in full swing, seemed daunting. Especially since her reasoning involved a crush that was urging her to help a woman, a literal stranger, backpack down Redwood Creek to install a useless rotary phone. And while Virginia had supported Aspen her entire life, she was still worried that even this was beyond her normal shenanigans. But even Aspen knew that if she really was going to help Mo, she was going to need a week or two off to make that whim a reality.

"I really am crazy," Aspen mumbled as she walked closer to the bar, bumping right into Virginia. "Oops!"

"Watch where you're going, kid. I could crack a hip," Virginia grumped, holding on to Aspen's outstretched arms to steady herself. The older woman took a few seconds to study her face, keenly commenting, "Wow, don't you look stupid in love."

"I am not in love."

"Your face is telling me otherwise."

"No," Aspen said, jumping onto the closest barstool. "I'm just distracted."

"Thinking about your girl?" Virginia asked, leaning against the side of the bar. "You know, she was calling around here last night."

Aspen couldn't help but perk up at that comment, her heart beginning to beat more rapidly. "What?"

"She was wanting to speak to you about some shopping or something…No fear, I did what you could not. I got her phone number," Virginia said smugly, waggling her eyebrows at Aspen.

"That's it?"

"What, did you want me to propose to her for you too?"

"You are actually insufferable."

"Nah." Virginia cackled, enjoyment clear as day on her wrinkled face. "I'm just old and I know things. Entertainment is hard to come by around here. Prolly why Sal and I wanna make this our last season."

"You say that every season."

"This really will be our last one," Virginia replied slowly, tilting her head to meet eyes with Aspen. "The old building is yours if you want it."

"Yeah, I know," Aspen acknowledged, even as her heart broke a little at the thought of truly being stuck in Orick. She expertly masked the pain she was feeling by adding, "Can't wait to run this place until I'm as old and rambunctious as you."

"I can hear you cussing at Butch now. She's cleaning the counter with an old rag while you sweep. You start naggin' at her about how the only things she cares about are changing out flat beer and flirting with tourists. Oh, love, it's a beautiful thing."

Aspen blew out air in frustration, leaning forward to place her forehead against the curved edge of the bar. The more Virginia made grandiose comments about Mo, the more Aspen worried her plan was made in a feeble attempt to garner intimate attention. And that idea made Aspen sick to her stomach.

"Mo isn't interested in me like that."

"Right…and Sal and I won the Mega Millions last night and are gonna buy a beach house down in Carmel-by-the-Sea," Virginia returned flatly, but Aspen stayed quiet, not taking the bait. "It don't matter anyhow, here's her phone number."

A few seconds passed before Aspen felt the sharp edge of a piece of paper being slid under where her head was resting against the bar's edge.

"Thanks," Aspen murmured but didn't move, instead just anxiously analyzing the way the paper felt against her forehead.

"She also asked about where the closest outdoor store was, which I thought was kinda weird seeing as there ain't a reason to be in Orick this long unless hiking in the redwoods is one of your passions. You'd think she'd stop somewheres before coming all the way here. Besides, don't y'all lesbians have built-in compasses to all things camping?"

"Stereotypes are harmful, Virginia," Aspen chastised, slap-grabbing the phone number before lifting her head to meet her eyes. "Also, I think you have the wrong idea about Mo."

"How so?"

"Just because she's butch doesn't mean she knows her way around hiking poles."

"Well, good thing I told her you were the expert." Virginia nodded toward the paper. "So put her in your damn phone and give her a call."

Aspen held back a smile at the thought of hearing Mo's voice, dropping her head to enter the contact information into her phone. "I'll call her tomorrow. I've gotta get the fruit cut."

"Fuck the fruit. Salvador will do it."

"He's terrible at bar chores. Besides, I'm on full shift tonight. Oh, and by the way…" Aspen saved Mo's number and tossed her phone onto the counter with a loud *thunk*. "I wanted to ask you about something important. Do you remember that talk about giving me time off for backpacking?"

"Done," Virginia responded immediately, moving around the bar toward the under-cabinet fridge.

Aspen blinked for a few moments, her lips slack before turning to ask, "Just like that?"

"Yeah, I assume you wanna go somewhere with Butch—"

"Her name is Mo."

"Butch, Mo…same difference. Either way, if you think she ain't cut out for hiking poles, you should probably go with her," Virginia said matter-of-factly, pulling out the bins of lemons and limes and tossing them haphazardly onto the cutting board built into the bar. "You know what? Take tonight off too."

"What?"

"Yeah, why not. Go grab her from wherever she's staying." Virginia grabbed a knife and brandished it in Aspen's direction. "You do know where she's staying, right?"

"Actually, yeah," Aspen said, excitement bubbling up in her stomach.

"So there is hope for you yet." Virginia violently cut a lemon in half.

Suddenly, the kitchen door popped open. Salvador strode through it with his left arm already slinking into one of the sleeves of his outstretched jacket. Stopping in his tracks at the sight of the women, he sheepishly grinned before announcing, "I've got some errands to run, ladies. Don't wait up f—"

"Oh no you don't," Virginia warned, taking another intense slice without looking up. "I gave Aspen the night off, so get back in that kitchen and help Ben roll silverware. Now!"

Salvador looked to Aspen for help, but she just shrugged, watching as he pulled his arm back out of the coat. "Yes, love."

"Thank you. Now, Aspen." Virginia met her eyes, her voice still commanding. "Go and pick Butch up, take her down to Eureka, and get her whatever she needs. Let me know if all she's good for is a hot lay. I can spare a few hundred to keep her from dying."

Aspen nodded, pulling her phone from her pocket and quickly dialing Mo's number. She performed an apologetic nod to a retreating Salvador as she slid out of her stool, moving toward the door before Virginia could change her mind.

Just as she thought she was going to catch Mo's voice mail, a sleepy voice answered, "I'm gonna make this real easy for you to understand. I sold my house. I'm selling my boat. I have all-weather liners in my Subaru. I no longer own a printer, so your ink is useless. And…I do not need a fucking vacuum. So please, for the love of God, take me off your list!"

"You own a boat?" Aspen asked, amused, waving back toward Virginia as she made her way out. "Thank you!"

"Don't get pregnant!" Virginia yelled back just as Aspen passed through the double doors.

"Aspen?" Mo replied, her voice softening significantly.

"Yeppity yep. Though, I didn't do any stalking for your number this time, thank you very much."

"Ah, so Virginia did write it down," Mo said, a tinge of disappointment in her voice.

Aspen picked up on it. "You didn't want me to call?"

"No, no, that's not it. It's, uh—"

"Complicated?"

"Kind of? I don't know, I just…" Mo danced around the subject, her voice getting more and more anxious as she rambled. "I just didn't…I didn't want to bother you."

"With your phone number?"

"Uh…"

"Or the fact that you needed directions to an outdoor store?" Aspen finished. Mo sighed, signaling that Aspen was dead-on. Her excitement overflowed at being right and she squealed, "So you are going to go through with my plan! Come pick me up."

"What?"

"I'm at Dry Creek, pick me up. Periwinkle overheats something terrible when I drive to Eureka, so your Subaru will be more than adequate for our little jaunt."

"Jaunt?" Mo asked hesitantly.

"Yep. To Eureka. I know the best place with the best prices, so get your butt over here. Virginia gave me the night off, so we don't even have to rush," Aspen blurted out, hoping Mo would give in.

"Okay," Mo said. "But you don't even know what I need?"

"That's fine, we'll figure it out." Aspen grinned, listening happily to the shuffling on the other end of the line, cluing her in that Mo was getting out of bed.

* * *

"Take the next right."

Aspen clapped excitedly as the clunky, heather-gray, sheet-metal-covered warehouse rolled into view. The industrial-style building was separated evenly between two stores. The left side had plain black painted lettering across the top denoting *Blau Outdoors and More*, while the right side sported a medium-sized light-up sign that read *The Thrifty Squirrel*. Aspen watched Mo careen her head close to the steering wheel to read the signs as she maneuvered the Subaru into the parking lot.

"I'm so excited," Aspen exclaimed, bouncing in her seat.

"You don't get out much, do ya?" Mo asked grumpily.

Mo had been a terrible car buddy the entire forty-five-minute drive to Eureka. If Aspen hadn't felt so strongly about Mo being open to the plan during their beach conversation, she would one hundred percent be canceling this right now. But even grumpy and cold Mo was somehow fun, so Aspen continued to bounce in her seat as Mo parked the car next to some used campers.

"You are going to love this place."

"Eh." Mo shrugged, seeming to look past Aspen and toward the store. "Nice Winnebago."

Aspen followed suit, walking toward the Winnebago in question. It was a classic boxy model in pretty terrible condition. The exterior was yellowed and brittle from the California sun, contrasting horribly with the new tires Blau's must have installed to tempt buyers. Just looking at it made Aspen's skin crawl.

"I hate it."

"I think they're pretty cool." Mo moved to stand next to Aspen. "I've always wondered what living in one would be like. I bet it's freeing."

"If you want to be free, you'd be better off living inside your Subaru," Aspen barked, darting toward the stores and hoping Mo would follow.

"Oh."

Aspen, trying her best to block out the memories that had soured her mood, forced out a happy, "Let's go. I haven't been to Blau's in like a year."

"I assume it's not a chain?" Mo played along, allowing Aspen a tad bit of relief.

"Nope, it's family owned and operated. They have similar stock to places like REI, but without the same price tags. The best part though…" Aspen turned to get Mo's attention before pointing at the adjoining business. "The Thrifty Squirrel!"

Mo finally caught up, matching Aspen's brisk stride. "Why does a thrift store make it better?"

"You need a phone, silly. How else would I complain to Annie about how annoying you are?"

Mo let out the first chuckle of the evening, which felt like payment in full to Aspen. She couldn't control her grin as she looked both ways before crossing onto the apron of the store, pulling open the front door with ease. The taller woman walked through, and Aspen watched her slowly take in the interior. Blau's wasn't visually pleasing like Bass Pro Shops or REI, but it had everything an outdoor nerd could possibly need. Plain, busy white-and-gray commercial tile floors, forest-green walls, and mismatched ceiling tiles with fluorescent lighting defined the inside. The center of the store was chock full of clothes, separated into the usual gendered sections. The perimeter was lined with outdoor gear for fishing, hunting, camping, cycling, water sports, hiking, and more. It was basic but clean and well-stocked.

"Not what I expected." Mo's voice sounded slightly nervous. "I thought it'd be more kitschy."

"I get that. A gigantic fish tank built into the side of a faux mountain is cool, but the water bill would keep prices high. Blau's is no frills," Aspen said calmly before gently touching Mo's bare forearm, the warmth instantaneous on her palm. "What are we here for?"

"Uh…" was all Mo mustered, but she almost seemed to push her arm into Aspen's hand.

"All right, let's start with needs. What clothes do you have?"

Aspen watched Mo's face crumple in distress, so she squeezed gently, hoping it would let her know it was okay to take her time. It was obvious she was thinking about Annie, but it seemed like something else was bothering her. The more Aspen watched her struggle, the more confused she became.

"I haven't backpacked since way before Annie died...so I guess I need clothes?" Mo's weight transferred from one foot to the other. "I need as many outfits as one would need to trek to the fork in the creek."

"Which fork?"

"I don't remember the name, just that Annie preferred this one fork."

"Well..." Aspen mentally flipped through her knowledge of the dispersed camping areas of Redwood Creek, trying her best to figure out which fork an avid backpacker like Annie would love. "Does Elam Creek ring a bell?"

"No."

"44 Camp?"

"Um..."

"Bridge Creek? Tall Tall Trees?" Aspen followed up, seeing no signs of recognition from Mo's profile as she kept her eyes on the shop. "Anything past those options, like Devil's Creek at the end of the park, would be expert level to get to this time of year. The water is only just starting to go down."

"Annie loved a challenge," Mo responded wistfully, shuffling forward to touch a display with paracord bracelets hanging from it. She pulled one off a hook and inspected it before offering it up to Aspen. "Is this a need?"

Aspen chuckled, grabbing it from Mo. "Not a need at all."

"But it has a compass."

"A pretty terrible one," Aspen replied, unsnapping the plastic buckle where the compass was situated to show the metal-edged tool sheathed underneath. "These bracelets are a great way to carry extra paracord, but this metal multitool thing on the buckle sits underneath the compass, which pretty much makes the thing useless. Anyone who used it while snapped would probably walk in circles before succumbing to the elements."

"So you'd just die in style, then?" Mo asked, her voice softer now, almost playful.

"Hopefully this is made of stuff that would biodegrade with your body, but yeah, I guess if that's how you want to go out."

"No, I think I have paracord and a compass already. I'm more looking for a good map of the park."

"It's all right, I've already got one up here," Aspen said, pointing to her temple. "And a paper one in my pack. I'll get us a backpacking permit for a week or two, so we'll have time to figure it out."

Mo turned, her voice becoming hard again. "You don't have to do that, I—"

But Aspen cut her off with a raised palm, reaching forward to grab her hand and pull her toward the men's section in the rear of the store. "I'll get you where you need to go. No ifs, ands, or buts. Now, you are only gonna need three outfits, a rain jacket, and a puffer, tops."

Aspen pulled her down the middle aisle past the women's clothes, enjoying the feeling of Mo's soft fingers along her own more calloused ones. Once in the men's section, she scanned for lightweight backpacking shirts and pants, finding them rather easily. She tugged Mo there, depositing her in front of a table display of men's hiking pants in a multitude of neutral colors.

"How did you know?" Mo asked, grinning down at Aspen.

"I know what looks good on you," Aspen replied, winking. "I recommend these here. They are made to repel water, are lightweight, and the lower legs zip off so they double as shorts."

"That's useful," Mo agreed, finally dropping Aspen's hand to lean forward and grab a tan pair. She pulled them up closer to her chest, feeling the fabric carefully between the thumbs and forefingers of her hands. "I think these will do."

"Cool, pick your three outfits out. You'll also need a puffer—"

"I've got one of those, actually. A Patagonia one from forever ago, but it's still nice."

"All right, then just grab a decent lightweight rain jacket as well. I'm off to get some sports bras, because I need new ones if I am going to come with you. Which I recommend you also get if you don't have any, so meet me there once you're done," Aspen instructed, turning to walk back toward the front of the store.

"Oh, uh…" Mo hesitated.

Aspen stopped, intuitively picking up on the fact that Mo wasn't quite ready for her to walk off yet. "Got a question?"

"No, I just, uh…you said you'd come with me and uh…"

"You don't even know which fork in the creek you want to hike to, so you'll need a good guide."

"I'm not saying you aren't a good guide, I just had a particular plan in…" Mo looked like she was in agony. "Never mind."

"You sure? I don't want to overstep."

"Yeah," Mo replied, nervously wringing her hands. Aspen found the display utterly adorable. "But I could use some more help here. With shopping, I mean, if that's okay?"

"Totally." Aspen suddenly moved behind Mo. "Can I touch you?"

Mo's breath hitched ever so slightly. "Yeah."

Aspen looked down where Mo's flannel laid over her chinos, and she tugged it up and over her waist, her fingers brushing against Mo's warm, lean back. It felt amazing to touch Mo like this, so she had to focus to not allow her fingers to spread out and explore. Quickly she slid her thumbs behind the fabric, between the rear belt loops and her soft skin, flipping out the tag. "Thirty-two by thirty-two."

"Oh, I'll probably need a thirty waist. I've lost a bit of weight and I just tighten my belt a lot," Mo explained, her voice wavering just a tad.

Aspen let go, removing her hands and flattening Mo's shirt back into place with care. It had been a simple gesture in theory, but in practice it only compounded Aspen's attraction. She hovered her hands for a few more seconds before returning to the task at hand, shifting to the display to grab three black pairs of correctly sized pants. But as Aspen swiveled to offer them up to Mo, she looked down at Mo's chinos and remembered she had only seen the woman wear some shade of tan on her legs.

"Oops."

"What?" Mo asked, her face blank.

Aspen returned the pants to the display before grabbing the exact same style in a color described by the tag as Saharan Desert. "Perfect." Aspen tossed them in Mo's direction, watching the woman react at the last second to catch them. "Now, you need some shirts."

"I have some cotton—"

Aspen cut off Mo with a snort, moving toward the sweat-wicking polyester shirts a few displays down. She grabbed two medium T-shirts, both cobalt gray, and moved toward the long-sleeved ones on the next rack. "Cotton would be terrible. Poly is a far better fabric and makes a great base layer for underneath your jackets. Gray okay?"

Mo pulled the T-shirts from Aspen's arms, grunting favorably in response. Skirting through the hangers quickly, a forest-green long sleeve with neutral horizontal speckles caught her eye and she pulled it out. After a few seconds of admiring the articulated pattern, Aspen turned and pressed the shirt against Mo's chest.

After the initial shock wore off, Mo asked, "Does it look okay?"

"Yep. Brings out the green in your hazel eyes. Did Annie like to dress you?"

Mo choked out a laugh. "Actually, no. Style, in any form, wasn't really her thing. If I had told her I was struggling choosing something, she would have just struggled right along with me."

That admission made Aspen smile as she tried to picture what Annie looked like and how the two of them would have done this together. She watched a goofy smile slowly appear on Mo's face, letting her know that this was definitely the shirt. "Well, I think Annie would agree with me. So you are getting it, no exceptions."

"Yes, ma'am."

The two held an earnest stare that had affection spreading deep inside of Aspen's chest. The deep green seemed to burst out of Mo's pupils, causing the golden-brown perimeter to look like the sky behind a wondrous fireworks display. Aspen felt like she could lose herself forever in those eyes, unable to look away. So she followed her gut, reveling in the feeling. Her lower lip crept between her teeth as she watched Mo's eyes drift to her mouth. Aspen found herself wishing their lips would meet, the middle of Blau's be damned. But before she could really expand the moment, Mo turned to face the displays, severing the connection. With disappointment, Aspen kept holding the shirt up in midair, where she used to have it against Mo, before allowing it to naturally drop to her side.

"Okay, so that is three and three. I need a rain jacket now?"

"Oh yeah, right." Aspen turned toward the jackets. "They're over there."

"Am I really going to need one?" Mo asked as the pair made their way over, Aspen's mind still buzzing about the lost moment.

"Uh…" Aspen righted herself, remembering the task at hand. "Yes. You should know that you always need a layer to protect against rain. Nothing ruins the fun of hiking like being soaked to the bone and miserable."

"You're right. I have lived more than a decade in the Bay. I should know that rain is a thing."

"I prefer Marmot for a midrange, waterproof jacket," Aspen explained, scrolling quickly through the Marmot rack. She found an offering in forest green, pulling out another medium, which she figured would size best with Mo's frame. But seeing it off the rack showed that it was a quarter zip. "Shit."

"What?" Mo asked, moving closer to her to glance at the jacket.

"Quarter zips are terrible. I was hoping it was a full zip," Aspen whined before taking in more of the jacket's features. "And no pockets or hood? Someone at Marmot has lost their damn mind. Ugh, I really love the color, though."

Mo didn't respond, instead moving to another rack nearby. Aspen sighed, rehanging it before continuing to peruse. Assuming quarter zips were the new craze with men, she considered moving toward the North Face rack when a gleeful cheer from Mo had her turning around.

"Is this what you were thinking?" Mo presented another forest-green jacket displayed proudly in her hands. "Has a full zipper, hood, and more pockets than I'd ever use."

"You do have an eye for style," Aspen exclaimed, walking over to inspect the jacket. It was exactly as described, and she quickly checked that the waterproofing matched her expectations. "That's a winner. Good job, Mo."

"I just followed orders, ma'am," Mo replied jokingly, standing at attention and giving her a quick salute.

"At ease, private." Aspen played along, rolling her eyes playfully. "What else do you need?"

"Uh…food, I guess?"

"I've got that in droves. Do you have any allergies?"

"No, but maybe since it's my trip I should…" Mo's face fell from its previous happy lilt.

"No worries, my stock of backpacking meals are to die for," Aspen said. "Well, live for. Do you have shoes?"

"Yes," Mo answered, almost too quickly.

"All right…I saw some of your gear the other day so you should be good with just this. I'm sure you'd know what you're lacking otherwise. Let's go get my sports bras then skedaddle over to The Thrifty Squirrel."

"Skedaddle?" Mo questioned, but Aspen ignored her, skipping toward the women's clothing.

CHAPTER NINE

The pair paid for their purchases and safely deposited them in the trunk of Mo's car before turning to make their way toward the thrift store. She watched as Aspen gave the campers a wide berth again, her eyes firmly on the ground in front of her. Studying her a bit longer, Mo noticed how her shoulders seemed to be turned in while her gait significantly quickened, like Aspen was a toddler who was just scolded for simply existing. Mo's limited experience with Aspen had taught her that the woman was pretty lively and carefree, so this kind of behavior was stark in contrast.

Something wasn't right.

"You good?" Mo finally asked as the two reached the front doors.

"Huh?" Aspen answered, obviously distracted. When their gazes met, Mo watched Aspen's face brighten in mere seconds, like a switch was flipped. "Yeah, totally. I'm just laser focused."

"On getting a phone?" Mo chuckled, pulling open the door for her, letting go of her previous concern. "It's just a phone."

"No, it's Annie's phone," Aspen replied warmly. "It has to be special."

Mo hummed in agreement, even as her chest tightened at the comment. She was truly torn. On one hand, it excited her to get to know Aspen in this way. A part of her was enjoying the woman's presence, her heart, and this adventure she had generously planned. But a different part, the part she had trusted for the past four years, was dreading Aspen's involvement. Mo had lied to this woman, and it had snowballed into a trip that she was wholly unprepared for.

"Hey, are you okay?" Aspen's soft voice broke through.

Mo blinked, smiling instinctively before assuring Aspen, "Yeah, sorry. I got lost in thought there."

"I noticed." Aspen squeezed her forearm before nodding toward the left side of the store. "I know it's not much, but the home goods are over there. Their clothes selection is eh, but they always have the most interesting odds and ends."

Mo moved in that direction, stuffing her hands into her pants anxiously. She finally looked around, taking in the rather cold and bland thrift store. The Thrifty Squirrel was as bare bones as Blau's, but instead of outdoor goods, Mo mostly found racks and racks of clothes. Taller shelves stuffed full of housewares, electronics, and other assorted knickknacks lined the left side of the store, indicating Aspen was correct in leading them there. A silence had fallen between the pair as they entered the section. Mo followed her down the last aisle, watching as Aspen would reach out to touch random items even as she glided toward the back. Mo enjoyed watching Aspen. Her movements seemed calculated yet careless in the same motion, a conundrum that just seemed to fit Aspen perfectly.

Before Mo could compute that her companion had come to a stop, Aspen was shoving an object in her face with glee.

"Frog phone!"

"A what?" Mo asked, startled by her sudden movements. Looking down, she found that Aspen was showing her a small desktop phone, very much shaped like a classic green and white frog. "That is indeed a frog."

"It's so cute," Aspen exclaimed in a cutesy voice, manipulating the phone to hop in midair like a real frog. "Oh my God, I love it so much. I would one hundred percent die for this frog."

Mo looked on in amusement, finding every aspect of Aspen adorable. After watching the frog jump for a few more seconds, Mo finally noticed that it lacked a cord. She reached forward to stop Aspen's movement. "Is it cordless?"

"They weren't when I was kid," Aspen said, opening the frog's mouth to display a set of buttons between the microphone and receiver. She then closed it again, turning to show Mo its butt where the cord would connect. "It would go here, I'm pretty sure."

"Must have lost its cord. Bummer." Mo sighed, watching as Aspen continued to absentmindedly play with the phone, opening and closing it as she regarded it thoughtfully. "I didn't even know they were a thing."

"You know," Aspen began, her voice more low and even. "When I was kid, I once got invited to a popular girl's house for her birthday. I'd never been allowed to go to anyone's house before, and I was over the moon that I'd even been invited. Thankfully, I was at Janice's at the time, and she was sweet enough to let me go. The girl's name was…Mary, I think? It doesn't matter, whatever her name was, she had one of these phones in her bedroom."

"In her bedroom? Damn, fancy."

"I know, right?" Aspen paused for a few moments before continuing, "All the girls thought I was so weird because I was obsessed with the phone. I named it, petted it, and even begged Mary to go to her neighbor's house and call, just so I could answer it. I wasn't invited back."

Mo reached forward, rubbing the side of Aspen's shoulder gently. "Kids are mean."

Aspen pulled away, laughing it off. "No, they didn't know better. I'm sure anyone would have found it weird. I was a strange kid."

"What did you name the frog?" Mo asked, noticing her deflection.

"Frog."

"You weren't a strange kid at all." Mo laughed. "Just unimaginative."

"Hey!" Aspen balked, pushing Mo's shoulder slightly with the frog. "Rude."

Mo shrugged but grinned deviously anyway before saying, "As lovely as Frog is, I don't think they will make a good wind phone. Kinda small, and it doesn't have a base."

Aspen nodded in agreement, giving the phone one more pat before depositing it back on the shelf. "Then let's keep looking. They actually have a decent amount of phones littered through all this crap."

They split from each other, sifting through all the random electronic goods to find the perfect phone. Mo began her search with a half-decent amount of drive, but after finding her fifth basic early-2000s cordless phone with base, she found herself becoming agitated.

"We might have to force Frog to be a tree frog. I can't find anything more than these stupid, boring cordless phones," Mo complained, moving a printer to peer behind it.

"Gotta have patience to pick," Aspen reminded Mo from her knees as she sorted through some larger stuff on the bottom rack. "Ooh, jackpot!"

Mo didn't waste time, moving to kneel next to Aspen as she pulled a see-through plastic wall phone from the depths of the shelving. Aspen flipped to sitting crisscrossed on the ground, already pressing each of the numbered buttons with fervor.

"Looks pretty sturdy," Mo commented, moving to kneel on one knee as she scrutinized the prize. It was a curved phone, with a button-laden cradle, and had minimal yellowing on the clear plastic surround. It even had a clear spiral cord, something Mo was sure was rare. Fun, indeed, but there was something off about it. "I don't know."

"Well," Aspen said, turning the phone to study the back. "It has slots to mount."

"Okay," Mo responded flatly, still looking at the phone as Aspen played with it.

"It's not Annie's vibe, is it?" Aspen finally asked, looking up at her curiously.

The ease at which Aspen could read her was daunting. But even as Mo stood, uncomfortable under the woman's keen gaze, she agreed, "No, it's not."

"No worries, then." Aspen placed it back on the shelf. "We will keep looking."

Instead of continuing the hunt, Mo stood there silently and watched Aspen perform her calculated tornado search of the lower shelves. At this point, she was more excited to see Aspen's happy reactions than she was for the phone itself. As Aspen crab-walked to the next cluster of shelves, Mo caught a glimpse of blaze orange behind a black microwave, piquing her interest. She knelt down, sliding the microwave to the right, which knocked a bunch of things over onto Aspen's hands.

"Avalanche!" Aspen giggled, stopping her search to put everything right side up. "I already searched through there—"

"Wait, I think I found something you missed," Mo said, leaning all the way against the shelving to reach the cold plastic of the item she had spotted. It definitely felt curved like a phone, so she pulled it out and sat back on the ground in the same motion.

It was the ugliest phone Mo had ever laid eyes on.

The blaze-orange base was wide, boxy, and bland. It had a stainless steel hang-up cradle for the receiver and a simple orange disk in the center that sported the slightly faded numbers. A clear but time-yellowed rotary dial was mounted over the top with finger holes stamped out over each number. In the center of it all was a removable piece of paper covered by a plastic disk that had the area code and emergency numbers typed out in Courier font. The tightly coiled cord was dirty and dusty from the shelf but was just as ugly an orange as the rest of the phone. Mo jiggled the cradle a few times before removing the receiver itself, noting how grimy the blaze-orange plastic felt in her hands. It was a classic receiver, boring in every way, and as Mo held it up to examine it closer, it felt as uncomfortable as it looked.

"Is this it?" Aspen politely asked, sitting down across from Mo.

"Annie's favorite color was orange," Mo began, unable to control her smile as she thought about her late wife's obsession with the color. "If she'd have been allowed, and I say that only because the limits of society are what stopped her, she'd have bought everything in orange. I mean, she drove us to our first date in her orange Ford Fiesta. The bridal party on her side had accents of orange in their clothes—in the flowers even. Her touring microphone had an orange surround. Our house was littered with random pops of orange. A chair here, a serving bowl there, an accent wall in our bedroom. I think if she'd have found a backpacking pack that fit her in blaze orange, she would've bought it so fast."

Mo looked up to a fully focused Aspen, who nodded silently for her to continue.

"I used to joke that in order for her to enter her final form she needed to get a part-time job at Home Depot."

Aspen laughed heartily. "The double meaning in that…"

"Orange is so ugly." Mo chuckled too, placing the receiver back on the cradle. "But it was her."

Silence fell on the pair as Mo continued to peruse the phone, her eyes burning as she kept thinking about how much Annie would have loved this thing.

"May I check to see if it'll work?" Aspen's voice was soft, reverent.

Mo didn't reply, instead handing it over and watching silently as Aspen did her thing. After a few moments, Mo said, "Opal told me to get something truly ugly. I think we found it."

"Opal?"

"My friend, well, she was Annie's friend too. She owns a killer tattoo shop back in Palo Alto. She's my best friend, Bud's, wife."

"Okay."

"Opal and Annie were close. Very close. I called her about the plan, and her only request was for the phone to be super ugly."

"Well, this one definitely fits the bill," Aspen agreed, handing the phone back.

"Yeah?"

"Yep. Opal sounds like a great friend, and judging by your reaction, this is meant to be Annie's phone." Aspen grinned warmly, her gaze spreading affection through Mo's chest. "Let's go pay."

"Okay," Mo agreed, standing to her feet before reaching down to help Aspen up.

She nestled the phone close to her chest and began walking toward the front counter. Aspen barely trailed behind, letting Mo set the pace.

"I hope I can do this," Mo said, surprised that she let it slip out, stopping to allow Aspen to cross in front of her.

"Of course you can. The weather is looking pretty good starting next week, so let's meet up Monday morning. I'm thinking about seven a.m. sharp, at your cabin. I'll call and ask Betty to meet us at the trailhead and we will confirm the install and itinerary. It's mostly approved, but Betty wants to meet you personally."

"Really?"

"Yeah. She's a great lady, don't stress it. Just be on your A-game," Aspen explained happily, stopping right before the queue for the register. "Sounds good?"

Mo hesitated before agreeing, "Yeah."

"Awesome." Aspen clapped. "Oh, and, Mo?"

"Yes?"

"On the trip, do you think you could tell me more about Annie?"

"What?" A quick pain shot through Mo's stomach as she considered the question. "Why?"

Aspen shrugged, making her way to the register. "No reason."

Mo didn't question her, deciding it was easier to just wander confused behind her.

* * *

Nothing like a weekend alone for Mo to fret about Aspen yet again. Her Saturday was spent sleeping, meandering, and anxiously reconsidering her choices. Her mood would swing in every different direction like a pendulum that refused to stick to the rules of magnetism. Every time she would begin to wonder about what it would be like to give in to her affection for Aspen, her mind would find some reason to shut it down. But even so, here Mo was, packing Annie's gear into the pack as best she knew how, mulling over her array of options.

"Maybe," Mo muttered aloud to no one, stopping her movements, and she thought seriously about driving back to Blau's to find last-minute backpacking food. "I could go without her…"

But she quickly thought twice about that, knowing Aspen would probably hike out and find her. Having that kind of attention would be beyond embarrassing for Mo, especially if she found herself in a pickle out in the woods. The wind phone idea was intriguing enough to give part of her hope, making the rest of the plan worth actual consideration. But the more she mulled over her options, the more obvious it was that she would have to endure Aspen, which excited and frustrated her all the same. A darker thought entered her mind, one where she went out somewhere else with no food at all.

Before that could fully manifest, though, her cell phone's ringer brought her back into the present. With a lean she looked at the face of her phone on her bed, Bud's name and laughing picture brightly displayed. Mo promptly ignored it, going back to shoving the things Opal had recommended inside the large backpack. Mo had separated out what she was told she wouldn't need, setting those items neatly in front of the old television. The ringing from her phone stopped for mere seconds before beginning again, causing Mo to whine, "Please, Bud, not now."

She ignored him again, instead moving to fill her water bladder from the kitchen faucet. The phone ceased to ring again as she turned off the water, cradling the bladder just so in order to close off the top. Right as she cinched the rod over the folded edge, her phone rang yet again. Something snapped inside of her, causing her to angrily stomp toward her bed.

"What?" Mo demanded, answering her phone quickly.

"So you are okay," Bud replied, his voice riddled with worry. "I was telling Opal that I might need to call local authorities to check in on you."

Mo took in a deep breath, releasing the air slowly from her lungs before stating as calmly as she could muster, "Sorry, Bud, I've been busy."

"With what?"

"Packing." Mo was curt, moving back into the kitchen to grab the bladder she had left behind. She moved her focus to reinstalling the hydration hose to the feeder outlet.

"You're coming home?" he responded gleefully, steamrolling any reply Mo had. "Oh thank the Lord Jesus Christ and all that bullshit, I've been worried sick. Opal keeps telling me to give you space and all, but I just knew you'd be up there all sad and shit. And you would 'member how much we mean to you and you'd be back down here in no time."

Mo closed her eyes, guilt mixing with her annoyance. Crushing Bud's usual overextensions was difficult for her on a good day, let alone one when she'd been feeling particularly down. "I'm not packing to come back to Palo Alto, Bud."

"Huh? Then what in the Sam Hell are you packing for?"

"The backpacking trip," Mo reminded him, moving back to slide the bladder into its pouch, feeding the tube around and up to where she could use it easily. "Remember the video call with you and Opal?"

"Aw shit, Imogen, all I 'member was you talking about some woman you met up there. I usually leave the hiking rigmarole to my beautiful wife," Bud explained, his voice returning to the worried lilt. "I thought y'all would go on a few hikes, get to know each other intimately, and you'd come on back with a new sense of life."

That comment went a little too far for Mo.

"Bud," Mo seethed, her frustration growing at his lack of tact. "You are treading on thin ice."

A silence stretched between them, and Mo continued her task, hoping Bud would apologize and find an excuse to hang up. Before she could find one of her own, she heard a long, sad sigh, followed by Bud clearing his throat.

"Opal likes to tell me I'm like a bull in a china shop."

"Mm-hmm," Mo hummed, her anger sitting painfully behind her eyes.

"Did I tell you that she tattooed a celebrity a few days back?" His high-pitched tone showed his nervous need to avoid. "I'm so damn proud of her."

"Yep."

"Uh-huh."

"Must be nice."

Bud didn't respond immediately, another awkward silence filling the space before he finally said, "I went too far again, didn't I?"

"Yeah."

"I'm sorry, I just..." Bud sucked in a breath. "I'm sorry."

Mo rolled her eyes, moving to sit on the couch. "It's fine."

"You sure I can't come get ya?"

"No, Bud, I need space."

"All right," Bud said, finally accepting the awkwardness. "But, uh...maybe give that lady a chance. For me. If ya wanna, ya know?"

For all Bud didn't know or pushed Mo to open up about, there were just some things he could say to her where no argument was created in their wake.

"I'm sorry, Bud. I'm just really—" Mo caught herself, considering her next words carefully. "I'll be fine."

"I'm not going to say 'you better be' or nothing like that, I just uh—" Bud coughed. "I love you a whole damn ton."

"I know."

"And you love me too?"

"I do."

"Alrighty then, I'll cut this off before I get in any more hot water. Be safe, and I'm sorry I keep pushing ya," Bud said sincerely. "Also..."

"Yeah?"

"Annie wouldn't want ya to suffer like this."

"Bye." Mo ended the call, tossing her phone onto the cushion next to her before sliding her face into her palms, her fingers covering her eyes just as tears began to form.

CHAPTER TEN

"Six thirty is an early start, so I really appreciate the ride."

"Anything for my second-favorite lady," Salvador responded kindly, his smile wide underneath his thick mustache. "Do you know the address?"

Aspen climbed into the passenger seat of Salvador's old truck, closing the door with fervor. As she pulled the seat belt over herself and locked it into place, she said, "No need, I can tell you how to get there. Just drive like you're going to the bar."

"Down 101 it is." He cranked the steering wheel shifter into reverse, rapidly pulling out of Aspen's driveway. "You oughta replace the roof soon, sweetheart. It's liable to leak next rainy season. Or even worse, fall in on you."

Aspen groaned, leaning her head back on the head rest and closing her eyes in one swift motion.

"I ain't trying to nag ya or nothing. Just a suggestion."

"I know. I think I just put off the cabin's issues so easily," Aspen confessed, knowing full well Salvador was right about the roof. "Because it was so cheap, you know? It's not a mover or a shaker, but it stands."

"You could buy our house in town…" Salvador said an octave higher, his voice lilting to incur favor from her.

"And what? Rent out the cabin? That's a lot of money, work, and time that I don't have, Sal."

"Ginny and I will help. Or you could sell that beaten-up pile of redwood to Odessa—"

"Or to Candy," Aspen corrected, her bias obvious. "The Pearsons aren't too fond of me."

"Yeah, Mr. Pearson has some sort of grudge against you." Salvador laughed, his tone more amused than upset. "Just the other day he was talking about you at the store and this tall woman put him in his place. She walked right up to the counter and saw through all his bullshit, like she had been there watching him since the day he was born. I thought I was watching one of Ginny's soaps."

"*Pretty Little Liars* isn't a soap opera." Aspen giggled. "And the tall woman, was she a local?"

"Naw, she was about your age, and you are the only young local I know of. Short hair, thin as all get out, grumpy disposition. Plus, it looked like she bats for your team, if you know what I mean." Salvador looked over at her quickly, waggling his eyebrows. "Bar is coming up."

"Turn left after the bridge," Aspen instructed, feeling tingly warmth spreading down her neck and arms at the idea that maybe Mo was the woman who had stood up for her. "I think that was Mo. She's also the woman you are dropping me off with for this backpacking trip."

"Mo?"

"Yeah, short for Imogen."

"Imogen got a last name?" Salvador's tone deepened as the truck rolled by the bar. "Social security number?"

Aspen laughed deeply. "She's harmless, I promise."

"I gotta protect my baby," Salvador replied, turning left after the bridge. "I didn't do a goddamn thing about Kyle, and look how that turned out."

Aspen's stomach dropped a tad, and she turned to see a rather serious expression on Salvador's face. She reached out and touched his shoulder lightly before reminding him, "I think my lesbianism killed that more than—"

"Don't," Salvador cut her off, slowing the truck significantly. "Kyle was a sorry excuse for a human. It doesn't matter if your wife is a lesbian, you don't treat her like the mud under your boot."

As they reached the sign for the horse trail, Salvador pulled the truck over to the side of the road, throwing it into park before turning to meet Aspen's concerned gaze. He studied her for a few moments, rubbing his mustache with his thumb and forefinger as his lip trembled. After loudly swallowing what could have been his pride, he said, "I'm so damn proud of you."

Aspen was rendered speechless. Her left hand instinctively went to her chest as bittersweet emotion puddled behind her eyes, one compliment away from cascading out as tears.

"I've seen your life, most of it, at least, and seeing you come into your own after everything your parents and Kyle put you through..." Salvador's voice tapered off, his lips turned down as he struggled to complete his thoughts. "Janice would be proud. Virginia is proud. I'm proud. They have nothing on you, and I just...I wanna make sure that anyone you hang around is worth your time."

"Thank you." Aspen reached out and took Salvador's hands, only barely keeping the tears at bay. She watched a few fall down his tan cheeks, making their way into his mustache. She broke the air with a choked laugh, leaning forward to wipe away the newly created tear lines. "I love you, Sal."

"I love you too, sweetheart," he said, grinning again. "I went and made it weird, ya?"

"Never." Aspen turned to look back at the road. "Her cabin is there, to the left."

He resituated himself, getting the truck back onto the road. "But for real, if she tries anything unsavory, you let me know."

"You'll be the first one to know. Well, after Betty, of course," Aspen assured him, her body abuzz with emotion now.

"Betty is on her case?" He turned into Mo's driveway, slowly moving to park behind her Subaru, which had its rear hatch open. "Well, no need for me, then."

"Thanks for the ride and…" Aspen grinned. "You know."

"I know." Salvador winked before nodding toward the truck bed. "Now grab your gear and have a safe trip. I'll keep Virginia in line while you're gone."

Aspen popped open the door and slid to the ground, turning to pull her pack and hiking poles from the bed.

"Hey?"

"Yeah," Aspen replied as she carefully placed her pack on the ground.

"I just want you to be happy. Wherever, whenever, whoever. All right?"

"All right."

"Love ya, Aspen."

"I love you too," she replied earnestly, closing the door before lifting her pack by the handle and backing away, allowing Salvador to reverse up the driveway. Mo came ambling out with her own pack on her back as Salvador honked, almost sending the taller woman off the porch in surprise.

"Sal dropped me off," Aspen explained with a newfound lightness, moving to put her stuff into the rear of the Subaru. "Are you ready for an adventure?"

"I'd rather a cappuccino from Blue Bottle, but beggars can't be choosers, huh?" Mo said, walking awkwardly toward Aspen.

Aspen immediately picked up that Mo's mood was farther south than its usual grouchiness, instantly dimming some of the confidence Sal had raised up. Aspen tried to press past it, putting on her largest smile before trotting over to help pull Mo's pack off her back to place in the Subaru. "Got everything?"

Mo only responded with an affirming groan, leaving Aspen with the pack and returning to the door to fling her flip-flops back inside before grabbing a pair of ankle-high hiking boots, blaze-orange laces catching Aspen's eyes. Mo dropped to sit on the uppermost step, slugging them on like a child made to wear rain boots on the day after a huge storm. Aspen ignored the obvious question, instead asking something a little safer. "Do you have any Crocs, by chance?"

Mo, in the middle of lacing, dramatically rolled her head up to catch Aspen's eyes. "Yeah."

"Are they in your pack?"

"No," Mo said curtly, going back to lacing, her fingers pulling in tight, rough movements.

"Can you grab them?"

Mo looked up and stared for a few seconds before nodding, returning to finish her task. Once she was done, Mo stood and trundled back into the cabin. Aspen awkwardly rolled back and forth on the balls of her feet, playing absentmindedly with the edge of her dark-blue puffer. After a few more empty moments, Mo returned with orange Crocs in hand, slamming her cabin door closed. She watched Mo quickly lock it and smiled her best smile as Mo made her way to the Subaru.

"Awesome!"

"Why?" Mo asked as they both climbed inside, a chill running down Aspen's spine due to the cool morning air caught in the vehicle.

"For hiking the creek," Aspen explained. "I had an extra pair at the bar if you didn't have any. Don't wanna get our boots wet when we need to make crossings and stuff."

"Oh."

"Yep."

Aspen watched Mo stare at the steering wheel, her hand hovering over the start button. Just as the moment stretched on long enough for Aspen to feel brave and ask why they weren't moving, Mo hit the button, starting the Outback. Once on the road, Aspen decided to fill the air with an easy, "The new clothes look great on you."

Mo gave her another positive grunt, feeding Aspen's anxiety.

"Take a right and follow 101 north. Then take a right on Bald Hills road."

Mo drove faster than Aspen remembered her doing on their ride to Eureka, reaching the turn quickly. She pointed it out, and Mo took the right at the last possible moment, causing Aspen to grasp the handle above the door. The Subaru skidded, tires squealing on the last bit of asphalt as it barely made it onto the dirt road safely. Looking worriedly between Mo and the road, Aspen decided it was best to just keep silent and hopeful instead of facing the regret that was creeping up in her.

"Next right is the trailhead parking, unless you wanted—" Aspen instructed as Mo took the turn, pulling into a tree-covered parking lot that consisted of twelve or so paved spots. "To walk the Lady Bird Johnson Trail."

"Not really."

The white park ranger truck was tucked in the back by the access road, and Aspen was happy to see Caroline leaning against the front, drinking timidly from her Nalgene.

"You can park next to the ranger truck."

But as they pulled closer, Caroline waved them toward the gated entrance of the access road, and Mo obliged. Aspen rolled down her window as they slowed to a stop, greeting Caroline enthusiastically. "Morning!"

"Good morning," Caroline replied, obviously not fully awake yet. "Betty wants you two to park down by the maintenance shed."

"Oh?" Aspen replied, confused.

"Yeah, this trailhead has more smash-and-grabs than Tall Tall Trees," Caroline said with a yawn. "I'll open it up and you can drive on through. Betty is down at the shed. You can't miss it."

"Okay, thanks, Caroline."

"Yeah, thanks," Mo added, her voice still low and terse.

Caroline moved to unlatch the gate, walking it back to open up the road. Once she was fully out of the way, Mo drove past the ranger and down the hill, curving around thickets and clumps of common deciduous trees. At the bottom of the curve sat a decently sized shed made from redwood, the front barn door already swung out. Mo pulled into an obvious space next to the shed, parking and turning off the car without much fanfare. The sour mood of the car was too much for Aspen, so she jumped out and trotted toward the open door.

"Betty?" Aspen called out as she rounded the corner, the darkness of the shed taking her eyes a bit to adjust to.

"I'll be out in a second," the high-pitched and brisk voice of Betty returned, bringing a small smile to Aspen's face.

"No rush," Aspen responded, looking back toward the car where Mo still sat. "Seems like we have time."

After a few small clatters and clangs, Betty emerged from the darkness, a small green box and hammer in her hands. "Good morning, Aspen."

"Morning," Aspen sang back, leaning down to hug the woman.

Betty Kellog, barely over five feet on a good day, hugged her back tightly before releasing her. Aspen noticed her straight black hair was in a braided bun today, contrasting nicely with her lightly golden pale skin. Her slightly wrinkled skin and random gray hairs lied to newcomers, barely letting on that she was proudly in her early eighties and going strong. Aspen swore the ranger outfit was sewn onto Betty years ago, since she had never seen her not wearing it. It was her daily decision on whether to wear the campaign hat that denoted the level of professionalism she wanted to exude on any particular day. Betty was one of Aspen's heroes, and not even Mo's mood could ruin a cherished interaction.

"I've been thinking," Betty began in her usual business voice.

"Good thoughts, I hope."

"About the wind phone in particular."

Worry flooded Aspen, and she looked toward Mo's direction, noticing the woman was now fiddling around in her pack by the trunk. If they couldn't install the phone, would Mo even want to continue the trip with her?

"I think that it's the monument I've been looking for," Betty continued, relieving Aspen's anxiety instantly. "I've told Chuck and Ben that I had more things to accomplish before retirement, and well, I've not quite been known for community outreach."

"That might be true," Aspen admitted. "But you've kept everyone together and the park maintained, even with not much in the way of facilities or staff."

Betty nodded in agreement. "Yeah, it's never been easy. I had to cut down on events and engagement, which was fine back in the day because people were amazed enough with tall trees. But nowadays, people want something more."

"Yeah."

Betty turned, pointing the hammer in Mo's direction. "That her?"

"Yep."

"Wind phone idea hers or yours?"

"Mine," Aspen said, her eyes firmly on Mo, who was putting on her new jacket. "But she is the inspiration for it."

"I think it's a good idea. A great idea, even. I'd say putting it near the Tall Tall Trees trail would be best—"

"Huh-uh," Aspen cut her off but kept her gaze fixed on Mo. "I'd prefer it be an adventure. Like maybe one of the forks past Bridge Creek?"

"Hmm. Make it an actual hike, huh?"

"Yeah." Aspen finally turned to face Betty again. "I can maintain it, even if I have to get permission to use an access road. It's just a phone on a tree, it shouldn't cause much in the way of disturbance. And if it catches on, we can place a marker on maps for dispersed campers to visit it. Maybe even build it a shelter of sorts? Nothing too drastic."

"Bridge Creek is six or so hours of straight hiking from here, not even an hour or two from Tall Tall Trees if you are experienced. Maybe make it one of the farther creek forks? Especially since we adjusted and opened more dispersed camping south of 44 Camp."

"I planned for a week or two of backpacking," Aspen explained. "Since she's not as experienced, I'm thinking of maybe backpacking as far down as Devil's Creek, going up into a few groves, and not going my usual breakneck speed."

"Shouldn't take more than a week unless you really lollygag," Betty said evenly. "Here."

Aspen watched as Betty held out the hammer and small cardboard box. She took them easily, letting the weight of the hammer drop to her side. "Tree nails?"

"Yes, ma'am," Betty confirmed. "No redwoods. Make sure the chosen tree is healthy and easily accessible. Take lots of pictures, if you can. That way I can get Caroline to make a slideshow for the bigwigs. They love slideshows."

"Thank you, Betty. I am so excited."

"Me too, actually. I might use it after all is said and done. Now…" Betty turned fully toward Mo, who was now quietly sitting on her tailgate. "I need to approve a backpacking permit."

Aspen turned to look at Mo, who was fiddling with a small object, a pained expression painted across her features. This part scared her. Aspen went to stop Betty to explain, but she was too quick, already marching over to Mo with purpose, so Aspen took charge in order to soften what would be Betty's grittier introduction. "Mo! This is Betty, the park ranger I was telling you about."

Mo didn't stand, only turning to nod in Betty's direction before holding out a weak hand to shake. "Mo Reeves."

"Ranger Kellog," Betty replied formally. "Do you have experience?"

"Uh…uh, well," Mo stuttered, shoving whatever she had just been messing with into her front pocket. "Yeah. Not as much as Aspen, but yeah."

"Got water filtration?"

"Uh…" Mo looked to Aspen, who nodded. "Yep."

"Food?"

"Aspen is bringing it."

"Bear vault?"

"Bears need vaults?" Mo tilted her head, confusion obvious.

"Trick question. I know Aspen has the food," Betty teased. "Are you a serial killer?"

"Not in this life, but maybe in a past one."

That reply got a small lip twitch out of Betty, and Aspen relaxed, knowing the trip would continue as scheduled.

"I'll risk it." Betty swiveled toward Aspen. "Think you could scout a good place for the memorial to that family from last season?"

"Two birds, one stone," Aspen said.

"I'm satisfied. You have your permit. Two weeks max. Call me after you both get back, and we will meet to discuss and look at the pictures," Betty finished, her short legs already moving her toward the parking lot. But just as she passed Mo, she turned and reminded her, "Get Aspen killed, and I'll send you to your maker myself."

"Yes, ma'am," Mo agreed, watching as Betty made her way up the hill. "Wow."

"You did it," Aspen congratulated Mo, walking forward to squeeze her arm before storing the hammer and nails in her pack. "All we have left is the hike. Got the phone?"

Mo turned and reached over her pack, grabbing the phone from the car. "Yeah, I didn't have room in my bag."

"I can hang it off my pack, if you'd like," Aspen offered, her lower lip subconsciously sliding between her teeth as she watched Mo's reaction.

"Okay." Mo placed the phone next to Aspen. "Doesn't need to work, I guess."

"Oh, it'll work," Aspen replied happily, easily stringing some paracord through the mounting holes and to the rear of her pack, making sure to use one of her better knots.

Mo scoffed loudly, lifting her pack to a sitting position before maneuvering herself in front of it. The noise was almost painful for Aspen, reminding her all too well of her time before Orick. Before she only had Virginia, Salvador, and the trees. She rolled her shoulders in an attempt to shrug it off, but she kept her eyes on Mo even when she knew she should be getting ready to go.

She watched as Mo adjusted the pack's straps before attempting to put it on, her hands dancing around the buckles and snaps in confusion. Aspen held herself back from correcting her, still feeling the frustration from being brushed aside all morning. Mo's lanky arms were twisted in weird directions as she leaned backward to slide her pack over her shoulders and onto her back. Aspen thought Mo looked more like a gangly dog adjusting to booties than a decently experienced hiker. The pack was sitting entirely too high on Mo's shoulders, looking more like a weird growth than a bag. She had to hold herself back from helping as Mo completely ignored the waist strap, instead only snapping the chest one.

"What?" the taller woman gruffed, annoyed confusion all over her face.

"Nothing." Aspen smiled tightly, reaching to properly put her on her own pack. As she worked her own straps in the correct process, Mo wandered back and forth while constantly adjusting the pack. Once the weight was properly distributed to her hips instead of upper back, Aspen grabbed her hiking poles from the side strap and engaged them to the proper height.

"Ready?" Mo asked impatiently, rolling her shoulders in discomfort.

Aspen wanted to help her—she really did—but this was a lesson Mo was going to learn the hard way.

CHAPTER ELEVEN

"Last chance for Lady Bird Johnson Grove!"

Mo didn't reply, instead running her thumbs under the edges of her shoulder straps in a downward motion, frustrated that they were already digging in under the weight of her pack. So far, the pair had only hiked back up to the main parking lot and then down from the trailhead to the edge of the creek, passing easily over a small brook. It was less than half of a mile, so why did her back already hurt? There weren't any crazy elevation changes, and the path itself was flat and well maintained. It was downright irritating.

Beautiful and spirited Aspen, however, was humming an unknown melody, happily hiking along like she wasn't also weighed down by a ginormous pack. Mo desperately wanted to demand why it was so easy for her. How was she not also grimacing in pain? But that would probably mean she would also have to admit her lie to Aspen—which she wasn't in the mood to endure. She had barely found the spoons to get out of bed this morning, let alone deal with whatever judgment Aspen might have for her fib.

A fib Mo didn't even have to create.

"Hold on," Aspen stage-whispered suddenly, stopping quickly in front of Mo. "Look."

Mo, feeling shooting pain in the arches of her feet at the abrupt halt, followed Aspen's pointed finger to the edge of Redwood Creek, studying the rocks for whatever she was pointing out. "What?"

"It's a bird."

"A bird?" Mo couldn't help but scoff, rolling her shoulders in pain.

"An American Dipper," Aspen replied quietly, her excitement evident. "The small, darkish gray, and pudgy bird there by the driftwood and large rock."

Mo used those clues and scanned the water's edge, finally spotting the bird, which was no bigger than a robin. It was standing in the moving water of the creek, submerging its head for a few seconds before popping back up, the water rolling on and off its plumage with each swift movement. She watched it dip in and out for a few moments, noticing how skilled it was at diving, like if a songbird was raised by ducks. It was then Mo realized that this was the first time she had looked somewhere other than at her shoes since she had parked the car.

"They aren't super common," Aspen said, breaking the silence. "I see one maybe once or twice a summer season, if that."

A half-assed "Cool" was all Mo could add, and Aspen cleared her throat, adding punctuation to her feeble attempt.

"All right, let's let them hunt." Aspen sighed, the joy from her voice totally gone. "We should follow the trail for most of today—the creek level is only now starting to drop. I'm thinking we should take a quick side quest in a little bit, up one of the little-known overgrown offshoot trails. I wanna show you some of the more unseen parts of the Ladybird Grove that have been cut off by wildfires in the past."

Mo only nodded, adjusting her pack for the millionth time before finally looking around. The shorter, more windblown coastal trees around Route 101 were mostly gone, leaving Mo to peruse more of an evergreen forest. The steeper elevation on either side of Redwood Creek was covered in Douglas firs, canyon oaks, and other related trees. The farther south that they followed the water flow, the taller the trees looked. The creek itself was moving at a decent pace in narrow sections, with larger pools of flat water ballooning out at the wider edges. The signature smooth, water-tumbled stones littered every surface near and around the creek, allowing for only random peeks at dark-tan sand. It was easy to tell where the water had been at its fullest, and Mo felt comfort in knowing the trail ran along the creek, making getting lost rather difficult.

"Wanna go for a cool morning dip?" Aspen said, pulling Mo back into the present.

"Are you crazy?" Mo replied, not sure if Aspen was joking. Her mood had not been lightened by the beautiful scenery. "It looks so cold."

"Alrighty then." Aspen put her hands up in surrender, nodding slightly toward the trail. "Let's get to the edge of that grove, I guess."

Their forward movement from here on out was slow going. Aspen had decided to stop leading, instead moving to walk behind Mo. Every so often, Mo would stop and look to Aspen for direction, and the woman would just point encouragingly toward the trail. This gesture caused Mo's annoyance levels to rise. She took to stomping forward angrily, doing her best to figure out the reason why Aspen would decide to do this. Was this some kind of test? Did Mo not understand some rule of backpacking?

"Can I say something?" Mo finally asked, her voice dripping with indignation.

"Judging by your tone"—Aspen's voice was weary—"you don't need my permission."

"Why the fuck am I leading?"

"Were you ever a Girl Scout?"

"Huh?" It felt like Aspen wasn't taking this seriously, so Mo turned to shoot her a dirty look, resentment almost bubbling over. "Do I look like a Girl Scout?"

"Boy Scout, then?"

"Ha ha, very funny," Mo mocked. "No. I played guitar. Inside. Like a normal kid." She kicked a rock, her heel sliding down a small divot in the trail, causing her to almost lose her balance. "Shit!"

Aspen reached out, grasping her pack and elbow firmly. "Are you okay?"

"Yes," Mo snapped, pulling away. "What are you getting at?"

"Well, I was taught by a group of Girl Scouts to let the slowest member of the group walk in the front." Aspen smiled, gesturing for Mo to continue walking. "That way, they set the pace and no one is left behind."

Mo breathed in deeply, flexing her tired feet and throbbing lower back before returning to the trail. "I wish you'd left me behind."

"Do you now?"

"Yeah. I really do."

"That's not really a good idea…"

"Yeah, well, neither is butting into a depressed woman's life. But you had no problem doing that."

The sentence was out of Mo's mouth before her filter could catch it. The regret was instantaneous, but her pride kept her from turning around and seeing the aftermath of her words. Punishment seemed to be the goal of this trip, and Mo was speed-running to the end.

* * *

The better part of the next two hours were spent in silence. Mo would stop frequently to remove her pack, drink hastily from the extra water bottle on the side, and sit on a stump or log to rest. Of all of those stops, only once did Aspen follow suit. Otherwise, she would stand with her pack firmly on, sipping from her hydration tube, staring solemnly out at the water.

The scenery only got greener the deeper they hiked, and Mo found herself ignoring all of it, instead internally whining about how much pain her body was in. It only dug her deeper into her terrible mood. Just as Mo was about to find another place to sit and ponder how to get out of this relatively unscathed, Aspen picked up the pace behind her.

"It's up there," Aspen said coldly, walking past Mo and taking a left past a decent-sized Douglas fir.

Mo followed, stopping quickly as the trail ended at shrubs. "You want me to go in there?"

The sound of Aspen's legs plowing through the brush stopped, followed by a groan. "Do you want to see some good redwoods?"

So far Mo had only spotted them from afar, since the trail exclusively followed the creek. "Okay. Can I put my pack down?"

"Fine," Aspen said, turning to walk back toward Mo. "Do you have any food in there?"

"You didn't bring the food? I thought you were the expert."

Aspen closed her eyes for a few seconds before responding with a slow and calm voice. "You misunderstand. I have the food. But…" She pointed at Mo's pack. "If there is food in there and we leave it here, then it could attract a bear or some other wildlife. I'd rather your gear not get torn to shreds on the first day."

Mo grimaced at her miscalculation, but she still held firm. "No food."

"All right. Put it against that tree," Aspen instructed, her hands falling to a zipper on the band around her hips. As Mo removed the pack and leaned it against the base of the tree, Aspen tied a blaze-orange strip of cotton around the closest branch to the trail. "A reminder, just in case."

A quick glance at her watch let Mo know it was fifteen past one, and she pulled one arm over her chest and under her bent forearm, trying urgently to stretch out her screaming muscles.

"You aren't going to remove your pack?"

"No. Bears."

"Right." Mo frowned, catching Aspen's eyes watching her stretch. "My arms and back are killing me."

Aspen's gaze softened, but she didn't comment on Mo's discomfort. Instead, she gestured with her thumb toward the thicket-covered hill. "Up we go."

It was slow moving up the hill, but Aspen had them walking in a zigzag pattern, which seemed to help. The tiny bit of Googling Mo had done when she was feeling actual motivation for this excursion had informed her that deviating from a trail was a terrible idea. But Aspen seemed competent so far, and all Mo had contributed was sass and general assholery, so she didn't comment. Her grave seemed already dug.

After twenty straight minutes of climbing and pushing through ground cover, the hill plateaued. Once through a thick wall of short trees, the brush subsided, opening to a brown leaf-litter-covered floor with a smattering of ferns. In front of the women were about five or six gigantic trees, at least forty or more feet of space between each one. Aspen stopped next to the first grouping of yellowy-green ferns and turned to look at Mo, a small smile on her face.

"Look up," Aspen said.

Mo then noticed how much wider these trees were, their deep reddish-brown color and thick, flowy bark letting her know they had reached the redwood grove Aspen promised. She then followed Aspen's advice and looked up. The trees didn't seem to stop, their height akin to most small skyscrapers. There were bushy green puffs at the tops, like erasers on the ends of pencils, blocking out bits of the sky. The view up was disorienting but breathtaking, and Mo was enthralled by how small she felt in comparison.

"This is a small grove, not normally accessed by regular hikers. Betty and some of the other rangers showed me that little path up here, and I always try to stop at least once when I hike the creek trail."

Mo was unable to find words for Aspen, her mind in a struggle between the beauty and her own turmoil. She slowly let her head drop, taking in the width of these trees instead of processing the looming guilt she felt for how she was treating Aspen. "Can I touch one?"

"Sure." Aspen pulled her pack off with ease and leaned it against a jagged stump. "That one there is about eight or nine feet in diameter."

Mo walked to the tree in question, placing a hand against the interesting grain of the reddish bark. As she studied it, she noticed how it was light brown in places where the bark was rubbed off. She slowly walked around the base, gliding her hand along the uneven bark to feel the peaks and valleys as she moved. At one point she noticed a large black spot where bark was missing. It ran up the side of the tree so high that Mo couldn't tell where it ended.

"It's black here."

"Tannic acid. The trees produce it to combat bugs," Aspen explained. "On some trees, though, the black is where a tree has been partially burned during a wildfire or some other fire incident."

Mo touched it, feeling the edges of the grain. The black didn't take away from the tree's majesty, but it definitely put its fragility into question. Or in the case of tannic acid, its ability to persevere.

"Cool."

"Yeah."

"I love it here," Mo finally said, her head on a swivel.

"You do?"

"Yeah, I think…I think Annie would have loved this too."

"From what you've told me about her so far, I'd agree. I've hiked out here just to sit, relax, and even read. It's one of the few places I feel truly at peace."

"Hmm," Mo mumbled, her mind's eye instead focused on trying to imagine a blurry image of Annie frolicking amongst the trees. But all she could muster was a feeling of regret and deep-seated sorrow. Every day it was harder to remember what she looked like.

"How does it make you feel?" Aspen asked, stepping closer.

"I feel…"

"Safe?" Aspen offered, cocking her head to the side as she watched Mo turn.

"No." Annie's image disappeared from her mind. The thick, towering trees and their enormous footprint. The shaded grove floor littered with dead leaves, only a few plants having learned to thrive. It led her to one feeling, and one feeling only. "I feel… insignificant."

"Is that good?"

"It's familiar," Mo replied honestly, catching Aspen's deep-brown eyes gazing at her. Just as her feet tried to move her toward Aspen, her brain made her turn away. "I'm kinda hungry."

"Oh." Aspen sighed. "Right. I've got some energy bars in the top pouch."

Mo nodded, choosing not to reply as she reached for the zipper.

* * *

The pair didn't talk the entire hike back to the main trail. Instead, Mo just silently observed Aspen's careful descent, the orange phone almost taunting her as it bounced around. Her muscles were on fire, and she silently wondered if she would have even made it to the grove with her pack. How did Aspen make it look so easy?

Would it have been as easy for Annie?

"Must be marshmallows in her boots," Mo mumbled grumpily under her breath, gripping a tree for dear life as she tried to safely inch down the last small vertical slide before returning to the actual trail.

"Your pack is undisturbed," Aspen announced, lifting it easily and walking it to a stump closer to Mo.

"Thanks." Mo grimaced, pain shooting from her knees down through her shins. "Are we done?"

"Are you tired?"

Mo checked her watch, the time ticking closer to four. "We've been walking all day."

"True."

"Musta been miles," Mo complained, sitting on the stump next to her pack before rolling her fists along her aching calves. "I'm old."

"It's actually less than two from the lot, though I did take you three-fourths of a mile up an incline and back." Aspen checked her own watch. "Yeah, we should move out to the creek and find a spot for the night."

"Why not here?" Mo asked snidely, the idea of carrying her pack even ten feet more sounding like the end of the world. "It's flat-ish."

"Not allowed. We can only camp along the creek bed."

"That's stupid."

"No, it's not."

"Yeah," Mo snapped, sliding her arms into the shoulder straps begrudgingly. "It is. I hate it."

Aspen didn't answer her immediately, instead pulling out a map and analyzing it. "We are in the dispersed camping zone, I just need to pick a spot. Do you want me to carry your pack?"

That offer exasperated Mo more, and she scoffed. "I got it."

"Okay." Aspen turned and trotted back to the trail, leaving Mo to struggle with her straps.

A minute later, Mo caught up and followed her off the trail toward the creek bed, stepping carefully on sand instead of the more precarious rocks.

"The bridge everyone uses is over there." Aspen pointed to their left before moving right toward a bend. "Let's go find somewhere over here so we aren't right in the way of any hiker's path."

Mo followed Aspen along the rocky bank toward the bend, silently praying for Aspen to pick a spot, any spot. Right as they rounded it, Mo heard Aspen whistle and increase her pace, finally standing on a patch of sand free of large rocks.

"I think this is as flat as we are going to get."

"Finally," Mo exclaimed, dumping her pack to the ground as quickly as she could. "My feet are on fire."

Aspen followed suit, quickly sticking her hiking poles in the sand. Mo then watched her walk around the area, moving some rocks while bringing others to the middle. Once she was satisfied, she returned to her pack and began pulling out larger covered bags. As she opened her own pack and looked inside, Mo felt her lack of knowledge coming back to bite her in the ass.

"Tents?" Mo asked as nonchalantly as she could.

"Ground cover then tent," Aspen replied, her tone tense but patient.

"Okay." Mo looked through her pack, bringing out item after item, searching for the bag with the tent. She found a small, folded tarp, a tag on it denoting ground cover, and she felt a small bit of pride poke through her nasty mood. "Ground cover."

"Put it anywhere away from the rocks but not too far out. Flat is preferable, as you will be sleeping there," Aspen explained, already putting together rods connected by string.

Mo plopped the ground cover away from her things, returning to search for the tent. After another few minutes, she became worried. The only large items in a stuff sack were her sleeping bag and some thin rectangular pad that reminded her of naps during kindergarten.

"Everything okay?" Aspen asked, her deep-blue tent already taken shape.

"My tent..." Mo stated in annoyance, standing to her full height. "I don't understand."

Aspen slid the blue cover over her tent before strolling over toward Mo, asking tentatively, "Did you pack it?"

"Do I look stupid to you?" Mo immediately snarled, her chest now throbbing along with her tired muscles.

"Mo," Aspen warned lowly, slinking to her knees to look through her things. After careful inspection, she looked back up. "Yeah, it looks like you forgot—"

"This is your fault!" Mo yelled, her frustration finally reaching its boiling point. "You made me go on this stupid trip, to hang that stupid phone, to talk to my stupid wife."

Aspen kept her focus on the ground, her arms pulling in across her chest in a protective motion.

"Who fucking died. Why the fuck would she do that? And why the fuck"—Mo waved wildly around—"would she love this place? It's wet and dirty and fucking hard to walk to. My feet hurt, my back hurts, my everything hurts. And for what?"

Aspen was frozen solid, her face distorted as she listened to Mo's complaints.

"To be poetic? Yeah, some poetic final trip that will make me magically forget the love of my life. Like that is even possible… it'd be more poetic to die." Mo shook her head, beginning to pace. "No, this trip is something else entirely. I'm here to please some random woman who convinced—no, forced—me to go and be poetic—"

That comment made Aspen's head shoot up. "I resent that!"

"Do you?"

"Yeah." Aspen moved to stand, her eyes on fire. "I'm not the one who acted like I knew how to backpack."

"Oh, so you knew, huh?"

"Not officially, but now, yeah I do." Aspen's hands moved to her hips. "Even novice backpackers are taught how to properly wear a pack or"—Aspen pointed to her boots—"not wear someone else's hiking gear."

Aspen was right about that.

"I just wanted…" Aspen breathed in deeply, her lips beginning to tremble. "Whatever. We will sleep in my tent tonight, I'll take you back in the morning. I'm sorry I ruined…" She waved her hand around Mo's torso and head. "This."

And with that Mo watched Aspen return to building her tent, not another word said. All the anger seemed to drain from her body, leaving only anguish behind.

* * *

Mo was dumbstruck.

It was obvious now that the feelings Mo had for Aspen had led her to dumping years of built-up anger, resentment, and depression on a woman she had known for less than two weeks. And all Aspen did was apologize. Mo knew, deep down, that she was being incredibly ungrateful and downright mean. Aspen hadn't done anything remotely wrong to her, but Mo had selfishly decided she had. Now, a few hours later and a backpacking meal consumed in silence, Mo was seeing it all differently.

How did Mo turn a sweet woman, who was only trying to connect, into her personal punching bag? And even more, how could she make it right?

The rocks Aspen had gathered earlier were for a fire, one that was now burning between them. Aspen's eyes were firmly on it, while Mo's were on her. She kept thinking over and over that all Aspen had done was apologize. Mo, on the other hand, had blown everything out of proportion. So while Aspen's reaction was somewhat defensive of her own honor, in the end it was just apologetic. Like Aspen had done something wrong.

Mo had to make it right.

"Aspen?" Mo asked softly, watching the fire dance in her eyes.

Aspen sat unmoved and unanswering.

"I'm an asshole," Mo said with more conviction. "What I said was unacceptable."

Aspen looked up, meeting Mo's gaze.

"I've been really unfair to you and…" Mo gulped. "It might not mean much, and I respect whatever you decide, but…I'm sorry. I truly am."

Aspen looked back at the fire.

"I don't think there is an apology that fits. I'm gonna sleep out here on the ground cover tonight and, uh…I hope we can talk about it more in the morning?"

Like expected, Mo didn't receive a response. Instead, she listened closely to how the bubbling of the creek mixed with the crackle of the fire, and she pondered her regret.

CHAPTER TWELVE

Aspen didn't really sleep. Most of the night was spent rolling around inside of her sleeping bag, her stomach in knots. How had a fun, flirty trip turned into dragging a self-centered grump through the woods against her will? Especially one that she was actually interested in. If Virginia was here for the previous day's trip, she'd make some snide joke about Aspen's type being jerks. Which was correct; antagonistic people were her bread and butter. But there was something even worse going on here, something that Aspen had not quite experienced in her life.

Mo had taken responsibility.

In all the years of conflict where Aspen felt she was being treated unfairly, the other person had never apologized in the way Mo had last night. It was so unfamiliar that she had nothing to compare it to. Her parents had never apologized, always projecting their own mistakes back onto Aspen. Kyle had apologized, but only as a way of bringing back Aspen's affection and usefulness. Mo, on the other hand, let her know that she was fully in the wrong for how Aspen had been treated and placed the ball of moving forward into her hands.

And it had kept her up all night.

The birds had been singing for hours at this point, and the heat of the sun rolling around inside the tent finally urged her to move. With a deep breath, Aspen tried to suppress her anxiety as she made herself presentable before unzipping the door. Her eyes easily adjusted to the morning light as she stepped out into her Crocs, extending her back to full height in a stretch. After she took in another deep gulp of redwood air, Aspen finally looked in the direction of where Mo had decided to camp for the night. She couldn't help but smile at the woman, who was seated cross-legged on her sleeping pad, her hair pushed in four different directions.

"Good morning," Mo offered sheepishly. "Did you sleep well?"

Staying mad wasn't in Aspen's DNA, so she sighed and trotted toward her companion. "Morning. And, uh, no."

"Me neither."

"Mmm," Aspen hummed, wondering if she should sit on the ground cover with her.

Mo must have read her mind, patting the other end of her sleeping bag before asking, "If you are comfortable, I would love it if you'd have a seat with me."

Aspen dropped to her butt easily, mirroring Mo as she scooted to face her.

"I don't want to make any excuses," Mo began, her eyes dropping to her hands where she was absently picking at her cuticles. "I know better and I uh—I wanted to explain but I don't want you to think that it's an excuse, ya know?"

"Honestly." Aspen squirmed, her eyes also on Mo's hands. "I kinda get why you yelled—"

"Don't." Mo looked up, concern in her eyes. "You had nothing to do with any of what I said. I was frustrated. I've been frustrated for a long time, actually, and I blew up on you. Which is shitty and totally not what you deserve."

Warmth spread through Aspen's chest at Mo's carefully chosen words, and she met her hazel gaze, seeing conviction behind her eyes. "Yeah, it sucked."

"It did and I'm sorry." Mo's face was as genuine as Aspen had heard in her voice. "And I'm even more sorry I lied to you about being a backpacker. I—I don't know why I did that."

"To seem super hot and cool?" Aspen joked, breaking some of the tension.

"I wish." Mo laughed. "I'll be totally honest, I said it because I wanted you to leave me alone."

Aspen giggled. "That didn't pan out did it?"

"No, no it did not." Mo smiled crookedly before adding, "But that's all I lied about. Backpacking was Annie's thing and I came up here to…" Mo dropped off, her eyes now unfocused. "I don't know why I actually came up here."

"To honor her?" Aspen offered.

"No." Mo shook her head. "To die?"

The honesty in those two words hit Aspen hard. How would she go about talking to Mo about something like that? So she decided not to respond, instead allowing Mo the space to explain herself further.

"But, I think even that was an excuse." Mo nodded, her voice sounding relieved. "I just want it to stop hurting so much."

"I read you all wrong," Aspen said, pulling her knees up to her chest.

"How so?"

"A sad, attractive woman trying to grieve?"

Mo's eyebrows went up in contemplation before she nodded in agreement. "That might be more accurate than you think. I just like to complicate things and make everything harder than it needs to be."

"Losing someone doesn't mean the feelings die with them."

A small smile curved at the edges of Mo's lips. "You are too nice to me."

"Thank you for apologizing," Aspen said, her voice stronger. "And thank you for coming clean about not knowing what you were doing. I will admit, I let you suffer a little bit there."

"You did?" Mo chuckled, rubbing her hands together nervously.

"Yeah, I regret it, though. You probably fucked up your back a little in the process."

"Actually," Mo said, sliding her hands around the ground cover. "The sand wasn't as bad as I thought. My back feels a bit better this morning. And I've always been kind of a grumpy person. I think I just like to complain."

"That you do. It gets old real quick too."

"Sorry. Annie said my worst quality was my penchant for complaining. Even at the smallest things."

"Can I ask you a question about Annie?" Aspen leaned her chin on her kneecap as Mo nodded. "Why didn't you go backpacking with her?"

Mo's head rolled back in contemplation. "I wish I had a wild story about a freak accident or terrible experience, but much like Annie's dislike for my boat, I just was never interested."

"Oh, she didn't like your boat?"

"No, and I never really took it personally. When you love someone, you learn their boundaries and what they like and don't like. Annie took Opal backpacking once and got her hooked, and since I wasn't a fan, I never really considered it a bad thing to let them do their thing. We were in a band, so we had a shared hobby."

"You were in a band?" Aspen asked, remembering a bit about a guitar but not a band.

"Country and folk cover band. It's actually how we met." Mo smiled wide, obviously reveling in this memory. "To tell you about it, I have to give you a bit of a backstory."

"All right, how about you tell it to me over there while I get some coffee and breakfast going?" Aspen offered.

"Sounds good." Mo stood, stretching slightly before offering a hand to Aspen. "So I grew up in a little town outside of Boston, with normal Christian-adjacent parents. Nothing much happened until my best friend, Bud, who I think I've mentioned to you a few times, moved to my town from somewhere in the mountains of Virginia. We met in marching band, he played snare while I played the bass drum, but outside of school we would jam with guitars and stuff. We became fast friends, giving each other the support that our families were terrible at providing. When I applied to Stanford University to get away from New England, Bud followed suit in solidarity, even though he barely made it a semester before dropping out to pursue a career in big-rig repair."

"Hold on, let me go grab the bear bag." Aspen stopped her, moving to the tree down the creek to pull down the bear bag she had hung the previous night, all the needed items for breakfast inside. She quickly returned, humming in excitement at being allowed actual insight into Mo's past. "What was your major?"

"Computer Science," Mo replied. "But I thought about law school, so I took a lot of prerequisites for it. It's kind of how I ended up doing Internet fraud investigation as a career."

"Oh, I didn't know that."

"I'm sorry I didn't tell you." Mo stood by the fire circle, her hands sliding into her pockets. "Can I help in any way?"

"No, just keep talking," Aspen said, moving firewood she had collected to start a fire. "I'm happy to be learning more about you."

"Okay. Uh…where was I?"

"Stanford. You and Bud."

"Right. Well, Bud dropped out, but he kinda secretly lived in my dorm after my roommate decided to stay off campus with her boyfriend. So toward the end of my freshman year while I was in class, Bud was strolling around Old Union, which was like a place students hung out and studied. He had come across a flyer on one of the corkboards for tryouts for a folk and country cover band that would take pop songs and turn them into country."

"That sounds really fun," Aspen exclaimed, pouring water into a pot.

"Bud thought so too, so he grabbed tabs for us since they needed drums, guitar, and a keyboardist. He called and set up a tryout before I could even say no. The band was Annie's, something she started after her ex had told her she'd never be good enough to sing for a crowd." Mo finally sat on one of the large rocks near the fire. "One thing you'd never do is challenge Annie Reeves. She'd prove you wrong every time."

"Reeves?" Aspen looked up. "Did you take her last name?"

Mo smiled and shrugged. "Felt honoring her was meaningful, I guess."

"No shade. I like it."

Mo blushed slightly, sending a small shiver down Aspen's spine. She went back to tending to the fire, trying to get it to the phase best for adding the pot.

"Anyway, Bud pretty much forced me to try out. Which I am glad I did, because once I saw Annie on the poster, I totally forgot about my reservations."

"What did she look like?"

"She was beautiful. Dirty-blond hair, blue eyes, and confidence for days. Every room she entered, she owned. If I had my phone on me, I'd show you a picture. I was already pretty smitten by the time I got to her rented garage in Palo Alto. I was also thankful I had brought my steel guitar, showing off my skills a bit, ya know? Funny thing was, she wasn't impressed with me. Like at all."

"Really?" Aspen asked with a laugh, raising up to full height. "I can't really see that."

"I think she knew I was into her." Mo snorted, the memory obviously bringing her fond joy. "She had just got out of a whirlwind romance with some terrible woman, so I think she was protecting herself. Either way, Bud can convince most people to give anything or anyone a try, so in the end she agreed to both of us. And a few weeks later, local artist and Bud's kryptonite, Opal, joined the band as our keyboard master. She also plays a mad fiddle."

Aspen smiled, taken aback by this side of Mo. She was being so open, like a floodgate had broken. "Opal was the friend who would go backpacking with Annie?"

"Yeah. She ended up marrying Bud. We kind of broke the cardinal rule of being in a band. Don't fall in love with your bandmates."

Aspen laughed at that, finally deciding the fire was ready for the pot of water. "Do you like your coffee black or with some sugar? I also have some powdered creamer if you're game?"

"I'll take it black, thank you. Anyway, the band was successful in and around Palo Alto. We had such a good time that we kept doing gigs all the way up until…" A few moments passed in silence before Aspen looked up at Mo, who was now staring out toward the creek. "Until Annie got sick."

"So, I can infer…" Aspen began with trepidation, hoping to not derail the mood. "That she gave you a chance?"

"Yeah, I guess I kinda broke down her resolve."

"I don't think she'd see it that way," Aspen offered, setting up her travel pour-over for the coffee. "I think she knew exactly what she had found."

Mo hummed in realization before nodding. "Yeah, I guess I hadn't considered that."

"Good thing I'm here."

"Truly. And, honestly, if you are still okay with it. I want to keep doing this." She waved her hand around to point toward the trail and creek, confirming her intention. "But only if you are comfortable."

No one had ever asked Aspen that. She was taken aback again, awkwardly adjusting herself in front of the fire. Her apprehension must have been obvious, as Mo moved closer to the fire, squatting near her.

"It's gonna boil over." She pointed toward the pot.

"Whoops," Aspen squeaked, shaking herself back to the present. She grabbed the pot with her rolled up towel, pouring the water over the coffee in the pour-over. "My bad."

"It's okay if you wanna quit," Mo said. "I made a fool of myself and of this trip. I treated you really badly as well, so I want to make sure this decision is yours."

"Actually," Aspen replied. "I do want to keep going. We can't quit after a bit of squabbling."

"You don't have to sugarcoat it." Mo laughed, standing up. "I was a dick."

"Yeah, but you told me more about Annie, and she probably needs to know how much of a cranky asshole you've been in her absence."

Mo gasped. "Are you going to snitch on me?"

Aspen moved the pour-over to the other collapsible cup, grabbing the pot again. "Damn right I will. Annie needs to know that you've been misbehaving in her absence."

"Okay, I'll give you that. But I gotta know something?"

"All right," Aspen said, passing Mo her undoctored cup of coffee. "What's that?"

"Do you always apologize when it's not your fault?"

That wasn't the question she was expecting, and it sent her into a mild panic. "Huh?"

"Last night, when I was being unfair you just—"

"I knew you were projecting." Aspen waved her hands, hoping this excuse she was creating from thin air would work. "Do you want eggs? I got a few packs of powdered eggs. They actually taste pretty decent if you add salt and some nutritional yeast."

"You're changing the subject." Mo cocked her head, studying Aspen curiously.

"Sorry."

"And now you are apologizing again."

"I don't know, maybe I was a Canadian in a previous life?" Aspen grabbed a pack of powdered eggs as she mentally kicked herself for that ridiculous statement. "I'm making eggs."

The air was awkwardly silent as Aspen focused on making the food. Just as she thought she was going to need to come up with something to fill the air, Mo said, "Why is the food in plastic tubs?"

Aspen looked over at the containers. "They're bear vaults. Tested and rated by IGBC, or the Interagency Grizzly Bear Commission. Have to have at least one in order to backpack in the Redwood National Park."

"You mean hanging it up over there wasn't enough?"

"No, I just do that out of habit. But you should store your food away from where you sleep, to keep bears from bothering you."

"Okay." Mo accepted the explanation easily, her tone far calmer than the previous day. "You are the expert."

"I know." Aspen winked. "Now let's get these eggs made, I'm starving."

* * *

"So, Annie was a singer?"

Mo nodded in reply, snapping down the top cap of her pack as Aspen placed her own bag on the ground in front of her. They had eaten breakfast slowly, enjoying easy conversation and a shared disdain for the powdered eggs. Afterward, Aspen had taught Mo how to disassemble and pack her tent. Then they cleaned up their campsite to look like they were never there, the pinnacle of "leave no trace." The entire time Mo was open and receptive, a side of herself that Aspen had only previously seen in small glimpses. It was so jarring that Aspen would liken it to a night-and-day kind of transformation, leaving her wondering if it would be sustainable. But as she watched Mo smile easily up at her before fluffing her hair with her right hand, Aspen changed from wondering to hoping.

Because if Mo was attractive before, she was irresistible now.

"She was a smooth alto," Mo explained, standing up. "We countrified 'Waking Up In Vegas' by Katy Perry. She not only gave it the classic nineties twang but knocked it out the park."

"Oh man, I bet that was so good," Aspen guessed, already trying to imagine what the song would sound like done in a country style.

"I called it our 'hook' song. If a crowd seemed kind meh, that song would always get people up on their feet and engaged," Mo said before looking down at her pack. "So, back to the pain, huh?"

"Here is where I admit to something." Aspen hesitated but then continued, "I kind of am the reason you were extra grumpy yesterday."

"I promise, you weren't."

"I kinda was. I let you hike without setting your..." Aspen stepped forward, grabbing onto Mo's pack. "Well, it's Annie's pack, isn't it?"

"Yeah."

"Well, either way, I didn't help you put it on correctly. Which contributed to a lot of your pain." Aspen gave an apologetic look, bracing for a tongue lashing.

Mo only laughed, covering her face temporarily with her left hand. "Honestly, with the way I acted, I deserved it. But um…could you help me now?"

Relief flooded over Aspen, and she nodded excitedly. "Totally!"

"All right, what do I do?"

"Before we do that, let's rearrange how you packed everything." Aspen pulled items out of Mo's pack and reverently placed them on the ground. "I'm going to add one of the bear vaults to your pack and move your clothes and stuff like this."

Mo watched intently as Aspen placed each item back into her pack, careful to arrange the weight while also maximizing the space.

"And I will take out these books and put them in my pack. You'll find the bear vault weighs a bit less than all this, and if you get the urge to read, you can just ask me for them."

"Sorry." Mo shrugged sheepishly.

"It's okay, I'm not mad. You had a lot of space free since I was packing all the food. And now we are all packed," Aspen said, clicking in the last buckle. "Make sure every time you unpack this, repack it the same way. It'll do wonders for your back."

"Thank you." Mo smiled, rolling and stretching her shoulders in anticipation. "Now, how do I wear it correctly?"

"Well, first we have to loosen all the straps," Aspen instructed, waving for Mo to kneel next to her as she pulled each strap out enough to start from scratch. "Technically, this should have been measured for your torso, but we can't really do much about that now."

"She was only an inch shorter than me," Mo offered as Aspen finished her task.

"Good, then this pack will probably be fine." Aspen motioned for Mo to step forward. "Go ahead and put it on, and I'll show you how to adjust each strap."

Mo donned the pack with a slight groan. She stood awkwardly, obviously not enjoying the weight. Aspen swallowed nervously, knowing the next few steps would mean she would be in Mo's personal space.

"Now, can I touch you?" Aspen asked, stepping closer to Mo.

"Yeah," Mo agreed, her focus bouncing between Aspen's eyes.

"First thing first." Aspen moved even closer, instantly feeling Mo's hot breath on her forehead as she looked down at Mo's waist. With unsure fingers, Aspen reached forward and grabbed the hip belt hanging near Mo's sides. She clipped it together at Mo's hips, the backs of her fingers warm against Mo's lean lower abdomen. "Hip belt. This will take most of the weight off your back."

"Oh, I didn't have this clipped," Mo said, her voice a tad wavy. "My bad."

Aspen tried to keep her breath even as she slid her hand under the belt on one side, her knuckles now resting against Mo's right hip bone. She pulled on the strap until her fingers felt the pressure, removing her hand to tighten the strap more. She then moved to do the same thing on the other side, Mo's breathing slightly hitching at her actions.

"All right, hip belt done. Next are shoulder straps."

"Mm-hmm," Mo hummed but left her hands at her sides.

Aspen swallowed her nerves, electric energy bouncing around in her body. She cleared her throat before grabbing each shoulder strap, pulling down until they looked tight and even. "Does that feel good?"

"Oh wow, yeah," Mo responded, her eyes firmly on Aspen when she looked up to confirm.

"Good, load straps are next."

"Load straps?"

"Up here." Aspen reached her hands up and over Mo's shoulders, almost like she was initiating a slow dance. Her hands brushed lightly past Mo's neck and shoulders, causing Mo to groan ever so slightly. The power Aspen found in this easy movement was intoxicating, and she fiddled around a bit longer than normal, enjoying this closeness. "They are straps connecting the top of the load to the rest of the pack."

"Got it." Mo's voice sounded thick.

Aspen pulled down, her wrists making contact with Mo's shoulders, which in turn had Mo reaching out to steady herself on Aspen's hips. Her body reacted positively to Mo's touch, and it took everything inside of her to keep herself from rolling her hips in response. Aspen kept her arms around Mo's neck, moving closer so that their bodies were now lightly touching.

"Is that it?" Mo finally asked, slowly removing her hands.

"No," Aspen replied, making it seem like she was testing the buckles near Mo's neck. "Chest strap is last."

With that, she fished each section of the chest strap from the crook of Mo's arms and snapped it lightly over her chest, trying her best to avoid brushing against Mo's breasts. But Mo's body had other ideas, leaning into her touch so that Aspen's forearms could feel the softness of Mo's chest right below her wrists. Aspen, not wanting to make it awkward, quickly pulled on the strap until it seemed proper before stepping back away from Mo.

"Done." Aspen looked up, finding Mo's eyes closed.

Before she could comment, Mo opened them and smiled down at her. "Thanks."

"Does it feel better?"

Mo took a few moments to move around, like she hadn't been paying attention the entire process. "Yeah, much better. It feels almost...lighter?"

"Yeah, it's like magic." Aspen grinned before moving to grab her own bag, her body still buzzing from their closeness.

"Need me to help you?" Mo offered, causing Aspen to drop her pack in surprise.

"No." Aspen's voice was a few octaves too high, and she quickly adjusted her straps, hoping she hadn't made a fool of herself. "I'll get it situated, and we'll head out."

"Damn," Mo muttered so quietly that Aspen almost missed it. She was sure she heard disappointment in her voice.

Aspen couldn't help but grimace, wondering if she had just made a mistake in refusing Mo. But when she turned around to gauge Mo's facial expression, she found apologetic softness instead of the usual grumpy lines. Aspen breathed a sigh of relief.

"Let's get going," Aspen announced, nodding her head in the correct direction.

This trip was all over the place, and Aspen just hoped she could keep up.

CHAPTER THIRTEEN

Mo wondered if there was something metamorphic about sleeping beneath majestic redwoods, because she was definitely seeing everything in a different light. The trees seemed taller, greener, and way more interesting than when she drove up 101 a little over a week ago. The water glistened perfectly under the morning sun, lapping steadily against the rocks as it flowed toward the sea. She was finally noticing the wide array of birds, all different shapes, sizes, and colors. And even the ground cover, which Mo had barely glanced at before, was not only lush but had stunning wildflowers sprouting out amongst the bushes. Sure, there was still a sense of familiar melancholy sitting in her chest, but it was undeniable that Mo's perceptions were becoming more in tune with her surroundings.

The only other noteworthy factor, besides her surroundings, was Aspen. Mo knew she hadn't changed per se, but she was finally giving in to allow Aspen to take up space in her world without gripe. Along the trail, Mo would attempt to look back at Aspen every chance she got. It felt wonderful to finally allow herself the grace to see Aspen fully, without the negativity she had wrongly placed on her. Even if Aspen didn't feel the same, Mo knew she deserved better treatment than what she had been giving her.

And she wanted to make sure Aspen knew that.

"There should be another temporary bridge up ahead," Aspen said suddenly. "I don't know if the water has gone low enough for Betty's team to install it, though."

"Do they install a new bridge every year?" Mo stopped, confused as to why the bridge would need to be temporary.

"The water levels of Redwood Creek rise higher in the winter season," Aspen explained happily, turning to point back to where they had previously crossed. "Back there is where the trail ends for winter visitors due to the danger of crossing when the water is high. They remove the bridges around early November. May is usually when the water begins to lower, allowing the park rangers time to bring equipment out and put them back."

"Oh, I get it. Makes the trail safer for everyone."

"Exactly. Humans are known for overestimating their abilities, so even on a pretty flat trail like Redwood Creek, people have been known to hurt themselves and need rescuing." Aspen smiled broadly up at Mo.

Mo noticed again just how irresistible Aspen's smile was. "And that is why I am thankful you're here with me. I might have ended up being one of those people."

Aspen's cheeks reddened under her compliment, and Mo watched her bite her lip before looking away and adding, "Maybe. Having me does lessen the danger, but it's still there. I assume Annie was pretty experienced?"

"Yeah, I assume she was. Opal would probably agree since she learned all the stuff she knows about the outdoors from her. I was wondering, actually, if she ever met you at Dry Creek. Annie was also a big fan of beer…" Mo trailed off, moving down the path again.

"I doubt it. I've only been living in Orick for about five years," Aspen said, walking slowly behind Mo's tepid pace. "Unless I met her on the trail, but I doubt that."

"Why so?"

"Kyle," Aspen remarked, the lilt in her voice taking on an adverse tone.

"Kyle?" Mo turned to catch Aspen's gaze.

"My ex-husband." Aspen shrugged. "He was every rural girl's dream. Tall, muscular, dark hair, blue eyes, played running back for our high school football team. We were run-of-the-mill high school sweethearts, married only a year after we graduated."

"Were you in love with him?" Mo asked. Aspen stopped moving and Mo somehow sensed it, turning to stop with her. She studied Aspen's contorted face, worried she had made a mistake in asking. "I'm sorry, I didn't mean—"

"No, no. Don't worry." Aspen chuckled. "It's just...no one has ever asked me that."

"Oh." Mo laughed with her, watching as she moved both hiking poles into one hand in contemplation. "Glad to ask the hard hitters, then."

"I think I was in love with the idea of him," Aspen said, catching Mo's eyes. "I don't think I need to ask. You were definitely in love with Annie."

Mo smiled wide. "Yeah, I guess that's kind of obvious. Which might be why I asked about him, seeing as you are out now. Well, let me make that a little clearer—of course you're allowed to be a lesbian and have been in love with him. Those things aren't mutually exclusive."

"Yeah, you're right," Aspen agreed, pointing back to the trail with her poles so they could continue. But instead of following behind her, she chose to walk beside Mo now. "Kyle initiated everything in our relationship except, well, the ending, obviously."

Mo snorted at that, trying to imagine Aspen in a relationship with a man. "I'll be honest, I can't really see you with a guy."

"Yeah, me either, actually. But looking back, I think I was in love with the stability he brought me. Even if he did treat me poorly, his lifestyle allowed me a lot of flexibility that I enjoyed. It lasted longer than I thought it would, because he was a traveling electrician, so I didn't have to face my suppressed sexuality most of the week," Aspen explained, the sound of her hiking poles hitting rocks calming Mo in a weird way.

"What did you do when he was gone?"

"Housework, mostly. He was every stereotypical blue-collar man you've ever met. He wanted me to stay at home for when we had kids, a process that no matter how hard he wanted it, I rarely gave him the chance to do." Aspen's voice was slightly lower now. "I thought I was broken…Come to figure out, I was just sleeping with the wrong gender."

"How did you figure it out?" Mo asked, enjoying the closeness she felt to Aspen at this moment. "I kinda just knew at a young age. I've not really thought about how I'd figure it out in your situation."

"Well, for me at least, it's pretty similar to you." Aspen reached out and touched Mo's shoulder softly. "I always kind of knew. I just hid it out of fear, or maybe shame? And at some point, after years of being left alone in that house, it just kind of clicked."

A smile spread over Mo's face. "Like a light switch was turned on?"

"Yep. And I never wanted to turn it off again. It was so overwhelming that it was only a month or so before I finally found the courage to tell Kyle."

"How did he take it?"

"Badly." Aspen laughed softly. "I can laugh about it now because he's gone, but he was pretty cruel."

"Ah."

"But I had Virginia and Salvador, who I had come out to a few weeks prior. And this…" Aspen twirled around, her arms spread out toward nature. "My half-baked life with Kyle didn't compare."

"I'm proud of you," Mo said with earnest honesty, loving the twinkle of Aspen's eyes in return. "You chose you."

"I guess," Aspen replied, clearly embarrassed. "Kyle thought I was cheating on him and used being a lesbian as an excuse so he wouldn't figure out who the 'guy' was. After I processed everything he said to me during that time, I think I figured out his true motives. It seemed as though he thought that he had saved me and was owed some sort of reward for doing so."

"Saved you?"

"From my parents. My childhood." Aspen's voice was smaller than Mo had ever heard it. "Sorry."

"Why are you sorry?" Mo asked as Aspen looked toward her feet, avoiding her gaze.

After a few long, sullen moments, Aspen answered. "I didn't mean to make some of Annie's trip about me."

Mo laughed heartily at that, which brought Aspen's eyes back up to hers. "That might be the end goal here, Aspen, but you are allowed to share. I want you to share. This trip can be about more than Annie."

"Yeah, but Kyle is ancient history." Aspen matched her energy, quickly wiping away any of the insecurity she had just shown Mo.

"Speaking of him…you aren't a reward, you know?" Mo slid her thumbs behind her shoulder straps. "And no one is owed you just because they helped you in some way."

"Stop." Aspen bit her lip again, looking away as she blushed. "I don't have any fancy backpacking food as payment for all these compliments, ya know?"

Mo let her off the hook with a mock scoff. "What? I thought this act would get me a steak dinner."

"Steak, huh?" Aspen returned, moving to walk again. "At least ask for something fancier."

"Like what?"

"Caviar?"

"I'm gonna be honest," Mo said. "I like a lot of different fish eggs, in a lot of different ways. But caviar of the traditional Eurasian variety is overrated."

"Especially at that price," Aspen added, leading Mo sideways down a steep but short cut in the path. "I'm not really into a lot of fancy stuff."

"Me neither. You can teach me about the different forks and spoons, but I am most comfortable somewhere where I can put my elbows on the table."

"Hear, hear!"

Conversation naturally died after this, and Mo found herself relaxed, even with all the physical exertion the trail required. Her back and feet hurt significantly less today. Aspen's help with her pack and the high from making amends that morning had kept her soreness to a minimum. The lack of pressure, the winding trail being her only adversary, was leading Mo to just feel things as they came instead of actively trying to avoid them.

Her hands languidly dropped into her pockets, causing her to remember the existence of Annie's treasure. Unable to resist pulling it out, she felt the coolness of the cylinder against her palm, watching as the metal seemed to almost twinkle in the sun.

"You wanna hear more about Annie?" Mo asked suddenly.

"Are you pulling my leg?"

"I thought you wanted to hear more about her." Mo tilted her head, pocketing Annie's treasure before Aspen could see it.

"I did, I mean, I do. I don't know, I guess I didn't expect you to just…" Aspen waved her right hand dramatically out in front of her. "Give in?"

"I am full of surprises." Mo shrugged, trudging past Aspen before pointing ahead. "I found the bridge."

"Yep, there it is."

Mo strolled right up to the front of it, admiring its construction. The bridge was basic, just horizontal redwood boards placed along a strong base. They were held in place by wood columns that were installed every four or so boards. A rope was strung from these columns on either side, giving the appearance of an old-style rope bridge. Mo turned and grinned at Aspen. "Looks pretty sturdy."

"If Betty had anything to do with it, it is. Just watch where you step. It's over deep water in the middle."

Mo tested the bridge's sturdiness with her foot, feeling no give. With confidence she stepped on and strode across easily, enjoying looking down into the clear water. "Are there fish in here?"

"Of course," Aspen said, following Mo across. "I'm not the fishing type so I'm not sure on all the types, but Kyle liked the trout."

"He came out here with you?"

"Yeah, fishing was the only way to get him here. Though he preferred getting drunk and passing out in a rented cabin over sleeping in a tent," Aspen grumbled. "Enough about him, what was that Annie story I was promised?"

"Ah, right." Mo breathed in, reaching the end of the bridge and continuing down the trail. "Remember how I said that she wasn't actually interested in me when we met? Like, at all?"

"Aww, yeah," Aspen said. "Were you not her type?"

"I think I was too much her type," Mo returned, noticing that the trail was going up into the hills to their left now, obscuring their view of the creek. "Are we going the right way?"

"Yeah, the water is too deep here to wade, so we will follow the trail up a bit. It will snake back down to the creek eventually. Though I think there is a scramble we will have to traverse. I'm unsure if they cleared the downed trees from last year."

"I'm so glad you know." Mo beamed, relieved that she wouldn't have to worry about getting lost.

"My pleasure to serve you," Aspen sang brightly. "So, did she tell you to kick rocks?"

"Kinda? She agreed to Bud and I joining the band and almost immediately gave me, and only me, a speech about how she was done with dating in her twenties."

"I love that." Aspen sighed wistfully. "A woman who is upfront about what she wants."

"I did too, actually. I thought she was a breath of fresh air. First off, for knowing I was crushing on her and second off, for communicating her boundaries." Mo went on, smiling slightly at the memory of Annie's seriousness. "I respected it, obviously, but it made me like her more, not less."

"Ain't that how it always works." Aspen's voice took on a knowing tone. "We want what we can't have."

"Yeah, her included. She later told me how she was instantly infatuated but decided I was a terrible idea. I'm thankful, because it allowed us to get to know each other without all the crazy pretenses. I learned every little quirk during jam sessions in that garage, and instead of actively pursuing her, I just learned to let it be." Mo's breathing grew labored as they made their way up a switchback.

"So who initiated more?"

"Both of us?" Mo questioned the sky. "Her?"

"Which is it?"

"Both, I guess. She was the singer and the brain behind our entire band. She would pick a song and then bring it to us with ideas, kind of conducting the first changes we would make to countrify it. But she wasn't the best at any one instrument, so I offered to teach her more after a session," Mo said as they reached the first sharp turn in the switchback. "I asked her to bring her guitar, and she brought me this beat-up old Taylor, gouged to all hell right outside the pick guard. She would play all choked up like a—"

"Huh?" Aspen interrupted. "I'm not musical in any way so you've lost me."

"It's like…" Mo stopped and turned to Aspen, miming like she was holding a guitar. "You know how people hold a guitar and strum across the strings over the sound hole?"

"Yeah." Aspen nodded, stepping closer to Mo like she could actually see the imaginary guitar.

"Well, Annie played hers all choked up, so her strumming hand swung the pick over the strings closer to the neck and damaged the guitar."

"Ooh, I love her. She went her own way."

"And didn't care what anyone thought either. I was so confused by it that I had her hold the guitar and show me her technique and she played it all…" She mimed erratic and unskilled guitar strokes, making it look more like she was swinging a hammer than strumming a guitar.

Aspen snorted. "What did you do?"

"I asked her if she wanted me to show her a better technique. I will never forget how her face almost…" Mo tapered off, her hand moving as she tried to find the right words. "Fell? But like, in an affectionate way. Then she played a perfect rendition of 'Hallelujah,' her choked-up technique be damned."

"I'm not following…"

"She had kind of tricked me into thinking she was bad at guitar so I'd offer to spend time with her. I guess she wanted to be sure I was into her, previous baggage and all, and I was. But she ended up romancing me more with her version of the song than anything." Mo chuckled as they reached the end of the switchback. It looked like the trail went flat for twenty or so feet before a gentle descent back toward the creek.

"Aww," Aspen cooed, obviously smitten with Annie's antics. "That's a cute story."

"Ain't it? She was a character." Mo sighed. "Thanks for listening."

"No, thank you for telling me. I need to know as much as I can, you know," Aspen said with a lightness that was music to Mo's ears.

"Why's that?" Mo asked, taking the hill down to the creek at a steady pace.

"More for me to talk to her about when we get this phone installed. I can contrast how sweet you were then with how grumpy you are now."

"Hey now, that's not fair," Mo whined.

"I mean, yeah, you are a tad less grumpy today. But I am watching you."

Mo laughed a deep, steady laugh, enjoying their easy back-and-forth. The pair rounded a decent-sized redwood before the trail spit them back out onto the sand and rocks of the creek. Mo took a few more steps out and surveyed the new view, noticing the creek had widened even more since their last crossing.

"Let me guess, no bridge?" Mo asked as Aspen stood beside her.

"Nope," Aspen confirmed before pointing at the bank to their left, farther south. "There is the narrow point, but if you noticed, there are a ton of tall rocks we gotta get over before that point."

Mo nodded apprehensively before turning to look back at the brush. "No trail back that way?"

"Nope. You either swim, which is impractical, or you scramble."

"With the packs on?"

Aspen bumped Mo with her hip playfully. "With packs on."

"What if I fall in?"

"You won't." Aspen winked before leading the way. "Now come on, don't be shy."

The tall rocks, which were more like a few large rocks leading up to a boulder, covered most of the left side of the bank. Mo couldn't see the other side, only the shortened portion of the creek near the end. She watched as Aspen walked along the wall, finding the best place to climb up. After a minute or two of careful analysis, Aspen waved her over.

"Let's go up right here. I'll go first," Aspen said cheerfully, Mo doing her best to keep her fears at bay. "You've got long limbs, you can do it."

"But I'm shaped like a pencil," Mo complained.

Aspen stepped on a big rock to her left, stabilizing herself on the larger boulder before shimmying up to a ledge made by a few flatter rocks.

"And I'm fat and kinda top-heavy," Aspen replied, pointing to her larger breasts. "Use what you got."

Mo breathed in deeply, watching each expert move Aspen made until she was at the top, about twelve feet off the ground. Before she could truly chicken out, Mo started her own ascent, noticing immediately how the weight of the pack limited her movements.

"Take it nice and easy," Aspen instructed from above. "Grab onto the ledge to your right and put your foot on the dark rock."

Mo did as she was told, lifting herself to the first ledge before working her way to the second one. If she had come across these rocks herself, she would have gone back into the woods to find a way around. But Aspen had a way of making most things seem harmless, so here she was.

"This isn't a pile of rocks," Mo grumbled. "This is a mountain."

"It's not one solid mass." Aspen giggled, obviously enjoying watching Mo. "So pile of rocks is more fitting."

Mo contemplated her next move, pushing herself up to the last ledge before the top with her legs. As she did so, her foot slid a bit, and she gripped to the rocks for dear life. "Shit!"

"You're okay."

"I know," Mo shot back as Aspen was removing her pack up top.

"It's pretty flat up here, so I'm gonna come and help you with the last bit," Aspen yelled as she moved her pack out of Mo's sight.

"Okay," was all Mo could muster as she looked down.

"Take my hand," Aspen said, now on her knees above Mo. "Then put your foot over there and push up."

Mo nodded, following Aspen's directions. She put her foot on the ledge and grabbed Aspen's hand firmly before thrusting her weight upward. Aspen's grip was firm, and Mo overestimated the amount of force needed—meaning she launched herself clear over the lip. They both yelped in unison, Mo's entire body weight, including the pack, now on top of Aspen. Mo was practically straddling her, their faces squished together as the pack pushed her torso downward. Mo pulled her head and shoulders up and off Aspen, but her body lingered, and she looked into her eyes.

"Whoops!" Aspen chuckled underneath but made no movement to push Mo away.

"I made it."

"Yeah, you definitely did," Aspen replied, her voice a tad deeper now.

Mo smiled down at Aspen, locking eyes. They stayed like that for a few moments, Mo enjoyed their closeness. How their bodies, even in this state, seemed to feel like they belonged together. Mo looked to her lips, considering her options.

"This is nice but..." Aspen squirmed underneath Mo. "My knee is at a really bad angle."

"Oh, I'm sorry." Mo immediately moved to try to alleviate her pain.

"It's okay," Aspen reassured her, helping to untangle their bodies. "I don't usually like asking attractive women to get off my lap, but..."

"Yeah." Mo finally let out a laugh. "Knees are important."

"Indeed." Aspen chuckled, pushing herself back up onto her feet. Mo watched her move across the flat top of the boulder, treading carefully to reach her pack. She watched as Aspen put it back on, in awe by how at ease she was here, how easy everything in nature came naturally to her. And as Aspen looked back down at Mo, sliding a strand of escaped hair behind one ear, she crossed her arms playfully.

"Next time you find yourself on my lap," Aspen started, moving toward the opposing ledge. "You're free to kiss me."

Mo's jaw went slightly slack, unable to find a retort as she watched Aspen carefully turn and begin her descent down the other side.

CHAPTER FOURTEEN

Aspen's flirting had officially broken Mo. So much so that she hadn't said more than a few comments about the trail, allowing Aspen to set the pace by just trotting along behind her. Every so often Aspen would glance back, finding a slightly flushed Mo just doing her best to keep up. The effect she was having on the taller woman was addictive, and she was overjoyed that they had made up from the previous day's disagreement. But even as Aspen craved to just turn around, grab Mo by her shoulder straps, and pull her in for a heated kiss, she knew in the back of her mind that a part of her wanted more than just a quick fling.

And that idea scared the hell out of her.

"How is it already three o'clock?" Mo asked suddenly from behind Aspen, making her jump a little.

Aspen glanced down at her watch, confirming Mo's assertion. "Well, we have been going at an elderly person's pace."

"Really?" Mo sounded a tad tired and disheartened.

"We talked a lot, and I don't know about you, but I slept like shit last night, so I purposefully kept our pace kind of slow. It doesn't matter, though. This isn't a race by any means."

"Maybe not for you," Mo mumbled, obviously joking.

"Oh, so you're an expert again?" Aspen jabbed lightly before looking around at their surroundings and explaining, "We are just past 44 Camp. There is a sharp turn in the creek up ahead that is thin. We'll cross the water there, then camp right when it begins to widen again. Should only be another ten, fifteen minutes of hiking. Tops."

"Aye aye, captain," Mo agreed half-heartedly, adjusting her pack and nodding for Aspen to continue.

Aspen treaded toward the sharp turn, getting off the trail and onto the rocky bed of the creek. She spotted a decent-sized, rotting stump and beelined for it. "Let's sit on this stump and trade our boots for Crocs."

"Why?" Mo questioned harshly. Before Aspen could even react to it, Mo sucked her teeth at her own tone. Aspen watched as she closed her eyes, her handsome face going slightly slack before she breathed in deeply. Once she finished two deep breaths, Aspen watched her open her eyes and give her an apologetic look. "I didn't mean for it to sound like that. Why are we putting on Crocs instead of keeping on our boots?"

Aspen bit her lip, her heart pulling her toward Mo. She reached out and squeezed her forearm gently before consoling her. "It's okay. We're going to walk through the water, and it's a whole ton easier to just get our feet wet in the Crocs than our boots."

Mo's left hand went up to cover her eyes as she chuckled lightly. "Duh."

"No worries," Aspen said to soothe her. The feeling of being respected without asking for it was pretty new to Aspen. She shivered uncomfortably, deciding to remove her pack and start the process of changing her shoes to avoid lingering in the feeling for too long. But as she looked over her shoulder and caught a glimpse of Mo's embarrassed little grin, her plan seemed destined to fail miserably.

"So…your birthday is coming up, right?"

Aspen forgot she had told Mo that. "Yep. In a couple of weeks."

"What day?" Mo sounded casual, even as Aspen wondered if she was making plans to spend it with her. A fleeting wish that she knew she should not get her hopes up about.

"June fourteenth," Aspen said, removing both of her shoes and socks. "I think it's a Wednesday, but I'm not sure."

"You have plans? Are Virginia and Salvador gonna take you somewhere nice? Maybe a trip?"

"A trip?" Aspen snorted, removing her Crocs from the large carabiner that kept them secured to the side of her pack. "Do I look like I go on trips?"

"We are on a trip right now," Mo declared loudly, and Aspen turned to watch her motion to their surroundings with her Crocs.

"This is my backyard. It would be like me staying with you in San Francisco and you saying we are going on a 'trip' to the Golden Gate Bridge."

"I'll have you know," Mo began as Aspen slipped on her last Croc, moving to stand and watch her companion's response. "It's an hour from my old house to the Golden Gate—on a good day. Closer to two during peak traffic. Sounds like a trip if you ask me."

"You are infuriating," Aspen said, making her best faux grumpy face toward a smug Mo. "Now get your Crocs on."

The pair crossed the water easily, Aspen making sure to keep her eyes firmly on Mo, who was reacting with childlike wonder to the sensations, sounds, and sights of the creek up close. Once on the other side, she turned to watch Mo bend down precariously, still not used to the weight of her pack, and choose a rock from the creek to examine.

"Redwood Creek is one of Earth's best rock tumblers," Aspen noted, smiling from ear to ear as she watched Mo gingerly return the rock to its home.

"It's pretty cool," Mo stated, her voice filled with the same wonder as her eyes. "I think I am beginning to understand why Annie kept coming back here every year."

Aspen didn't know the best response, so she just waved for Mo to follow her as she started toward the location she had mentally picked for their campsite tonight. She had admired it previously, on one of her more rigorous backpacking trips, noting how nice the spot would have been if it were another two or so miles down the creek. Their lazy pace had guaranteed that she could finally enjoy this section of the trail.

"Wow, lots of sand here," Mo said, walking around the spot before stopping near the water's edge. "Is it deeper in there?"

"I believe so." Aspen joined her. "Looks more than four or five feet toward the middle."

"Wow, it's so weird in comparison to where we just crossed. That was only ankle deep."

"The joys of this creek. Well, and the danger. It's even deeper in the winter, especially if we get good rain," Aspen explained before finding a good place to take off her pack. "I'll get the tent set up if you collect rocks."

"Around the size of last night?" Mo asked softly, obviously trying to be more useful.

Aspen nodded at her. "Get enough to make a circle similar to what I made last night. Then I'll go with you to gather wood and tinder."

"Ooh, tinder," Mo said smoothly, putting her pack down next to Aspen's with a relieved sigh. She then looked Aspen up and down before declaring, "I'd swipe right."

Now Aspen was the one left a little dumbfounded, not expecting Mo to flirt so easily. Sure, it was obvious that Mo was attracted to her, but it was a different thing altogether to hear her verbalize it. Mo seemed to be waiting for a response, her eyes twinkling with affection that Aspen was unsure she had ever seen directed at her.

By anyone. Ever.

"Wow, that was easy."

"What?" Aspen managed to squeak out.

"Make you speechless," Mo said with self-satisfaction before backing up. "Now I'm off to find rocks."

Aspen watched her saunter away, her stomach tying itself into knots. Normally she'd love this kind of banter—sexy, flirty, and free. But currently Aspen only felt fear at what she had seen in Mo's eyes. There wasn't just lust. There was something else. And something else was not in the cards for her.

* * *

Setting up camp took far less time today than it had the previous night. Mo did a lot better than Aspen thought she would, excelling at gathering the fire-circle rocks and the wood they would need later. Aspen had just finished setting up the second ultralight camp chair as Mo was bringing in the last bundle of tinder needed to get a good fire going. After she deposited it close to the fire, Mo waddled over to her pack. Aspen watched her gingerly pull her sleeping bag, sleeping pad, and ground cover out from inside. The woman hugged all of the items as close to her as she could, standing to her full height but not moving toward the tent. Aspen crossed her arms curiously, observing Mo look around the campsite like she was trying to find the most respectful place to set up her meager lodging.

"You don't have to cowboy camp."

"Cowboy camp?" Mo looked confused.

"Just a thing people call camping on the ground with no cover." Aspen turned to point at her tent. "I have a good two-person tent over here. It's a little cramped, but you are invited—if you want."

Mo eyed the tent before twisting her lips in contemplation. "I don't want to intrude on your space."

"I don't see you as an intruder." Aspen took a step toward Mo. "Besides, the California sun can be tricky. It may feel good out here right now, but tonight the temperature is gonna dip. Which I assume you experienced last night. It's warmer in there with me."

Mo didn't respond, instead crossing over to the tent and kneeling to put her stuff just inside the already tied-open flap. She then went to stand next to Aspen, changing the subject. "Anything else we need to set up?"

"Don't think so."

"Should we start the fire?"

"No, too early still." Aspen looked up at the edge of the still-visible sun. "I probably could have shown you how to set up the tent—"

"It is kinda toasty out here, huh?" Mo interrupted Aspen, her eyes directed at the creek.

"Yeah?"

"We smell like shit." Mo turned to lock eyes with Aspen, a mischievous look plastered across her face. "That water is looking mighty inviting…"

Aspen instantly wanted to decline. She knew that even if the sun and air were warm, the water was going to still be pretty cold. But she watched the twinkle in Mo's eyes spread to her entire face, and she was powerless to say no outright. "It's really not warm at all, but…"

Mo didn't let her finish, instead bolting toward her pack. Aspen watched as she pulled out a lightweight backpacking towel, tossing it haphazardly in the direction of the water. Then, without much forethought, Mo began stripping off her clothes. Aspen stood in shock, watching as Mo expertly removed her hiking shirt, leaving only a crisscrossed black sports bra in its wake. Then Mo walked a few feet toward the water, unbuttoning her hiking pants as she moved before stopping to slide the fabric down over her small but round butt and lanky legs. Something dropped out of Mo's pocket as the pants hit the ground, but Aspen was too distracted by all the skin on display to let her know.

Aspen's eyes zeroed in on her butt, accentuated perfectly by her tight black boxer briefs. She couldn't stop her eyes from moving up Mo's lean back, letting her mind wander to thoughts of scraping her nails up and down the length of her. Mo turned in her direction, but instead of listening to whatever the woman was saying, Aspen let her eyes wander over Mo's small but round breasts and down her lean stomach. She wondered what it would feel like to run her fingers underneath the band of Mo's boxer briefs, how Mo's muscles might react to her touch. The thought of it all was arousing Aspen in an almost painful way, causing her to squirm where she stood.

"Aspen?" Mo's worried voice finally caught her attention.

"Yeah?" Aspen croaked back, looking up to meet Mo's eyes.

"Are you coming in fully clothed?" Mo asked, a disappointed look behind her cheeky smile.

"No." Aspen laughed softly, reaching her hands down to grab the tight fabric at her waist.

She pulled up easily, awkwardly removing her hiking shirt. Aspen had been ashamed of her body in her teenage years but found herself more comfortable in it as she aged. Her ex-husband had never had qualms with her weight, instead being very vocal about how much he loved her butt. But after her divorce, she had a few fleeting moments of wondering if she should be trying to slim down. The first woman she had slept with had washed away all that worry, kissing every inch of her with a reverence that Aspen had never experienced, allowing her to finally fully love the way she was.

Fat and all.

"Do you mind if I take off my bra?" Mo asked, her fingers under the band in the front.

"Not at all," Aspen assured, licking and biting her lip in anticipation. "If you don't mind—"

"No, no! Please do." Mo had read her mind, pulling her bra off and tossing it back toward her pack before moving toward the water.

Aspen didn't want to be left behind, so she stripped off her pants before reaching around to unclip her own sports bra, letting it drop where she stood. She then followed Mo into the water, shivering as soon as the coolness reached her midthigh. "It's just like I thought. So fucking cold!"

"Nah." Mo leaned down so only her head was above water. "I think it feels good. Especially after all that hiking."

"Hot springs water would feel good, this is..." Aspen moved forward slowly. She looked up and saw Mo watching her intently, the woman's eyes fully on her chest. She could feel herself blushing under the attention. "This is just cold."

"You are..." Mo began, her eyes still on Aspen as she reached where she was kneeling. "Absolutely stunning."

"Thank you," Aspen responded, kneeling down next to Mo as her body slowly acclimated to the water. Mo grinned wide, just staring happily at Aspen in the afternoon sun.

Aspen giggled, feeling beyond comfortable just wading next to her at this moment. "God, you are so cute."

"We should have brought soap. Wait, can we even use soap?"

"Not directly in the water, no," Aspen said, shifting slightly closer to Mo. "I have some biodegradable stuff we can use to freshen up or clean the dishes, but we use that outside of the creek. I can show you how to leave the least amount of impact on the environment."

"Ooh, talk nerdy to me."

Aspen threw her head back in laughter.

"All joking aside," Mo said, moving even closer to Aspen, only inches between them. "I am thankful you're here."

"Even if you tried to scare me away?" Aspen asked, a tad breathless, moving so that she was fully facing Mo, their bodies now touching ever so slightly.

"I'm sorry about that."

Mo's breath was on Aspen's face as she slowly swallowed her nerves, her heart beating rapidly at how close they were now. Under the water her thighs were touching Mo's, so she slowly moved her arms to hover over her shoulders before asking, "Can I?"

"Please," Mo murmured, allowing Aspen to hang her wrists over Mo's shoulders and against her neck.

This pulled their torsos together, and Aspen let out a tiny moan at the feeling of being pressed against Mo fully, the warmth of her body staving off the coolness she had just been complaining about. Mo's hands snaked comfortably onto Aspen's hips, just above the band of her boy-shorts. She looked up, curious to see what Mo's reaction was. The attraction Aspen found in the taller woman's eyes was intensely alluring, and her focus trailed down to Mo's lips, soft and inviting. They stayed like this for a few long moments, both of them obviously enjoying the closeness. Her hands moved to feel down her neck to her shoulders, then back up again, stalling around Mo's jawline, where her fingers lightly played with the short hairs behind Mo's ears. Mo closed her eyes, her breathing beginning to quicken.

"Can I—" was all Aspen could get out before Mo leaned forward, ending her question with a light kiss.

Aspen deepened the contact, moaning at just how good Mo's soft lips felt against her own. Like they belonged together. She couldn't get enough, working diligently to deepen the kiss, loving that Mo was already moving her hands up and down Aspen's back, leaving a trail of goose bumps in their wake. Just as much as Aspen's body pushed her to continue the kissing, hoping desperately that it would lead to something more, her mind was telling her to slow down. To check in verbally with Mo about what this meant.

About how this changed things.

Their mouths parted naturally, and Mo leaned in close, allowing Aspen to feel her smile against her neck. "That was…"

"Good," Aspen finished for her, languidly trailing her fingertips along Mo's neck.

"Better than good," Mo corrected, pulling back to look into Aspen's eyes. "But I gotta tell you something."

That phrase had Aspen's nerves rapidly coiling in her chest, so she nodded nervously.

"You were right, it is fucking cold." Mo chuckled before tilting her head toward shore. "Do you mind if we stop and get warm? Maybe start dinner?"

Aspen was both relieved and disappointed. "I told you so!"

Then she leaned in and gave Mo a chaste kiss before reaching down to grab her hands and tug her toward the shore.

* * *

Dinner was pretty uneventful, which was fine by Aspen, as it allowed her a bit of breathing room from their kiss in the creek. Aspen knew it was inevitable. The two of them had enormous amounts of chemistry, held back by their individual willpower. What she hadn't known was that she was going to love it this much. Or that Mo, a woman wounded so deeply by the death of her wife, was going to be this blasé about it. Mo acted like this was something they had been doing the entire time, nary a hint to how she was feeling about it. And it bugged Aspen.

The last piece of wood had finished burning up in the fire. They were sitting in the comfortable silence that the cool air provided, watching the final embers dim down to almost nothing. It was a little past nine o'clock, and the wind made forty-eight degrees feel like thirty-eight. Aspen took in a deep breath before looking toward Mo, watching her watch the fire for a few precious moments.

"The wind is pretty cold without the fire," Aspen stated, attempting to keep her voice as neutral as Mo had been since their kiss. If she had gone with her initial thought, Aspen would have just walked over to Mo, pulled her up from the chair, kissed her gently, and then dragged her to the tent. But she was still unsure where Mo was mentally, and even more so, where she was at emotionally. "Ready to turn in?"

"Yeah, I'm kind of beat." Mo nodded, finally meeting Aspen's gaze. "Though not nearly as sore as yesterday, thanks to you."

The comeback wrote itself, but Aspen held her tongue, instead replying, "I still feel bad about not telling you that."

Mo stood, stretching her arms high into the air before letting them fall lazily to her sides. "I don't. I was an ass."

Aspen giggled then stood herself, grabbing the back of her camp chair and tipping it over on its side. Mo followed suit, even though Aspen knew she had no idea why, but this time she didn't ask. She just trusted Aspen. It felt incredible.

"I'm going to go to the bathroom," Mo said, grabbing something from her pack. "I gotta pee, just in case you were about to explain that damn trowel to me."

"Someone told you about the trowel?" Aspen exclaimed, doing her best to sound disappointed. "Damn, other people get to have all the fun."

"There will be other embarrassments," Mo reminded her, her voice trailing off as she clicked on her headlamp and walked quietly toward the woods.

Aspen had already used the bathroom and showed Mo how to brush her teeth, so she didn't have anything to keep her dallying outside of the tent. So instead she just sucked it up and climbed inside, adjusting their sleeping bags so they were barely touching. After she was most of the way inside hers, she pulled on her gray skullcap beanie, making sure to stuff any wayward strands of hair up inside of it. Then she waited, cross-legged and nervous, by the light of her headlamp for Mo to return.

"Miss me?" Mo asked just outside the tent before carefully climbing inside, making sure her Crocs stayed outside and underneath the rain fly.

"This is a nice sleeping pad!" Aspen blurted out, grimacing slightly at how loud and strange she sounded.

"Annie was particular about her gear." Mo smiled, patting the pad before getting into her own sleeping bag. "Or at least that's what Opal told me."

"Was she like that about the stuff in the house?"

"Yes and no. We never had disagreements about what to buy or what style the house should have. But she definitely enjoyed spreadsheeting each time we needed to compare appliances or furniture." Mo slid down to lie flat with her head on her fluffed-up backpacking pillow. "Do you like spreadsheets?"

"I'm a Gemini," Aspen said, sliding down onto her own pillow and clicking off her headlamp.

"I assume that means no."

"It actually means hell no."

Mo snorted heavily, squirming until their shoulders were touching. Aspen held her breath for a few moments, then after it seemed like Mo had found a comfortable spot, she released. Aspen considered going to sleep, but the thought from earlier still lingered.

"Can I ask you something?"

"Sure," Mo replied instantly, rolling to her side to look at Aspen.

"Something…personal?"

"Uh, yeah. I mean, if I don't wanna answer, I won't."

"All right." Aspen swallowed. "We kissed."

Mo didn't reply, causing Aspen to turn and look at her. She watched Mo's blank expression refuse to change. Her anxiety began to build before Mo relieved it with a simple, "Oh, sorry, thought there was more to that. But yeah, uh, we did."

"Is that okay?" Aspen finally rolled to face Mo, deciding she'd rather look into her eyes than the top of the tent.

"Of course it is, wait…" Mo suddenly looked concerned. "Was it not okay for you?"

"No, no. It totally was okay with me, I just…" Aspen chuckled a little. "Annie."

"Oh." Mo's eyebrows went inward, confusion apparent in her eyes. "Are you worried about Annie?"

"No, I'm worried about whether you were struggling with kissing me because of Annie."

"Ohh, now I think I'm tracking."

Aspen bit her lip. Feeling slightly embarrassed for bringing it up. "I'm sorry—"

"No, don't be sorry. That's a good question." Mo smiled lazily. "I think I can explain."

"Okay."

"You aren't the first person I've kissed since Annie died," Mo said simply, her face soft and understanding. "I had a one-night stand, about two years ago. And yeah, I did have a bit of a breakdown about it in front of that poor woman."

Concern welled up in Aspen, and she removed a hand from her sleeping bag, placing it gently on Mo's arm. "I'm sorry."

"It's okay. I'm really glad you asked. Because, yeah, I wasn't in any way ready for that intimacy," Mo said. "You aren't the first person I've kissed since her."

"That's—" Aspen started but Mo's hand covered her own, stopping her from finishing.

"But you are the first person who has actually cared about Annie. Well, at least in the way I deal with being without her." Mo's voice was almost a whisper, causing the hairs on Annie's arms to stand up. "Thank you for that."

Aspen didn't know what to say, so she just turned her hand in Mo's and squeezed as hard as she could.

CHAPTER FIFTEEN

The sun's rays hitting the tent slowly stirred Mo from her slumber, a far better alarm clock than she was used to. Her eyes slowly opened as she took in Aspen's tent, which was a nice, deep-sea blue with the sunlight filtering through. The sleeping bag was an iota too warm, so she gently rolled on to her back, yawning and stretching in unison. Birds trilled cheerily outside the tent, mixing perfectly with the lackadaisical babble of the creek. Mo could feel the warmth of Aspen next to her, but her easy breathing let her know the woman was still fast asleep.

The urge to turn and look at her companion was overwhelming, so Mo lightly rolled to her side, finding an amusing view of Aspen's eyebrows peeking out between her beanie and sleeping bag. Mo stifled a laugh, instead just feeling affection spread warmly through her chest at the sight. How did Mo's desire for Aspen change from a simple crush to something more enticingly deep? Her question from the previous night had taken Mo slightly off guard, but in the end she was pleased that Aspen had asked it. Even more so because it gave her courage to ask some questions of her own.

As if Aspen could read Mo's mind, she began to stir, emitting a rather lazy-sounding yawn from beneath her sleeping bag. Mo waited patiently, watching as she pulled the edge of her bag down below her chin and opened her eyes to meet Mo's.

"Morning," Mo greeted, making sure to speak softly. "I promise I haven't been staring."

"Good to know." Aspen giggled slightly, her voice crackly in the morning air. "What time is it?"

"No idea," Mo replied, enjoying how adorable Aspen looked just waking up. "Are we in a time crunch?"

"No, thankfully," Aspen said while checking her watch that she had slipped into a pouch installed on the side of the tent. "Already nine forty-five. Ya hungry?"

"I could eat." Mo punctuated her words with a yawn. "But that involves getting out of bed. Which, I must admit, it's a ton more comfortable here in the tent than out there. You were right. Again."

Aspen sported a slightly proud smile, pushing herself up to a sitting position before removing her beanie. Mo watched curiously as she fluffed her shoulder-length hair, the highlights taking on the blue from the tent. She then pulled it up into a lazy ponytail, yawning again as she made sure she got all the strands inside. Aspen pulled up her sleeves before turning to Mo, her soft features pulled in slight embarrassment before she asked, "What?"

"Nothing." Mo smiled, watching as Aspen pulled her lip in between her teeth nervously. "Just admiring you is all."

"Okay." Aspen turned slightly pink, looking away. She crawled out of her sleeping blanket and unzipped the tent flap, turning to put on her Crocs. "I'm gonna go to the bathroom and get breakfast started."

"Sounds good. Do you need help?" Mo began to pull herself up into a sitting position.

"I think I should be good. I'd say just relax for a bit. I'm hoping to get us to the fork of Bridge Creek today. I was going to have you look at a few spots around there to see if any of them were to your liking."

"Sounds…" Mo trailed off as Aspen quickly exited the tent, not waiting around for her answer. "Okay then."

Mo removed the sleeping bag from her body, yawning as she quietly considered what she was going to do next. Just as she began to focus, Annie crossed her mind, and she reached toward her hiking pants for the treasure. When she grabbed at its usual pocket, Mo found nothing but the feeling of crumpled synthetic material. Dread flowed through her body like ice water, and she frantically began searching, no idea about where it could have gone.

"Mo?" A concerned Aspen asked from outside the tent. "You good?"

"No," was all Mo could muster, frustration growing as every treasureless moment passed. The flap reopened slightly and Mo looked up, meeting the eyes of a worried-looking Aspen. "Annie's treasure."

"What?"

"I can't find Annie's treasure," Mo snapped loudly, picking up the pace of her hasty search. Aspen's breath caught in her throat loud enough for Mo to hear, and she stopped moving, attempting to contain her anger. "I didn't mean to yell at you Aspen, I—"

"S'okay," Aspen replied. "Where did you last see it?"

"My pocket, yesterday."

"Wait." Aspen pulled the entire flap open, letting the breeze in. "I think I remember something falling out of your pocket yesterday and God, I'm sorry I should have told—"

"Goddammit." Mo groaned in annoyance, moving to slide into her Crocs and join Aspen outside of the tent. "Where?"

Aspen's face was filled with guilt, but she pointed toward the rocks near the creek. "Over there, I think? I think in the same spot you took your clothes off?"

Mo power-walked over, her head moving back and forth as she scanned the ground for it. As she darted around, she rolled her ankle slightly. "Shit!"

"Are you okay?" a tiny voice asked gingerly from beside her. Mo turned to see Aspen looking rapidly between the ground and her face, the woman's obvious anxiety pulling painfully at Mo's heartstrings.

It made her stop and sit, regretful that her panic had caused that kind of stress on someone else. "You can stop."

"Huh?" Aspen asked, her voice still small.

"It'll probably take hours to find it in all these rocks," Mo replied, halfway smiling as she tried to convey her apology. "I'm sorry, I didn't mean to make you feel like it was your fault."

"But it's important, right?" Aspen replied, returning to search. "If it was Annie's, I will find it."

Mo hummed warmly, touched that Aspen wanted to keep looking even after she had let her frustration show again. "Please come sit next to me."

Aspen seemed to slow to return. Mo let out a defeated sigh, which seemed to call Aspen back to her side. She sat down on the ground, pulling her knees to her chest.

Mo placed a light hand on her kneecap. "I promise, even with how I acted, you weren't the reason I lost it. And if I'm being honest, I didn't even know what it was to begin with."

"What do you mean?"

"It was some hiking thing…I have no idea what it was and I didn't ask. Opal gave it to me, said it was Annie's, and I just…" Mo huffed air out, turning to catch Aspen's eyes. "I put too much weight in something insignificant."

Aspen didn't reply, instead lightly covering Mo's hand with her own.

"And I took it out on you. Again."

"What did it look like?" Aspen asked quietly, and Mo turned to meet her soft gaze.

"It was a little cylindrical thing with like a twisty circle on top but like to the side. Metal and wood, one side was kind of grooved? It had little leaves stamped into it. And 'AR' engraved, her initials, I assume."

"Was the little twisty thing textured and like off to the side of the cylinder?" Aspen probed, her voice taking on a wave of understanding.

Mo thought about the treasure before nodding. "Yeah, I think so."

"Sounds like a fancy ferro rod," Aspen said, looking back toward the rocks. "They're made to help start fires."

A wave of affection flooded over Mo. "How do you know that?"

Aspen shrugged before standing up again. "I'll keep looking…"

But Mo suddenly didn't want to anymore, instead reaching up to stop Aspen. "No, no. It's okay. I think I should let go of it."

Aspen nodded in response, but Mo noticed the anxiety had returned to her face.

"Aspen?"

"I'll make breakfast, then," Aspen said quickly before moving back toward the tent, leaving Mo to sit with the regret.

* * *

Mo was back to setting the pace. They were no longer following the trail; instead, she was leading them along the rocky creek bed. The trail was very overgrown in places, so Aspen had them wearing their Crocs today, explaining that they might need to trudge through the creek for some of the hike. After that she had gone silent, causing Mo to wonder if she had done something to offend her. They had been holding that silence for over an hour, and as they reached another shallow crossing, Mo decided to stop and allow Aspen to come up alongside her.

"Are you all right?" Mo asked, turning to look at Aspen.

"Yeah." Aspen shrugged, but her eyes were clouded with what Mo could only describe as guilt.

"I am going to go out on a limb here and say you aren't."

"I am, I'm just…" Aspen took in a deep breath, slowly releasing the air. "I'm sorry. I guess I woke up in a mood."

"That's okay," Mo assured her. "Moods are allowed. Obviously."

"Are you okay?" Aspen asked, her voice softer than it had been all morning. "With everything?"

"With us?" Mo cocked her head. "Or Annie's treasure?"

Aspen seemed to pull back in on herself, so Mo stepped forward before gently asking, "Can I hug you?"

"Why?"

"Just because." Mo took another step into Aspen's space but kept her arms at her side. "But it's up to you."

"Okay." Aspen chuckled.

The tension that seemed to have built between them rapidly dwindled as Mo enveloped Aspen, sliding her arms between her pack and midback. Aspen reacted awkwardly for a quick second before leaning into it, resting her forehead against Mo's collarbone and gripping the side of her own pack. They stayed locked in the warm hug for a few moments before Mo finally pulled back, looking down at Aspen with a big smile.

"Okay?"

"Actually, yeah. I'm sorry I got all weird," Aspen replied, her eyes a bit brighter.

"No worries." Mo nodded. "Do you want to talk about it?"

Aspen turned to look in the direction they were heading before looking back at Mo. "Not really…"

"Want to ask more questions?" Mo moved to cross the creek again. "Like the beach day?"

"Sure," Aspen said, only taking a few seconds before continuing, "You mentioned wanting to die…"

"Well," Mo began as she gently ambled forward, carefully watching where she stepped through the clear creek water. "It wasn't like the movies or what you hear from a television commercial warning about suicide. I just kind of decided to let it take me. If it wanted me, I guess?"

"It?" Aspen asked curiously, her voice calm and free of judgment. Mo lifted her arms up and out, twisting slightly as if to display her surroundings to Aspen. "So that's why you put up a fight about me coming with you?"

"Uh…" Mo thought for a second, stopping once she reached the shore. "Yes and no. I didn't really plan anything out. To be honest, I haven't planned anything since before Annie died. I've mostly drifted from moment to moment, hoping I'd stumble upon an answer of some kind."

"Have you found that answer?"

"I don't know." Mo motioned toward a large redwood stump forty or so yards down the creek. "Can we sit and have a break?"

"Of course," Aspen said brightly, and Mo felt a surge of happiness at the return of that side of her.

The pair hiked up to the stump, and Mo surveyed its many rings as she removed her pack and propped it against the side. She leaned over the stump, running her free hand along the surface, noticing the differences in size and color.

"The tree's history," Aspen murmured next to Mo, leaning against her as she mirrored Mo's position. "This," Aspen said gently, pointing at the center of the tree. "It's the tree's first year of growth. Each of the white lines show growth during the rainy season and the dark ones show growth during the dry."

Mo gulped at their closeness, tingles running along her scalp and spine as she watched Aspen explain. "How do you know its age, then?"

"You count the dark rings from the middle out. The wider the white rings, the better the growing season was. Dry seasons are denoted by little growth and smaller rings. And this"— Aspen leaned in closer to Mo to point at a dark blemish on the side of the stump closest to her—"is probably scarring from a forest fire."

"Wow."

"Yeah, a long life automatically archived," Aspen said reverently, turning to sit. "Right until the end."

Mo mirrored her movements, sitting close to her on the stump and mulling over Aspen's words. A few minutes passed before she decided to reveal more. "Annie was diagnosed with breast cancer right after Christmas 2016. I will never forget how strong Annie was. So sure, so just, so embattled under the weight of that kind of news. She seemed to take it like a champ while I was a bumbling mess. I really struggled to understand how this was happening to her. To us."

Mo paused, her eyes drawing up to the evergreen canopy, admiring the wind shaking the leaves slightly, the way the trees seemed to create a barrier from the outside world.

"The chemo was scheduled soon after. My active, albeit clumsy, wife was morphed into a slow-moving, nap-taking homebody. And while the cancer and chemo stopped a lot of things, it never stopped our love. We both took leave from work. I cared for her during the entire process, enjoying the time we spent trying to make her better. Our interests changed to indoor fun. Board games, video games, audiobooks, podcasts—hell, even small jam sessions in bed. Well, until she couldn't sing anymore. Then I would just play one of my guitars as she hummed along. Annie was such a good sport, down for whatever shenanigans I could think of to keep us both occupied as she became more and more bedridden. God, I tried so hard to make her better, but…"

Aspen didn't push, instead reaching for Mo's hand and squeezing lightly.

"But it metastasized in her lymph nodes and lungs. They confirmed it after her double mastectomy. I was distraught. But she was eerily calm, taking that moment to ask the doctor if that meant she could eat sushi again." Mo laughed, rubbing her forehead with her free hand.

"I don't follow…" Aspen said softly.

"Annie couldn't have certain things during her aggressive type of chemo. Sushi, raw veggies, raw eggs. You know, stuff like that. Don't ask why, I honestly never looked into it. But…" Mo swallowed harshly. "I did go to her favorite sushi place and got all her favorite rolls. I also begged the place to let me borrow one of their gigantic wooden sushi boats. I must've looked pitiful, because they agreed. I remember the exact look on her face when I came bursting in with the full sushi boat, sake slipped under my arm. We had a feast in the hospital room that night."

"Sounds wonderful."

"It was. We did one more round of aggressive chemo before Annie asked to stop. She was ready."

Her words seemed to enhance all the sounds around them. The creek babbled loudly. A few birds chirped with newfound gusto. The wind blew harder through the foliage, rocking the trees back and forth. Every syllable she released was not only heightening her senses but making her feel lighter—like they were a heavy weight, and she was becoming buoyant again.

"We had a lot of conversations about what I was going to do after she was gone. But for the life of me, I don't remember one request she had. I thought she was going to live all the way up until she died. I never lost hope."

"And maybe that's why you torture yourself so," Aspen said. "Because a part of you still hopes that she will recover. Even though you know she's gone."

"Probably, yeah," Mo choked out, tears forming in her eyes. "And she'd hate that."

"She might but—but I understand. It's hard to let go of hope. Especially with something like life or death. It's hard to hope it will actually change for the better." Aspen moved their intertwined hands to her lap, using her free hand to lightly rub along Mo's knuckle. "But I don't think Annie would be mad at you. She seems the forgiving type—being married to you and all."

Mo laughed a wet, coughing laugh as her tears fell. "You're right."

"Per usual," Aspen softly stated. "But for real—it's hard to let go of what-ifs. Stop torturing yourself over feeling something human."

"Thank you." Mo wiped her eyes before turning to meet Aspen's, a question lingering between them. After a few moments Mo decided to ask it, assuming Aspen would shut it down but hoping she'd actually answer. "What aren't you letting go of?"

Aspen blinked rapidly, the question apparently catching her off guard. Mo watched as she went through a few different emotions before taking a deep breath and giving her a guilty smile. "I guess I'm easy to read, huh?"

"If someone is paying attention." Mo squeezed her hand lightly. "But you don't have to share if you don't want to. But I…I want to listen."

Aspen's foot began to wiggle as her lips twisted in thought, her head wobbling in contemplation. "All right. Your struggle with letting go of Annie's…Annie. It, uh, hit a chord with me."

"How so?"

"Life's not always been the kindest, I guess? A lot of people have let me down over the years. I've always waited patiently, hoping those people would make a change. But that change… it never seems to come. But I still look for it. Even now," Aspen shakily admitted, looking up the creek and away from Mo.

"Kyle?"

"Kyle." Aspen nodded before adding with the smallest of murmurs, "My parents."

"I've avoided asking about them, even though I wanted to. Any time they are mentioned you get a particular look in your eyes."

"Growing up was…hard. My parents were what some people would stereotype as traveling hippies. They were high school sweethearts, both from around Eureka but they rarely stayed there. Instead, they drove their RV up and down the coast, from Vancouver down into Mexico. I was an accident. A night where birth control was laid to the wayside, I figure. But for some reason or another, they decided to keep me."

Mo slid her leg up under herself, turning to fully watch Aspen as she relayed the story. She could feel the weight of it all sit between them, like this was something Aspen rarely shared.

"They bought another RV and permanently parked it in Eureka, kind of making that our home base of sorts. When I was really little, I was easy to take with them. Anytime they wanted to be free of me, they would just feed me and put me to bed, locking me inside that hunk of metal. It worked. Up until I needed further care and teaching. And just like children do, I learned to talk, think, and was required by the government they despised to go to school. So they would leave me in Eureka for most of the year. Sometimes overnight, sometimes on the weekends."

"By yourself?" Mo gruffed, appalled, finding herself angry at Aspen's parents.

"Technically, yeah. Janice, Virginia's mother and our closest neighbor, decided to watch over me. She would make sure I ate, went to school, and had everything that I needed to survive. When I was a kid, I kind of saw her like a grandmother, so I didn't really understand why I couldn't just live with her. But she was feeble and unable to care for me full time, so she did her best with what my parents selfishly left for her." Aspen shrugged.

"I'm sorry." Mo studied the side of Aspen's head. "That's terrible."

"I was really lonely. I waited patiently for my parents to come home and was incredibly clingy when they would, only causing them to push me away more. A vicious cycle that I self-medicated with books and an overeagerness to make friends. Unfortunately, Kyle was the only one who actually showed me real affection so…"

"You took to him," Mo said.

"Figuring out myself and leaving that world behind…it's the best I've ever been. But yeah, I still need my parents. Even though I have no idea of how or where they are, I still want them to show up and accept me. Love me the way I should have been loved, I guess." Aspen chuckled sadly, turning to give Mo a defeated smile. "So yeah, while what they did is different, I understand."

Mo's focus bounced between each of Aspen's eyes, her heart tugging her forward. With a little shuffle, Mo leaned her forehead against Aspen's, pulling her into a slight embrace. They breathed each other's air for a little while before Mo finally said, "Thank you for telling me."

"Thanks for listening. I'm sorry I hijacked another—" Aspen began but was cut off by a light kiss from Mo.

"Don't. It's all right. Besides, I am glad to finally know the backstory behind your obsession with *The Parent Trap*," Mo joked, laughing when Aspen sighed dramatically at her.

"You are infuriating!"

"You keep telling me that," Mo returned, peppering another kiss between responses. "I'm starting to love hearing it."

Aspen rolled her eyes before adding, "You must have driven Annie crazy."

"On the contrary." Mo leaned back, smiling lazily. "She drove me crazy."

"Is that so?" Aspen scooted away to grab two granola bars she had stashed in the top of her pack that morning. With an exaggerated flick of her wrist, she offered one to Mo, who gladly received it.

"Ooh, thanks. And of course she did. Annie was the queen of a million tiny annoying things."

"Like?" Aspen ripped open her treat, doubt clear on her face.

"She would set her alarms to odd numbers, like 7:47 a.m.," Mo said, remembering fondly. "She liked extra, extra sauce on her pizza."

Aspen giggled heartily, choking a little before exclaiming, "Eww, what?"

"She ate cereal out of our mixing bowls and would leave them scattered around the house. Including on the back of the toilet. Because she did this horrifying thing where she'd eat in the shower," Mo declared loudly, pointing her bar toward Aspen. "Like, who eats cereal in the shower?"

"I've eaten in the shower…" Aspen replied. "Not cereal, but I've done it."

"Blasphemy!"

"It isn't that serious." Aspen huffed playfully, waving her off. "Annie sounds, I'm gonna be honest, really fun."

"Of course, don't mistake my annoyance for hate. I loved every little thing. But, like, she'd put milk in everything. Was afraid of getting animals because she couldn't give them enough of her time. Ooh, she hated cream cheese on everything but bagels. She would do the robot at the drop of a hat."

"That's just sensible," Aspen declared, even as Mo scoffed.

"Do you like Thai food?" Mo suddenly asked. "Annie was obsessed with ordering everything Thai hot but cried profusely into it. Every. Single. Time."

The towering redwoods just swayed lightly in the breeze as the pair were consumed in conversation, nothing pressing them forward. The energy was electric. Everything small was important, every joke hilarious, and every memory precious. But Mo eventually remembered she had been focusing too much on herself for a second, stopping to reel in her steady stream of Annie tidbits.

"You were married. Did Kyle have any weird things he did that annoyed the crap out of you?" Mo prompted, watching Aspen think.

Aspen's hand dragged down the side of her own face and neck as she considered an answer, driving Mo a tad wild. She squirmed on the stump but leaned in, waiting patiently.

"Weirdly enough, no. I mean, he was pretty terrible to me, but that was more than just a regular annoyance. I never really got to know him like you knew Annie. I only think our marriage worked for as long as it did because I didn't see him daily, which masked his self-centered nature and traditional expectations." Aspen gave Mo a half-hearted shrug before punctuating her reply with, "He was pretty blindsided when I left him, but I am sure he thought everything I did was annoying."

"His loss." Mo scooted even closer. She locked eyes with Aspen as the two naturally leaned in toward each other, a familiar yet new magnetism that had Mo utterly hooked. A thought popped into her head, and instead of squashing it down, Mo whispered it just loud enough for Aspen to hear. "I want to learn everything about you. Every last idiosyncrasy, even if it drives me mad."

Aspen launched herself into Mo, claiming her lips instantly. Mo moaned into the kiss, her hands wrapping around Aspen and grasping firmly to her midback. This kiss was more intense than the others they had shared, like a hunger had been released between the two of them. Aspen sucked lightly on Mo's lower lip, her hands moving from around Mo's ears down over her chest, where they slowed near her breasts.

Mo knew she was silently asking for permission, so she momentarily broke their kiss to rasp an enthusiastic, "Yes."

"Fuck yeah," Aspen returned, her hands moving to cup both of Mo's breasts through her shirt.

The feeling was incredible. Mo shifted on the stump to get her body closer to Aspen. As she did so, she trailed her own fingers along the small of Aspen's back. With practiced ease, Mo slightly lifted the back of Aspen's shirt and ran her fingertips lightly over the skin of her back, eliciting a deep moan. The sound brought a whole new wave of wetness between Mo's legs, and she moved to straddle Aspen on the stump, hastening their kiss.

But as she did so, Mo noticed Aspen got a tad rigid. This set off alarms in Mo's brain, causing her to pull away and look into Aspen's eyes. There in the deep brown of her eyes was a mixture of lust and fear, so Mo kissed her lightly before moving off her lap and asking, "Are you okay?"

"Yeah, sorry. I just—I'm not sure, is all," Aspen replied, following Mo to seemingly kiss her again, but Mo gently grabbed her hands and stilled her.

"Don't be sorry, it's okay." Mo nodded, smiling wide. "And if you aren't sure, that's totally fine. We can keep moving."

"Are you sure?" Aspen seemed pleased but also hesitant.

"Totally." Mo stood, offering her hand to Aspen. Once she took it, Mo helped her to her feet and added cheekily, "I only want to if we both one hundred percent want to. But I will have you know, I enjoyed every second of that."

"Thank you."

"No problem." Mo grinned, turning to meet Aspen's eyes, where she found softness instead of hesitation.

CHAPTER SIXTEEN

Aspen zipped closed the tent, the early-morning air cold against her skin. The wind had picked up during the night, and the unsettling sound had woken her up around six, howling unnervingly through the tops of the redwoods. The trees creaked and groaned under the strain of the gusts, leaving her alone with her thoughts. She genuinely tried to quiet them, but Aspen's inability to deal with her spiking anxiety next to Mo's slow, rhythmic breathing had led her to quietly dress, grab her satellite phone, and exit the tent.

Yesterday, the pair had reached the point where Bridge Creek flowed into Redwood Creek. After setting up camp, they used the little bit of daylight left to scout around, trying to see if they could find a good tree. Unfortunately, this particular area was thick with young redwoods, and nothing seemed to be suitable for the wind phone. Mo had become a tad frustrated with the lack of available space for Annie's phone but was in better spirits overall. She had been flirting and joking instead of wallowing in her frustration. It was stark in contrast to Aspen, who was now crumbling under the weight of her deepening affection for Mo. To help block her anxiety out, she had assured Mo they would hike all the way to Devil's Creek if they had to. Mo didn't seem too fazed, exclaiming that she was just happy to be here with Aspen.

With Aspen.

Her brain had taken that, plus their increasingly arousing interactions, and ran wild. Now, as she power-walked away from their campsite and into the woods, Aspen was hoping Virginia would be able to help her sort through all of this. Once she found some brush that blocked the wind but still had a decent view of the sky needed for reception, Aspen quickly found Virginia's number in the phone's address book and hit send.

"Pick up, pick up. Please pick up," Aspen whined, crouching to sit haphazardly in the leaf litter. She adjusted herself manically, trying her best to get comfortable.

After what felt like an hour but was probably no more than thirty seconds, a tired voice answered. "Aspen?"

"Oh thank God you're awake," Aspen almost yelled, cowering and looking toward the campsite, worried that her voice would carry. "Hi."

"You dying?" Virginia's morning voice grumbled.

"No, no. I just, uh…I'm having a problem?" Aspen's voice wavered, unsure if she could properly explain her predicament. "You're always the first person I think of when I'm in a pickle. And Virginia, oh am I pickled—pickling? Oh, I don't know, something like that?"

"Butch not good in bed?" Virginia responded, shuffling noises apparent in the background. "You don't need to call me and give me a play-by-play. I coulda just waited for you to come back."

"That's not, uh, my problem."

"All right. Well…" Virginia cleared her throat. "You're calling me damn near seven, so somethin' musta happened. What's wrong?"

"Well, I think I kinda…well, you see, we started to do the thing but I just…" Aspen was losing her composure. How was she supposed to make this sound plausible when she herself was confused? "I just feel all kinds of anxious and weird and—"

"She bad at it? I had to teach Sal. You know, orgasms are—"

"Oh God, please no," Aspen interrupted. "No, no. We haven't done that."

"Oh." Virginia's voice lightened from its usual gruff lilt. The older woman held an eerily long silence, which only ratcheted up the anxiety ping-ponging around in Aspen's chest. "You're in love."

"No!" Aspen yelled this time, exasperated. "Well, more like…attached?"

"In love. It happens to the best of us, honey."

"I am not in love. Granted, I've never been in love so I don't know how it feels, but I severely doubt it feels like this. I'm a literal mess, Virginia. I've had flings with tons of women, but for some reason I can't just sleep with her. Why can't I just sleep with her? And to top it all off, it's not like I'm not interested, I'm just…broken?"

"Kyle was wrong—"

"I know," Aspen groaned, rubbing her hand up and down her face. "But what if this is better?" Aspen's heart skipped a beat at the thought. "I don't know. I want to go back to the way life was. I make the connection, we have some laughs, we do the deed, and then she leaves. She is supposed to leave…right?" Aspen ranted, pulling her knees to her chest and resting her head against them. "Help me?"

"Sounds like you are doing just fine to me," Virginia replied, a chuckle in her voice. "Just relax a bit and go with the flow. It's kinda like tubing down the creek—just let the water take ya along. No need to try and paddle against it."

"This isn't like tubing. I feel crazy! And God, she's just so amazing and I don't know what to do. This is too much."

"You've got this, I…"

Aspen didn't hear the rest of what Virginia said, instead alerted to a distant snapping of twigs. Her head flung up and she squinted, recognizing the telltale poof of Mo's hair as she trudged through the woods toward her. She quickly whispered, "Fuck she's coming, I gotta go."

"Tell her how you—" was all Virginia got out before Aspen hung up, scrambling to reach a standing position before Mo got to her fully.

"Hey!" Aspen shouted too loudly, her body practically buzzing with awkward emotion. She had no idea what to do with her hands, so she waved before letting them fall to her sides, shifting in and out of her pockets. "'Sup."

"Morning," Mo returned smoothly. "You weren't in the tent, and I got a bit worried. Thought I'd use the bathroom and look for you. Two birds, one stone, ya know?"

"Totally. Sorry, I was on the satellite phone. I called to check in and make sure people knew we were okay."

"That's thoughtful," Mo said, bracing herself against a tree. "With how windy it is and all."

"Yeah." Aspen nodded, her free hand going into her hair. She looked down and noticed the trowel in Mo's hand. "Make sure you find a place to go where your butt is protected from the wind or you won't be warm for hours."

"Thanks for the tip." Mo grinned before nodding toward a semidistant tree. "Guess I will go and uh…"

"Right," Aspen replied, bowing weirdly as she moved to walk back toward camp, embarrassment flooding her senses. She waited until she was a few hundred yards away before exclaiming to herself in a stage whisper, "Goddammit, you are the weirdest person on the planet, Aspen Anderson."

* * *

The phone call with Virginia did nothing for Aspen's nerves. She had been so distracted that she knocked over the Jetboil. Twice. Mo politely took over, finding a flatter rock to rest the Jetboil on, and boiled the water for their coffee and oatmeal instead. Packing up was just as difficult. Aspen had forgotten little things, struggling to stuff-sack items she had put away a million times before. It was a wonder they had returned to the trail before noon at all.

Mo had been sweet and patient the entire time, not once making Aspen feel stupid for her apparent scatterbrain. So nice, in fact, Aspen had almost pushed her into a chair and flat-out told her what was bothering her. Unfortunately, a seemingly new kind of fear had stopped her each time. So, instead, Aspen just followed clumsily behind a leading Mo, desperately trying to make sense of her tumultuous feelings. The most bothersome of them all was whether or not Virginia was right.

"Am I?" Aspen whispered to herself, unable to say the infamous three little words out loud. She pulled her arms in close to her as another gust of wind swept by. "Can I?"

"Huh? What did you say?" Mo turned and said over the wind, obviously picking up that Aspen was talking.

"Nothing," Aspen cried back, watching Mo smile and nod before continuing to lead.

Aspen blinked a few times, slowing her pace a tad to look up at the swaying redwoods. Their loud creaking under the stress of the wind was as majestic as it was frightening. Aspen had seen plenty of windy days worse than this one, and she figured by how clear the sky was that the wind wouldn't bring any rain with it. She shrugged it off distractedly, her focus dropping to the ground as she continued to follow Mo. Her thoughts raced again, occupying her energy and focus.

"Am I on the right side of the creek?" Mo was suddenly beside her, leaned down close in order to ask.

"Yeah," Aspen muttered, barely looking up to take in where they were.

"Okay," Mo replied, wavering only for a second before moving forward. "Do you hike the whole length of the national park a lot?"

It was a long minute before Aspen's brain notified her of Mo's question, and she quickly mumbled, "Totally."

"Huh?" Mo asked, raising her voice to be heard over another gust of wind.

"Totally!"

"Cool," Mo answered. "I wish I knew if Annie did."

Aspen didn't fully register that comment, instead working her way through her anxious thoughts, her body on autopilot as it navigated the rocky terrain.

"When you are with someone for a long time, especially when you start that relationship young, you think you know everything there is to know about them. But as time moves forward and comfortability sets in, those things you thought you knew are nothing more than well-practiced assumptions. Your brain does its best to hold on to basic facts. Like their favorite food, color, flower, song. What they do at work, how they like their coffee, what they do in their free time. But some benign question from some well-meaning coworker or acquaintance will stump you. And either you will shrug it off, at peace with not knowing the answer, or it will refocus your attention back to your partner. On the essential details that make your partner who they are." Mo spoke slowly, leading them down the creek as she waxed philosophical. "Reminding you that constantly learning, or even relearning, about your partner isn't a bad thing. No, it shows an extra kind of care. One where you take the time to make sure you aren't taking them for granted."

"Mmm," Aspen agreed absentmindedly, barely listening.

"And if you're lucky, they are doing the same for you," Mo finished, stopping in front of an overhang of trees where the creek had widened significantly. "You know?"

"Huh?" Aspen asked, her focus returning to the conversation at hand just as she walked into the back of Mo, grasping her pack to keep her footing. "Whoops."

Mo chuckled before looking over her shoulder and inquiring, "Do we wade along the bank, or cross?"

Aspen did a triple take between the bank and the wide expanse of the creek. The bank in front of them was jutted right up against the water, an overhang of thick trees and brush making it impossible to walk along the ground. In order to move forward, they would have to wade through the water next to the low overhang, which would bring them to a rocky outcropping that Aspen could make out ahead. The second option was crossing the creek itself, as the other side was just a sand- and rock-laden creek bed. But the creek was too wide here for Aspen's liking. It would be too hard to tell the depth, which made it way more risky. The third option, which Aspen barely gave credence to, was to hike backward to a shallower crossing. She definitely wasn't in the mood for a backtrack, so she turned to Mo and shrugged half-heartedly.

"We wade."

"Cool." Mo nodded, shrugging off her pack with more practiced ease. "I assume Crocs and making my pants into shorts?"

"That's what I'm gonna do," Aspen responded, removing her own pack and cursing as her finger was crushed between the plastic on the strap buckle and her collarbone. "Fuck!"

"Careful! We aren't in a hurry."

"Yeah, yeah," Aspen grumbled, pinching the hurt finger with her opposite hand as she focused on the pain. "Stupid pack."

"You sound like me from a few days ago," Mo joked while she leaned over, unzipping the bottoms of her pants to create shorts. "Is it deep here?"

"Should be fine along the bank," Aspen explained, even as her focus was still on her finger.

Aspen sulked, walking herself and her hurt finger to the closest oversized rock to sit and ponder while she slowly kicked off her hiking boots. She took her sweet time removing her socks, still deep in her own feelings. Mo, however, was already pulling her pack back on.

"I'm gonna go on ahead. I think I see a perfect place to look for a good tree." Mo tightened her shoulder straps before snapping closed her chest strap. "See you in a few!"

Aspen only nodded in return, standing to remove the hiking pants she kept on over her workout shorts. Mo grabbed a long stick from next to Aspen, walking out of her view and toward the water's edge. Once her pants were off, Aspen slid on her Crocs and slowly tied the pants to the top of her pack. As she did so, she considered just being friendly with Mo. Ending the trip once her goal was complete and giving her a sweet goodbye, wishing her well with her life back in the Bay. It would create minimal anxiety, and she could return to her own way of life, sticking to what she knew.

"That could definitely work," Aspen whispered out loud to herself, bobbing her head back and forth in consideration. She internally decided that was her best course of action. If she couldn't resolve these issues easily, why push herself now? So Aspen took in a deep breath, centered herself, and brought her focus back to the task at hand. "Wade across the creek and find a suitable tree."

Aspen looked up. Mo was wading forward in the almost knee-deep water, checking the depth with her stick before advancing. She was pleased the woman had taken some of her advice to heart, so she turned her attention to her pack. But just as her fingers grasped the top handhold, a large gust blew in from the direction they had come. The trees loudly groaned under the pressure, and a loud crack caused Aspen to jump. She watched helplessly as a limb from one of the trees above Mo came hurtling down toward her.

"Mo!" Aspen screamed, but it was too late. The limb hit Mo squarely in the shoulders, launching her sideways into the deeper water away from the bank.

Aspen raced forward, slamming hard into the water in an attempt to get to Mo as quickly as she could. She could see Mo's arms and legs flailing in and out of the creek, splashing haphazardly as she struggled under the weight of her pack. Fear and worry exploded in Aspen's chest, pushing her to swim to get to Mo faster. She pumped her arms, the shocking cold of the water stark in contrast to her panic.

"Mo!" Aspen screamed again, watching as both of Mo's Crocs floated to the top. "I'm coming!"

In mere seconds but what felt like minutes, Aspen reached where she had last seen Mo on the surface. She dove under while extending her hands out, luckily finding one of Mo's arms. Aspen grabbed her bicep firmly and pulled, feeling around for the handle at the top of her pack. Once she had a firm grip, Aspen pushed her feet off the bottom of the creek, propelling them both back toward the bank. Aspen used all her strength to pull Mo's head above water, causing Mo to choke and wretch, spitting up whatever she had pulled into her lungs when she had been knocked in.

"Mo?" Aspen was desperate, looking between Mo's sputtering face and the bank she was pulling her toward. "Talk to me."

All Mo returned was a raspy coughing fit, so Aspen focused on getting her safely to shore, cursing herself for not paying more attention. Mo's butt dragged along the bottom of the creek as they reached the edge, pushing Aspen to pull harder. Once Mo was completely out of the water, Aspen moved to hover over her, quickly unsnapping the pack from her body.

"Oh God, I am so fucking sorry. I was in my own little world, and I forgot to tell you to unsnap your straps. The weight of the pack…" Aspen sucked in a breath, fretting audibly as she closed her eyes. "That was so scary."

Mo let out another deep cough, spitting up more water before smiling crookedly and replying, "Honey, you've never looked better."

"Really?" Aspen pushed her shoulder lightly, causing Mo to laugh and cough before sitting back and making an exasperated noise. "This might be the only time I ever get angry at someone quoting *The Parent Trap*."

"I thought it would be better received than a—Ah!" Mo grimaced loudly, sucking breath through her teeth as her left hand flung up to her right shoulder. "I'm fine."

"You are not fine!" Aspen yelled at her, returning to kneel over her. "A branch fell on you. Did it hit you in the head?"

"No, no. Just my shoulders. Mostly my right one, I think."

"I want to check that, but we need to get you out of the creek and out of these wet clothes." Aspen took a deep breath, her resolve hardening. "Can you stand?"

"I'm only a little wet." Mo moved to get up, sliding a tad under the rocks. "My pack, however—"

"Forget the pack. Let me help you to the rock over there," Aspen commanded, leaning over to grab Mo around the middle of her torso. She helped her to her feet and walked with her until she got her seated on some sand, her back against a rock. "I'll check your shoulder after I get your pack out of the water. I need to see if any of your clothes are dry. Once we get you changed, I'll start a fire and set up camp."

"Aspen."

Aspen ignored Mo, striding briskly back to the water to grab her pack, moving it next to her own before unsnapping the top, hurrying to remove items from inside. "Oh fuck, a lot of it got wet. I'll have to sort through it all. Did you pack your clothes at the bottom?"

"Aspen."

She finally found Mo's clothes, thankfully dry, folded in the bottom underneath her rolled-up sleeping pad. Aspen pulled out what she needed and rushed back to Mo's side, laying each piece out in preparation.

"We got lucky, your spare clothes are dry. Let me help you out of your wet—" As she turned, Aspen found a worried face staring at her. "What?"

"I'm right here, Aspen. I'm okay."

"I know, I just—"

"It wasn't your fault." Mo reached out and squeezed her wrist before adjusting her positioning against the rock. "It wasn't anyone's fault."

Aspen took a deep breath in, nodding in response. Mo started to move to remove her shirt before groaning in pain as she attempted to lift her arms above her head.

"Your shoulder?"

"Yeah."

"I'll help." Aspen's anxiety finally came down a tad. She reached forward and helped Mo get her shirt off. Once it was removed, she crab-walked closer to Mo's right side. "Let me look."

"Okay," Mo agreed, bending forward to give Aspen a better view. "Am I gonna die, doc?"

"God, when are you not insufferable?" Aspen replied, a playful lilt to her voice. She examined her shoulder, noticing the redness and welt that extended from the tip of her shoulder and across her trapezius muscle. She touched it lightly, but Mo didn't pull away. "Does this hurt?"

Mo shook her head.

"Can you move and rotate your arm?"

"I can try." Mo slowly rotated her arm, grimacing but making a full rotation. "I don't think anything is ripped or broken, but it definitely hurts."

"I agree." Aspen stood, crossing to her pack. "Keep trying to remove all your clothes. I'm gonna get the ground cover, emergency blanket, and my dry sleeping bag. We gotta get you warmed up."

"I can set up the tent…" Mo began, moving to stand as she unsnapped her shorts.

"No! You almost died. I need you to chill out and just take off your clothes. I'll set up everything after I get a fire started to get you warm."

"Eh." Mo shrugged, tilting back to shimmy her shorts from her body. "Dying wouldn't be the worst thing."

"The fuck it wouldn't, I—" Aspen yelled but stopped herself short, letting out an exasperated grunt instead.

"I'm sorry," Mo said. "You're right."

"Thanks," Aspen responded flatly, crossing near Mo to set up the ground cover on the most even stretch of ground she could find. Once it was laid out, she fluffed and placed down her sleeping bag before unfurling the tiny emergency blanket she had stashed in her backpacking first-aid kit. "Got your clothes off?"

"Yep, like the day I was born."

Aspen moved to hand her the pile of dry clothes, only taking a quick glance at Mo's naked body. She took in a deep breath before asking, "Need help?"

"Just with my shirt." Mo chuckled. "That was my only bra. I Googled that most backpackers only take one, so you know, seeing how I am one of those pros…"

Aspen tried to stay focused. She scrunched the shirt up so she could easily place it over Mo's head. She took extra care with the woman's right arm and shoulder, gingerly helping her get it situated through the arm hole. Once she was clothed, Aspen scooped up the blanket and wrapped Mo in it, her focus on the task and not the sheepish features of her companion.

"I'm a burrito," Mo declared after Aspen finished.

Aspen couldn't help but laugh a little, loving how her laugh brightened Mo's eyes. "You've got another layer, burrito."

"Ooh, I'm a three-layer burrito, then," Mo continued, taking Aspen's direction to lie down in her sleeping bag.

Mo let Aspen help her get fully inside, no complaints or attempts at doing it herself. Once she was zipped up to her head, Aspen gave Mo a few pats before asking, "Good?"

"Yeah, I feel much warmer."

"I knew you were cold!" Aspen pointed disappointedly at her before taking another deep breath. "I'm going to get everything set up, okay?"

"All right. I trust you."

Those words echoed in Aspen's head as she walked toward their gear to get changed herself. This was going to be hard.

CHAPTER SEVENTEEN

The wind died down a little after dusk, leaving a mixture of embarrassment and relief sitting squarely in Mo's chest. She had spent most of the day beside the fire, only moving inside the tent at the behest of an insistent Aspen. The same Aspen who had made a lame excuse to stay out there in order to ensure it was properly extinguished. There had been an uneasy awkwardness between the two all day, and Mo was unsure how to alleviate it.

Should she bring it up? Or should she let it slowly ripple away with time, allowing whatever was going to happen just happen? Mo didn't know. So instead, she just watched as Aspen's shadow paced back and forth, her lit headlamp the only light left.

"Are you still okay?" Aspen finally called out, breaking the silence. Her question was followed by another loud scrape that Mo assumed was her anxiously picking at the fire. "Like physically—well, overall-y I guess?"

"Yeah," Mo yelled back, trying her best to sound light and happy. "I think the Tylenol is finally kicking in. Too bad it can't also dull my embarrassment."

Aspen didn't respond immediately. Mo heard the telltale *whoosh* of the door to the tent being unzipped. She watched Aspen smile slightly as she entered, reaching to tilt her headlamp up and out of Mo's eyes before turning to kneel, zipping the door shut behind her. "I doubt it could do anything for my regret either."

"It was a fluke thing," Mo tried to assure her, adding a joking flair. "Prolly just God trying to smite me again."

Aspen choked out a laugh, her back still to Mo even though she had closed the door fully. After a few moments she finally turned, her face relaxed and soft. Not as tight and concentrated as it had been when she pulled Mo from the creek. Aspen crawled closer, sitting cross-legged next to her. "I think I'm starting to understand how you deal with all the heavy stuff that happens to you."

"That's good. My rule of thumb is that it's only funny if I'm in distress," Mo explained, reaching out to touch Aspen's knee. "But yeah, I'm okay."

"I hope so."

"Thank you, though." Mo scrunched her face as she locked eyes with Aspen. "Jumping in and saving me. I really appreciate it. I appreciate you."

"It's not a big—" Aspen began backtracking, her eyes flicking to the side.

"No," Mo interrupted firmly, squeezing Aspen's knee for emphasis. "You saved my life and I—I appreciate that. More than you know."

Mo caught her gaze again, and she watched revelation bloom over Aspen's features as she caught on. The weight of those words brought Aspen closer, seemingly pushing her knee into Mo's hand. Mo wondered if this was it, glancing down to Aspen's lips, licking her own in anticipation. But she remembered Aspen's apprehension, so she used her uninjured left arm to push herself up to a sitting position, mirroring Aspen. With a gentle tug, Mo removed the headlamp from Aspen's head and set it down in the front corner, allowing it to illuminate the tent with an indirect glow.

"Is it okay if I'm honest about what I want?" Mo asked, searching Aspen's eyes for permission to explain.

"I think I know what that is, and I…" Aspen leaned closer to Mo. "I want you to know that I do. I want to have sex with you, I really do."

"But…" Mo filled in for her.

"But…" Aspen swallowed visibly, taking in a deep breath. "That's all it will be. Just sex. After all this, you're gonna go back to the Bay and I'm gonna go back to the bar. A meaningful trip and an experience that we will share, but nothing more."

The tent went silent. Disappointment burned its way across Mo's chest, making it difficult for her to breathe. Was this what she wanted? It was hard for her to process with Aspen sitting in front of her looking so serious. Mo found herself hoping that she would continue to explain herself and everything would just fall into place. Suddenly, like Aspen could read her mind, she covered Mo's hand and began to lightly draw anxious circles on her skin.

"Right?" Aspen added, her face twitching as she desperately searched Mo's face for confirmation.

That look was all Mo needed. It immediately transformed the burning disappointment into a dull, disheartened ache. That familiar ache was confirmation in full that she would be unable to let Aspen down. Even if it meant pushing her own feelings to the side. This connection was enough for Mo.

This connection would have to be enough for Mo.

"Of course," Mo assured her, sporting her best smile. "There isn't any pressure for anything more. Besides, if I remember correctly, that was all we planned for back on the beach. A little fun, no strings attached."

"Oh, good." Aspen's shoulders dropped in what Mo assumed was relief, and she watched her create an out for her. "But I mean, you still don't have to, if you don't want—"

Mo cut her sentence short with a light kiss, pulling back slightly to give Aspen the chance to decide where this would go.

"You still don't have to either. I want you, Aspen. But I only want to do this if you want to, you know?"

Aspen launched herself forward, kissing Mo with ardor, almost pushing her flat on her back. Between heated kisses, Mo let out a moan that was a mixture of pleasure and pain as she had to use both hands to steady herself under Aspen's excitement.

"Are you okay?" Aspen pulled back slightly to ask, her eyes turning toward Mo's shoulder.

"Never better," Mo confirmed, shifting her weight to her left as she kissed Aspen back with the same amount of enthusiasm.

"Good." Aspen sighed happily into her kisses, relaxing her body as they continued their fevered mutual exploration. "Because I want you too."

Mo was hooked. She craved more, desperate to feel all of Aspen underneath her. She began kicking the sleeping bag off her legs, rotating her knees under herself. With a quick movement, Mo broke their kiss and gently grasped Aspen's shoulders, lightly turning her while simultaneously straddling her lap.

"Lie back," Mo said, her voice low and tinged with growing arousal. Aspen did as she was told, her bottom lip pulled between her teeth. Mo looked deeply into her eyes, noticing how dark they had become. "Can I touch you?"

"I hope so," Aspen replied flirtatiously, lifting herself back up off the ground to remove her zip-up and shirt in one fell swoop. She grabbed the top of the sleeping bag, pulling it underneath her before she lay back down.

"Oh, yeah, that'll do." Mo hummed, taking in the soft expanse of Aspen's bare torso. Mo's eyes raked over her soft, ample belly and up to her gorgeous full breasts. She watched as Aspen's nipples grew hard under her stare, a mixture of how Aspen felt about this moment and the cold of the Northern California air. "You must've also read the same professional hiker article I did, bringing only one bra—"

"Shut up," Aspen interrupted her, grabbing a handful of Mo's shirt and tugging upward in a clear directive. "Off."

Mo gingerly removed her shirt, careful to not aggravate her damaged shoulder. She wanted to make another joke, but Aspen was now crouched forward off the ground, her right hand warm against Mo's lithe abdomen, above the button to her pants. Mo let out a surprised groan at the touch, rolling her hips down into Aspen. This seemed to be exactly what Aspen desired, and she moved her hand higher, lightly grazing over her belly button and in between her breasts. Mo's breathing became more ragged, but she stayed still, her eyes closing in enjoyment.

"You're so beautiful," Aspen murmured, her hand now gliding across one of Mo's breasts.

Mo could only let out a whimper as Aspen closed her hand over her left breast, squeezing lightly before teasing a nipple between her thumb and forefinger.

"Fuck." Mo moaned deeply, her hips rocking forward again. "When did I lose the control?"

"You had control?" Aspen teased, her hand now trailing across Mo's chest again, squeezing her right breast with the same intensity.

Mo smiled wide at that, loving the feeling of Aspen teasing her breasts. But she needed to feel Aspen in the same way. That urge spurred her to grab Aspen's hand with her own, intertwining their fingers before pushing it up and over Aspen's head. Mo made sure to grind her hips into Aspen as she did so, leaning forward to kiss her hard again. She moved her left hand off Aspen's, cradling her weight next to her head while she used her right hand to touch Aspen's stomach where their bodies met.

"Oh, God," Aspen rasped, kissing Mo harder.

Mo hummed happily into her mouth, continuing the energetic pace of their kisses as she trailed her hand up Aspen's curves to her breast, squeezing just as she took Aspen's lower lip lightly between her teeth. Aspen's hips rolled up into hers, and Mo continued her ministrations, wetness pooling between her legs as she did so. Aspen's hands seemed to finally remember they existed, and Mo felt her grip onto her back, lightly feathering up and down on either side of her spine. That slight touch slowly turned to light scratching, and Mo couldn't help but moan again, her arousal only growing with every glorious drag of her nails. Finally, Mo slowed the pace before pulling away to look down at Aspen.

"God, you are so fucking sexy," Mo uttered, her eyes roaming across Aspen.

"Thank—Oh," Aspen gasped as Mo moved to nip at her neck and along her collarbone. "That feels so good."

"Good." Mo moaned, shimmying her good hand under Aspen's arm so she could kiss down her chest and toward her nipple.

"Please," Aspen asked, the tone of her voice clear she already desperate for more.

Mo obliged immediately, taking Aspen's right nipple into her mouth, rolling her tongue over the tip as she lightly sucked. Aspen pulled in air through her teeth. Mo couldn't help but smile into her breast, excited that Aspen was enjoying this as much as she was. She wasn't in a hurry, making sure each move she made with her mouth and free hand were intentional. Mo paid particular attention to anything that made her whimper and squirm, wanting nothing more than to make Aspen feel like the center of Mo's world.

And in that moment, Aspen was.

"You are killing me." Aspen gasped for breath, digging her fingernails into the back of Mo's arms as she held on for dear life. "I need you to take off my pants and fuck me, please."

That request sent lust shooting out across Mo's body like little pulses of electricity. Mo sucked in a ragged breath, more than ready to oblige. She left a few butterfly-light kisses on Aspen's sternum before pushing up and off her, her hands going to her own pants. She unbuttoned them, watching as Aspen reached for her own.

"Let me," Mo demanded, stopping to cover Aspen's hands. "I'll get mine off first, then yours. I want to. Please."

"Okay." Aspen nodded, her face clear with need. "Hurry. Please."

"Patience, beautiful," Mo said, even as she picked up her pace. She sat back briefly, making it easier for her to remove her underwear and pants. Once done, she crawled back over Aspen and gave her a quick kiss before beginning to remove her clothes, excited at the prospect of seeing Aspen fully naked.

"Look who isn't patient, though." Aspen pouted slightly as she watched Mo discard each remaining article of her clothing.

"I can go slower…" Mo licked her lips.

"You better not!"

"Then, shh," Mo commanded, finally hooking her fingers under the band of Aspen's underwear. She pulled them down, Aspen helping her out by lifting her hips off the tent floor. Mere moments felt like minutes as Mo observed a naked Aspen, taking in every little detail from head to toe. "Wow."

Aspen didn't respond, instead grabbing at Mo's left wrist and pulling her forward. Mo complied, gently laying her body on top of Aspen, enjoying every new sensation of bare skin on bare skin. They kissed lazily, both of them reveling in the feeling rather than attempting to rush to an end. Mo loved that she could feel how wet Aspen was on her stomach and decided to move slightly to the side, straddling one of Aspen's legs. Pressing downward, Mo rubbed herself against Aspen's thigh, not only repaying the kindness to her but rejoicing in the glorious pleasure she received by the movement.

"You are so wet," Aspen said breathlessly between kisses, her hand again tugging at Mo's, attempting to bring it to her center.

Mo switched which thigh she was straddling, deciding to push through the pain of her shoulder so she could touch Aspen. After her adjustment, she began kissing Aspen again, increasing the fervor once her hand lightly grazed Aspen's inner thigh. Mo moved it up and down the skin of her thigh, matching the rhythm of her kisses as she teased her, getting closer and closer to Aspen's center with each lap. Aspen moaned in protest but did not break the kiss, instead rolling her hips up in an attempt to get any friction off of Mo's thigh, which hovered very close but not close enough.

Mo decided to stop her teasing, finally moving her fingers up the curve of her thigh and down between her folds, lightly touching Aspen's clit for the first time. She was rewarded with an immediate moan from Aspen, and Mo slowly explored, keeping her touch light and thoughtful as she figured out what Aspen liked best.

"Please," Aspen gasped, breaking away from their kiss. "You're only teasing me."

"How about this?" Mo asked, looking into Aspen's eyes as she upped the pressure of her fingers, adding another as she danced up and around her clit.

"Oh, fuck yeah." Aspen groaned, laying her head back as she closed her eyes. "Faster."

Mo complied, loving the sights and sounds her ministrations were producing. She focused on consistency and Aspen's face, leaning up to take pressure off her arm and focus on the task at hand. Mo loved the way Aspen squirmed, her hair splayed in all directions, her breasts lightly bouncing with her movement. Mo experimentally dipped her fingers lower, and Aspen immediately moaned and bucked her hips.

"Oh, God yes," Aspen cried, opening her eyes before begging, "Inside, please."

Mo couldn't refuse, entering her slowly with one finger while her other hand came up to thumb at her clit. Aspen was soaked, but Mo still went slowly, checking her facial expressions for anything amiss. Mo tested a few strokes, making sure to lightly skim upward with each pass. Aspen was undone now, her breathing ragged and her eyes pleading up at Mo. She added another finger, slowly entering her again with a careful pace.

"Oh my God, Mo," Aspen responded, her voice low and needy. "Faster, please!"

Mo picked up her pace, making sure to keep to a rhythm, loving how she seemed to be pulling Aspen apart at the seams. Sweat slowly rolled down Mo's back as she focused, hyper aware of her own throbbing center pressed against Aspen's thigh. She kept up her pace, watching as Aspen seemed to slowly creep forward toward oblivion. As Mo noticed Aspen begin to tense, Aspen opened her eyes, gazing up at her with need.

"I'm gonna come."

"Please," Mo begged, leaning down as far as she could without breaking her tempo. "Please, come for me."

As if on command, Aspen let out a guttural cry, and immediately Mo felt her pulse around her fingers. Mo stopped her movement but left her fingers inside, riding out Aspen's orgasm as she leaned closer. After a few moments of watching pure ecstasy cross over Aspen's features, Mo slowly slid her fingers out of her, slumping in a pile next to her.

"Well, fuck," Aspen gasped, her breathing still quick.

"That was amazing," Mo added, rolling so her body was halfway on top of Aspen's. "More than amazing even. Incredible."

"Incredible?" Aspen giggled, turning to meet Mo's gaze. "I haven't even shown you anything incredible yet."

"I don't know, watching you come undone like that…" Mo grinned devilishly before letting out a hearty laugh. "Seemed pretty incredible to me."

Aspen rolled her eyes endearingly before shifting, pushing Mo onto her back, her hands immediately finding purchase over Mo's nipples. Mo's laugh caught in her throat as Aspen expertly cupped both breasts, her mouth moving to Mo's collarbone as she mounted her in one motion.

"Oh," was all Mo could say, her smugness quickly shifting to pleasure as she felt Aspen suck in the skin at the nape of her neck.

"Do you like that?" Aspen asked, one of her hands now trailing goose bumps up and down Mo's front.

"Yes." Mo nodded, craning her head to watch as Aspen tweaked one of her nipples.

The pleasure sent a sharp jolt down to her center, and she let her head fall back, closing her eyes as Aspen worked her magic. Mo loved that Aspen seemed right at home with her body, taking her time to kiss and suck along the free skin of her neck and chest. Just as Mo bucked upward, seeking any kind of friction against her center, Aspen pulled her own hips away, instead kissing her way underneath Mo's small breasts and along a jutting rib.

"May I?" Aspen asked softly, shuffling down Mo while kissing along the flat expanse of her stomach.

Mo swore her own wetness doubled at the request, and she found herself nodding wordlessly, unable to vocalize her approval.

"Is that a yes?"

"Yes," Mo finally got out, receiving a moan of approval from Aspen in reply.

Mo's eyes slipped closed as Aspen's mouth explored along her waist, kissing and nipping as she went. Aspen situated herself so her arms slid under Mo's thighs, her mouth lazily kissing up and down the inner skin of Mo's thighs but never over where she wanted her. Frustrated, Mo let out a growl and lifted her hips off the sleeping pad, hoping Aspen would hurry.

"See? Patience isn't as easy as you thought."

"Do as I say not as I do," Mo clapped back, thrusting her hips up again.

Aspen nipped a tad harder at Mo's inner thigh but kissed closer to her center, feathering them lightly on her outer folds. Mo groaned deeply when Aspen's tongue slipped between, drawing lightly up to her clit then back down to her entrance.

"Shit," Mo hissed, her eyes slamming shut as she pressed herself against Aspen's mouth.

Aspen explored her for a bit before adding more pressure, circling Mo's clit in a tantalizing motion. The pleasure was immense and was quickly ratcheting up, especially after it had been built up under Aspen's teasing. This was going to be quick, but by God, it was going to be fantastic.

"I'm already so close," Mo warned, her hands coming down to thread lightly in Aspen's hair. "Please."

Aspen raked her tongue down, dipping inside her entrance before coming back up to her clit. Then, with what felt like practiced ease, Aspen used the right amount of pressure as she pulled her tongue up and down in a motion that was quickly driving Mo over the edge.

Before she knew it, her orgasm had built close to the peak, and she fought every muscle in her body to not clamp down too hard on Aspen's head. Within mere delicious moments Mo's orgasm hit, and she bucked against Aspen's tongue. A low moan escaped her lips as she rode Aspen's face, taking in each precious wave as they hit her square on. After what felt like hours but was barely even a minute, Mo was brought back to the present by a wet kiss from Aspen. She groaned, finding herself becoming aroused again at the taste of herself on Aspen's lips.

"You are a goddess," Mo said, pulling Aspen down on top of her, loving how warm and soft their bodies felt pressed against one another.

"You were right." Aspen grinned, kissing the side of Mo's jaw as she settled her weight against her. "Incredible."

Mo chuckled, the word rolling around in her mind as a familiar feeling swelled in her chest. She turned to meet Aspen's pleased gaze, and she wanted to say it. To give that sprouting swell of emotion a voice. But Aspen's eyes were almost glowing under the minimal light in the tent, and the words caught in her throat. So instead, Mo shot Aspen a lopsided grin before catching her lips in another deep kiss.

This was all they would be. Right?

CHAPTER EIGHTEEN

From the second that Aspen's eyes opened, lazy and heavy in the midmorning glow, she could feel her soul yearning. Usually when Aspen woke up after a night of sex with a woman, she was satisfied. Light, centered, emotionally ready to return to her regular activities. But in this instance, all she wanted was for this moment to never end. To have more of Mo.

Aspen assessed herself. She was naked, overly warm, and slightly slick from the humidity of the tent. Even so, she was beyond comfortable in the gentle arms of a softly snoring Mo Reeves. The same Mo who spent most of the night giving her unfathomably good orgasms. That would have been good enough for Aspen a few weeks ago, but Mo had stepped it up by also making her feel like she was the most important person in the whole world. It was an experience that Aspen hadn't even considered possible, seeing as all her intimate moments always naturally came to their logical end. An exchange. A transaction. Nothing more, nothing less.

"Morning, gorgeous."

Mo's words had a bittersweet ring to them. Aspen moved only as much as needed to look into Mo's hazel eyes, delighted to see affection reflected back at her. "It's hot."

Mo shuffled a bit, looking toward the tent flap before asking, "Want to go outside?"

"No." Aspen giggled, shifting closer into Mo's arms. "Too comfy."

Aspen felt Mo's gentle chuckle at her indecisiveness before she pulled her in even closer. Aspen rewarded the action with a contented sigh, reveling in the wonderful feeling of warm skin on skin. She never wanted it to end. But even as that urge sat front and center in her mind, another thought pulled itself forward, pushing all her feelings to the side.

"I think today is the day," Aspen announced, giving perspective to the thought.

"Huh?" Mo mumbled into her hair.

"Today is the day you talk to Annie."

"Is it?" Mo pulled back a tad, rolling their bodies so she could get a good view of Aspen's face.

"I feel it." Aspen smiled softly up at her, watching as Mo searched her eyes. "Somewhere close by is Annie's perfect tree, and I am going to find it."

The left corner of Mo's mouth curled slightly, and Aspen resisted the urge to kiss it, instead lightly kissing the tip of Mo's chin. She pulled away from her, disappointment chilling her body as she shimmied out from underneath the sleeping bag. With a quick movements, she threw on a shirt before she fumbled around in the tent, looking for her pants.

"I believe you," Mo finally replied, and Aspen heard shuffling behind her, letting her know that she was following suit.

"Thank you," was all Aspen could think to say as she pulled up her pants, not worried about finding her missing underwear. "Southwest egg scramble sound good? It's one of my favorite dehydrated meals, but I only had one more when I packed for this trip. I've been saving it for phone day."

"I can whip it up this time, if you want."

Aspen swung around just in time to watch Mo grimace as she pulled her arm through her sleeve. "Oh, no you're not. You still need to rest."

Mo pouted. "In here?"

"No, you can sit out there with me, but you shouldn't be doing anything but looking pretty." Aspen pushed herself to her knees, the deep ache of the previous night's fun radiating from her arms and thighs. "Which reminds me."

"That you're the pretty one?" Mo interjected playfully.

"No. I will need to call for reinforcements. There's no way you're hiking back out of here in your condition, so I'll need to contact Betty." Aspen unzipped the tent door. "I looked at the map a little bit last night, and if I'm right, we're pretty damn close to one of the access roads. I'll arrange for her to come and get us tomorrow morning. I can hike both of our packs a few miles without issue, but I definitely don't want to hike out the way we came in."

"Are you sure?"

"Totally. Won't be difficult at all." Aspen gave her best confident grin, hoping her eyes didn't give her away, before grabbing her map and satellite phone. She then scrambled out of the tent and off toward the creek to make her call.

For some reason, instead of going straight into the woods, Aspen's feet took her right to where Mo had almost drowned. She stopped just inside the cool creek water and closed her eyes, feeling it trickle in through the holes in her Crocs. She reveled in the coolness, allowing herself a few deep breaths before she opened her eyes again. Aspen scanned the shimmery surface, unable to find the exact spot where Mo was struck. Nature was funny that way, its violent change always blending in seamlessly afterward. After a few moments, she cleared her throat before lifting up her phone, dialing Betty's number.

"Aspen?" Betty's concerned voice answered in under two rings.

"Hey, Betty." Aspen tried to sound calm and in control. "We hit a bit of a snag—"

"A snag? Are you okay? Did she—"

"No, we are both okay. Well, actually, the windstorm from yesterday injured Mo's shoulder." Aspen felt the guilt creep up again. "A large limb fell directly on her, and while I don't believe her shoulder is broken, she's injured enough that she can't carry her pack. I checked the map, and we're very close to an access road that ends near the stream past Bridge Creek—"

"Coordinates," Betty demanded gruffly, and Aspen heard papers being shuffled and a few clicks of a pen.

"According to my satellite phone we are at—"

"Actually, just give me the decimal degrees. I'll look them up on my computer."

"Got it. Uh…41.189597, -123.971968. That's where we are currently, but where I want to meet is close by. It's the access road that ends at the stream behind us and to the west," Aspen said, hoping Betty would check on the computer.

"Ah, yes. There is Bridge Creek flowing southwest, then there is a smaller stream flowing south…" Betty trailed off, clicking her tongue as Aspen imagined her surveying the map. "Well, I'll be damned. Access road drives almost right up to it."

"Yeah, my map doesn't name the stream or the road, but it would be the easiest way out." Aspen hesitated. "If you are willing to come and get us, of course. Or you can send someone, I'm not picky."

"Naw, I'll do it. Let's make the meeting time around one-ish. I'll go to 44 Camp and get some stuff done in the morning," Betty said.

"Thank you, thank you, thank you." Aspen almost squealed. "You're my hero, Betty."

"Naw, kid. You're the smart one. Injuries happen. But rarely do the injured parties plan their own rescue. I'll see you in the morning."

"Sounds good. Thanks again, Betty."

"Don't mention it," Betty finished curtly before hanging up.

* * *

"Are you sure you can hike?"

"Aspen," Mo warned. "My legs work just fine. Besides, you cooked breakfast, made me a makeshift sling out of one of your shirts, and packed our little day pack. I should be good."

Aspen put her thumb between her teeth, anxiously biting at the cuticle as she considered Mo's words. "You're right. I'm sorry, I just—"

"It wasn't your fault," Mo reminded her, stepping a few feet closer. "Now, where were you thinking we should look?"

"Uh…I have it marked," Aspen mumbled, kneeling down in front of the day pack. She flipped open the top, pushing the blaze-orange phone to the side to grab her map. Aspen unfolded it completely, then refolded it so their area of the trail was visible, and found her penciled star. "Around the bend on the opposite shore is a little stream. If I remember correctly, there are plenty of big-leaf maples and coastal Douglas firs over there. They kind of hug the stream and are surrounded by redwoods, but they have a nice view of the river bend."

Mo looked toward the bend for a few moments before asking, "Is it toward where I was hit?"

"Uh, yeah. Darn, I didn't consider that. So, actually we don't—"

"No. I want to." Mo smiled confidently down at Aspen, offering her uninjured hand. "Let's go."

"All right. Yes, ma'am." Aspen took it, letting Mo help her to her feet. She slid the map playfully under Mo's slinged arm, then pulled the small bag onto her back, nodding toward the wading point. "Shall we wade?"

"Totally, but you are taking point this time." Mo laughed, following Aspen to the edge of the water.

The levels were a tad lower today, but Aspen still rolled her shorts up, taking a quick glance up at the treetops before entering. She walked the same path as Mo had, turning to look back at her companion every so often to make sure she was okay.

"I'm good," Mo announced, reading Aspen perfectly. "It'll be good to finish it. Wouldn't want the river to think I'm a wuss, ya know?"

"Oh, too late for that." Aspen snickered. "Mother Nature almost had you. And just so you know, she never forgets."

"Well, that's comforting."

"I can think of worse fates."

"Mmm," Mo replied absentmindedly.

"Fuck," Aspen swore under her breath, understanding how Mo received her words. "I'm sorry, Mo."

"Don't be," Mo replied, a lightness in her voice. "You are a lot of the reason this trip wasn't that."

Aspen slowed her pace, even as the dry bank was right in front of her. A warm, fuzzy feeling welled up in her chest at Mo's words, leaving her a tad speechless. The sloshing sounds got louder as Mo came alongside her. Aspen felt a warm hand slide up and down her left arm, and she looked over at Mo, tears welling behind her eyes. "I'm glad. I'm glad I could help."

"Me too." Mo smiled, her face filled with gratitude. "I'm gonna tell her."

"Huh?" Aspen blinked a few tears away, picking back up her pace.

"Annie," Mo said with certainty.

"Oh, well I'm sure she would be grateful that you didn't… you know." Aspen waved her hand around, turning to walk backward across the sandy bank and watch Mo exit the water.

"Kill myself?" Mo filled in, her voice deep.

"Yeah."

"That wasn't really what I was planning to tell her, but yeah, I don't think she'd be too happy."

"Oh…" Aspen faltered but didn't add anything more. Instead, she pointed toward the small bridge ahead that crossed to the opposite bank. "That's our bridge."

Mo nodded. "Lead the way."

The sand wasn't nearly as rocky as their campsite, making it easier to traverse. Their journey was silent, save for the light twittering of small birds and the occasional shrieks of a Steller's jay. The churn of the river over the rocks got louder as they closed in on the bridge. Aspen shook the bridge to test its stability before getting on, turning quickly to make sure Mo was still behind her.

"Still here." Mo raised her voice to be heard over the water.

Aspen grinned, crossing the bridge with care. On the other side her eyes went straight to the tree line, skimming it for anything promising. She quickly found where the small stream went northeast off of the creek, and she decided to move toward it. After crossing the bank, she found an easy upward slope to move up into the tree line.

"Over here," Aspen called out, her eyes studying the trees.

"What's up?" Mo replied, catching up.

"There are plenty of maples and firs along this stream," Aspen said, pointing at the slope. "We can go up in—"

"Look!" Mo exclaimed, interrupting her.

Aspen turned toward where Mo was now moving, and that's when she saw it. Right at the mouth of the stream was a small but majestic big-leaf maple. It was guarded on both sides by huge, towering redwoods. Deep green moss climbed up its body as its beautiful, snaking limbs sat lopsided between its overly sized neighbors. Aspen watched as Mo almost skipped toward it. Her excitement was contagious, pulling a huge smile from Aspen.

"Wait up!"

"Nope, you gotta hurry," Mo replied, her voice almost childlike with wonder. "Man, she's gorgeous."

The tree was. As Aspen got closer, its tiny, mossy frame was striking sitting between the two wide and tall redwoods. Mo made her way to its base and put out her free hand, softly touching the trunk.

"Can we?" Mo asked, low enough that Aspen almost missed it.

Aspen trotted right up next to Mo and quickly studied the quintessential maple leaves, brown bark, and winding limbs. "Totally. It's a big-leaf maple. We were told to avoid redwoods."

"She's huge," Mo commented, now looking straight up the trunk.

"It's actually kind of small. Most big-leaf maples get much larger than this."

"She's perfect." Mo's head dropped, and she softly moved her hand back and forth over the light moss. "Right?"

"Well," Aspen replied, turning slowly to see the tree's view. "Wow."

Mo followed suit, taking in the same picturesque view as Aspen. The tree wasn't blocked by brush, instead just wonderfully shaded by its redwood neighbors. It looked out over the rocky bank and the creek's thinner bend to the right and the deep, rushing water on the left. Many gorgeous redwoods were across the creek, looking absolutely statuesque as they seemed to guard the river.

"It's absolutely perfect," Mo whispered, turning back toward the tree. "I think we found it, Aspen."

"We did." Aspen smiled, her chest tightening with a mix of emotions. "This is it."

"I can't wait to talk to her," Mo said, turning toward Aspen. "Can I—"

"Nope." Aspen glared at her, removing her pack. "I will install it. I don't want Annie to be angry at us because you injured yourself trying to put her phone in."

"Wouldn't be the first time."

"I'm sure." Aspen flipped open the top of her pack, energy already flowing through her at the excitement to get the phone installed. She removed the phone, the blaze orange a stark contrast to the mossy green and brown of the tree. She pulled out the nails and hammer, her mind already chastising herself for not grabbing something to create an awning or sign for the phone. "A future trip. Definitely."

"Huh?"

"Nothing." Aspen shook her head, organizing her items as she mentally planned out the task.

"What are you gonna tell her?" Mo asked, kneeling next to Aspen.

"What?"

"Annie, duh," Mo added, tilting her head as she met Aspen's eyes. "What will you tell her?"

"I'm going to talk to her?" Aspen asked, anxiety creeping up in her chest at the thought.

"Totally!"

"Oh, uh, I-I was just joking before," Aspen stammered, standing up to full height with the items cradled in her arms. Mo followed suit, her gaze burning holes into Aspen, which caused her to blush slightly. She leaned her arms toward Mo, nodding down toward the phone. "Here."

Mo grabbed it with her free hand.

"Hold on to it while I get the nails in," Aspen said, turning to gauge the best height. "Right here?"

Mo stepped forward, holding out the phone to the spot Aspen had placed the nail. "Yeah, that's a good height. If you're short."

Aspen snickered. "Well, hopefully this will become a fixture that lots of hikers use. So yeah, that includes us shorties."

"Got it."

"I'm sure she wouldn't care."

"No, she wouldn't. She'd probably love this, honestly. She struggled with verbalizing her feelings, ya know?"

Aspen scoffed lightly, that comment hitting close to home. "What?"

"Nothing, I just—" Aspen took in a deep breath. "Same."

Time crept by as both women just stared at the tree, deep in their own thoughts. Aspen could feel the words she wanted to say, the impulse to let go of all her pretenses. To explain. Before she could build up the courage, Mo cleared her throat next to her.

"I'm really happy for you, Mo," Aspen uttered instead, cutting off anything Mo was about to say. Then she lifted the nail back up to the tree. "I'm glad you had that kind of relationship. You know, the kind where you really know them and they really know you. I'm thankful you brought me on this trip and allowed me insight into your love with Annie, even if it did only scratch the surface. That kind of love should be celebrated."

Mo didn't respond right away, so Aspen raised the hammer and hit the nail into the bark until only a small sliver of the head was sticking out. Aspen turned, gesturing for the phone.

"Can I hang it?" Mo asked softly, holding the phone against her chest.

"Sure can. I just need it for a second to make sure I hammer the other nail correctly."

Mo agreed with a murmur, handing the phone over. Aspen worked quietly, making sure not to hang the phone as much as use it to get the other nail situated in the correct spot. After she was finished, she went to hand the phone back to her companion.

"I would—" Mo started, softly taking the phone under her arm. "You deserve that kind of love too."

Aspen froze for a few seconds, hammer in a ready position. An empty sensation spread across her chest and down into her stomach. She took a few extended blinks before slamming the hammer against the nail, letting the action speak for her.

CHAPTER NINETEEN

You deserve that kind of love too.

Her own words continued to echo through Mo's mind as she watched Aspen hammer in the final nail. Before Mo could backtrack the implication, Aspen met her eyes, allowing her to see the eager glint. Aspen raised a single finger to her mouth before theatrically displaying the tree to Mo, Vanna White style.

"Annie's waiting," Aspen exclaimed, her voice soft and joyful.

"Thanks," Mo replied, implicit words weighing down her tongue.

Aspen only nodded, turning to trot quickly down to the bank. Mo wanted to yell after her to stop. To stay. But the words stuck in her throat, so she just turned to look at the tree, the nails waiting patiently for her to hang the phone on them. Mo balanced the phone against her chest as she rotated it, wanting to mount it properly. She moved in closer to the tree, leaning her cheek against the rough bark as she delicately slid the back of the phone onto the nails. With a downward thrust of her palm, Mo secured the phone to the tree. She then backed up a few steps, letting her eyes take in the sight of the bright-orange phone hanging perfectly in the center of the trunk. Like it has always been there.

Like it would always be there.

"All right," Mo mumbled, resisting the urge to turn and look for Aspen. "I guess it's time."

She didn't move, though. Instead, Mo's mind went blank, her eyes firmly on the receiver. She wanted to ask Aspen what to do next. To have Aspen stand with her as she made the call. But this was a moment only for her, even if a part of Mo wanted it to be their moment. She took a deep breath, then stepped forward. Lifting her free but weirdly heavy hand to grab the receiver, Mo cradled it gently between her cheek and shoulder, blowing anxious air from her lungs. The lack of a dial tone was loud, and she resisted the urge to hang up.

Mo stuck a finger from her good hand into the rotary slot labeled with a slightly worn number one. Adjusting the way she was cradling the phone slightly, she pulled it down to the phone's metal stop with a rattle. The rotary slid back to its original position with a slight *thunk*, so she moved to the next number, picking up speed as she entered each of Annie's numbers. After she was finished, Mo waited for a ring that would never come. She chuckled before adding in the sound effects herself.

"Ring, ring," Mo mimicked, bringing her hand back to the receiver to more comfortably hold it up to her ear. "Annie?"

Obviously her wife didn't respond, but Mo instinctively looked up the length of the tree toward the sky. The sheer height of the two redwoods was even more apparent from this angle. Her head had to roll as far back as it could to see their bushy tops, making the much smaller maple pale in comparison. But that didn't detract from the beauty it created. Its brevity allowed Mo a beautiful view of the sky between the two much taller canopies. In that moment, as her eyes focused on the tiny window that the trees created, Mo swore she could hear Annie's voice answer in the receiver.

"Yellow?" the sweet, familiar voice said in her mind, mimicking her wife's signature way of answering the phone.

"Hey, babe. It's me, your wife," Mo choked out, trying her best to hold back the tide of emotion that this moment was creating. "It's been a while since we've spoken. Well, obviously, seeing as how you died." Mo chuckled harshly, stepping even closer to the trunk. "Which, by the way, was very rude of you, and I feel like I am owed some sort of compensation."

She paused, allowing Annie space to reply if she wanted to.

"I'm not calling you from the house phone. I actually got rid of that stupid thing pretty soon after you died. I always hated it. You knew that, though. I will admit, it was an easy compromise. Even when I would pick at you for never answering the damn thing. There was one thing you were right about—giving that number out really cuts down on the telemarketing calls. Just another thing you were smarter about than me."

Mo grinned at her random monologue, leaning her forehead against the base of the phone before continuing.

"Continuing after you died has been shit, but I guess I've made it this far. I wanted to thank you for not having any expectations of my life without you. It's really kept me from feeling too guilty." Mo grimaced at her words. "That was a lie. I've felt nothing but guilt."

She let silence hang for a few moments, giving time for Annie to respond.

"Unfortunately, I've been a bit lost. I wish I had thought of talking to you before this trip, but honestly, I've been kind of… selfish? Self-centered? I don't know. Bud and Opal asked me to do this, and instead of thinking about how I could remember you, I thought I'd just make it my end. You know, the big end. Come and see you, if that's how the afterlife works."

A deep laugh rolled out of Mo at that, embarrassment following.

"I know what you're thinking, but I—I felt guilty. Guilty I'd never come up here with you, shared this magnificent place with you. Guilty that I was stuck perpetually spinning my wheels. Instead, deciding to damage it and your memory with the easy way out." Mo stopped herself, leaning back to look at the phone again. "Not the easy way, but a less fulfilling one? And I knew you would definitely be disappointed. But I couldn't help how I felt. Feel? You left a huge hole, Annie. And it's one that I am only just starting to learn I don't have to fill. Because you aren't truly gone. Aspen taught me that, weirdly enough."

Mo adjusted the phone into the cradle of her neck, her hand moving to rub at her injured shoulder.

"Aspen Anderson. The whole reason I didn't go down the other path. Though I am sure she would say it was me. But without her pestering, I don't know where I'd be. Probably still in my cabin, covered in dirty clothes and discarded takeout boxes. Well, maybe not…I wasn't really eating either."

Mo took in a deep breath, her mind mimicking the soft and all-knowing hum that Annie would have made at hearing her say such things. She released it, tightening her grip on the phone. "I'm sorry. I really am. I know you tell me not to apologize and just do better. But this is an apology you actually deserve to hear.

"I think you'd love Aspen, though." Mo moved on, her face warming at the thought of her. "She's strong-willed, like you. And I think she finds me just as, if not more, annoying than you did. Oh, and she loves hiking too. Though I think she might be like an expert, expert. Like you were with singing."

Annie's singing voice filled Mo's mind, and she leaned back into the phone, basking in the bliss.

"I wish she could have heard you sing live. And, I guess if I looked at the odds, you two were far more likely to meet than us." Mo turned, glancing back down to the creek where Aspen sat calmly on a rock. "I think I might be falling in love with her, Annie."

Tears welled up in Mo's eyes at the revelation.

"I'm sorry about that. I don't think I expected to ever feel that way for someone other than you…Honestly, I feel terrible about it. Even though I know you'd be far angrier if I just kept myself depressed and single."

Mo waited silently, still hoping to hear Annie respond. It was heartbreaking to feel so close to her but be unable to hear her perspective. To know Annie's thoughts on Aspen. On herself.

"Do you want to hear about her?"

Mo watched as Aspen slid below the rock she was sitting on, now leaning against it as she looked out over the creek.

"She's gorgeous, like you, but different. Her personality fills a space, giving anyone in proximity little else to do but smile. She's broken. But aren't we all? I don't know if I really should point that out when I kind of added to it." Mo sighed deeply before continuing, "She caught the bad end of frustrated Mo. I remember when I let it get the best of me in front of you. You let me have it, as you should've, and I think I felt just as bad this time around. I picked the habit back up after you died. Bud got the shit end too. Even though he is more used to it than all of you, he didn't deserve it. I've not been the best to anybody in a while, and while I doubt I'm healed overnight, I've gotta do better. You would expect better." Mo's eyes closed briefly. "Aspen deserves better.

"All of this to say, I don't think a thing with Aspen is something she wants? I don't know, I haven't done this kind of thing in so long. I'm kind of lost on how it works? I really did think my days of falling in love were only going to be filled with you. Please don't feel bad, though. You didn't die on purpose. And even if you did, I wouldn't hold it against you. You knew what was best for you, and I loved you."

Mo's grip on the phone tightened and loosened.

"Whatever you wanted, I was willing to make it happen. But like…I hope my new feelings don't hurt yours. I don't think I could deal with that."

A swell filled her throat.

"I miss you, Annie.

"I love you, Annie."

Tears were flowing steadily now, but Mo didn't try to fight the feelings she felt pouring out. Her gaze stayed on Aspen, even as her mind considered Annie. And as if Aspen could hear her, she swiveled her head and locked eyes with Mo.

"I don't know what's going to happen, but…" Mo swallowed harshly, watching as Aspen stood and stared. "I'm going to try to live without you exactly like I lived with you."

Mo wiped at her tears, sniffling a bit before adding, "If that makes sense?"

Aspen tilted her head to the side before stepping closer to the hill, almost like she was silently asking if Mo was okay. Mo took in a ragged breath, the tears still flowing, as she adjusted the receiver once again.

"Do you wanna speak to Aspen?" Mo asked gingerly, waiting for Annie's answer. Silence was all Mo needed, so she waved her bad arm as much as she could before yelling down, "Aspen! Annie wants to say something."

Mo expected Aspen to question that remark. To maybe stand still down by the creek, studying her sanity up by the trees. Instead, she watched as Aspen quickly make her way up the hill, a slight smile on her face.

"Annie done talking to you already?" Aspen quipped, stopping next to Mo.

"Never." Mo sniffed, grinning. "She's stuck with me forever, I think."

Empathy crinkled Aspen's smile sideways, and she transferred weight between her feet before reaching out to squeeze lightly on Mo's wrist. "I think she's fine with that."

"She wants to talk to you," Mo said. "Goodbye, my love. I promise I'll come back and annoy you real soon. I love you so much."

With that she held out the receiver to Aspen, who took a few seconds' pause before taking it.

"Thanks," Aspen almost squeaked, holding the phone to her ear. "Hello?"

Mo took a step back, wiping at her eyes before turning to walk down to the creek bank. But she felt a hand at the crook of her elbow, soft but firm. She turned and caught Aspen's eyes. They were begging her to stay, so she nodded, watching Aspen's arm fall back to her side.

"I know we've not met, but my name is Aspen Anderson. I guess you could say I was Mo's guide on this trip. Do you mind if I call it a quest?" Aspen couldn't help but laugh at her own joke, pulling a small smile from the corners of Mo's mouth.

"I was wondering…did you call her Mo or Imogen?"

A tiny laugh bubbled up from Mo's chest. "Mo. Unless I was in—"

"Unless she was in trouble?" Aspen finished for her, like Annie had done it over the phone. "So Imogen, got it."

"Ha, ha."

"Anyway, I'm glad I could get her here. I'm sorry that she isn't in the same shape she was when we started. That wasn't really part of the plan, but what can you do? Nature has a way of dropping branches wherever it wants. I'm just glad it wasn't directly on her skull." Mo watched as Aspen drew in a deep breath, her free hand sliding into her pocket. "I don't really have much to say other than I wish we could have met. You sound like someone I'd really want to be friends with, on the trail or off of it. The universe is hella cruel to take you so soon, especially when you had someone terrific like Mo to share it with."

Mo leaned against the redwood, the pain in her shoulder be damned, watching as Aspen spoke with Annie. It was a sight she didn't know she wanted, let alone needed.

"Sure, Mo hasn't had the best time of it since you died, but I can see she's trying to find the balance. And I can't fault her for that." Aspen pulled something small and metal-like out of her pocket, and Mo craned her head to catch a glimpse. "So, I don't know if she told you or not, but Mo lied to me when she got here. Said she was an experienced hiker. I must admit, I knew deep down, from the get-go, that she wasn't. And that led to some interesting stuff that almost kept us from getting here and talking to you. I was so wrapped up in helping someone heal amongst the redwoods like I healed, that I kind of didn't see that she didn't need me for that.

"She just needed to see you. Well, talk to you. To figure out where you fit in her life now that you've passed on. I am just glad my meddling didn't end up with her dying too. I'm sure you'd have hated to see her so soon." Aspen looked up, catching Mo's eyes. "So, thanks, Annie. Thanks for letting me share this moment. I just wish you could be here for it."

Aspen turned and hung up the phone, the sound of the receiver hitting the cradle echoing out over the creek. Then, with a slight turn, Aspen held out her gripped fist. Mo reached her good hand out, upturned, allowing Aspen to drop a cylindrical, warm object into her palm.

"I found the fire starter," Aspen whispered. "A little after breakfast the day you figured out it was missing. I didn't know if you wanted it, after what you said. But I think that Annie would want you to have it."

"Really?" Mo exclaimed quietly, observing Annie's treasure as she twisted it lightly in her hands.

"Well, yeah," Aspen said, backing away. "You'll have to start the fire with it tonight. In her memory, you know? Commemorate the hanging of the phone."

Mo turned to look at the phone, its blaze orangeness bright against the bark. A small part of her told her to put the treasure on the phone, to leave everything here along the bank. But another part reminded her she wasn't ready to give everything of Annie's to this place.

"Thank you, Aspen."

"For what?"

Mo held up Annie's treasure and took a step toward Aspen, who in turn took a step back. The pain the action brought forth was instantaneous. Mo slid the treasure in her pocket, her mind racing on what to do. How to proceed forward if Aspen was moving backward. As she looked at Aspen's distracted gaze, her brain screamed at her to leave it alone. To let what was, be.

Mo couldn't let it go.

"You do know you were a huge reason I made it here, right?"

"No, that was all you." Aspen's voice was heavy, but with a forced lightness. "Now, let's go back to camp. Unless you aren't done—"

"No," Mo interrupted, giving in. "We can go back to camp."

"Awesome. Follow me," Aspen exclaimed, trotting down the hill.

Mo looked one final time at the phone, confusion swirling, before following Aspen down toward the creek. The weight she felt lifted moments before was replaced by another one. An unfamiliar weight that she was unsure how to shoulder.

CHAPTER TWENTY

Aspen's focus was locked in on the small creek ahead of her, not once turning to look back at Mo. This task was turning out to be far harder for her than she initially thought, and none of it had to do with the added weight of Mo's pack. She had made her decision, sitting there against the rock while Mo talked to Annie. Whether or not she could keep to it was a whole other task.

"Even with a couple of snags," Mo began behind her. "This has been a wonderful trip. It's a bummer we can't hike back out the way we came in. I kind of wanted to spend more time under the trees."

Aspen internally agreed but kept quiet. She hoped the creek would break into the access road at any moment, freeing her from the guilt that was far heavier than both the packs combined.

"Is Betty going to meet us at the end of this?"

"No, at an access road at the end."

"Oh, okay," Mo mumbled, her voice sounding concerned. "Are you sure I can't carry—"

"Nope," Aspen cut her off, crossing over a few rocks to walk along the opposite bank where the brush wasn't as overgrown. "Just watch your footing. This might be a small creek in comparison to Redwood Creek, but wet rocks are slippery rocks."

"Okay." Mo's voice was even smaller now.

Aspen adjusted the front pack in response, the weight taking a toll on her knees. She pulled it off in one motion, deciding to sling it over one arm to cool herself down. She expected a protest from Mo, but her companion kept quiet, moving to walk in front of her now. Aspen watched the woman closely, noticing that while she held her hurt arm rather gingerly, her body seemed to drag. Like something worse was ailing her.

It took everything in Aspen not to ask.

"The creek is getting smaller," Mo commented, turning to catch a peek at Aspen. Aspen flipped her eyes to the ground, tightening her grip on Mo's pack. "I assume that means it's about to end."

Aspen lifted up her free arm, checking the time. 12:34 p.m. stared back at her. Betty was either waiting for them or was traversing her truck over the dirt access road now. She then turned to look at the creek, which, if she was being generous, she would now call a brook. Her eyes followed its length, ending at a clearing past a huddle of firs. That's when she caught the glimpse of Betty's ranger truck, relief mixing with her guilt.

"Betty's up ahead." Aspen trotted up next to Mo and pointed. "You can finally go to the hospital down in Eureka."

"Are you coming with me?" Mo asked, slowing her pace.

Aspen could feel her stare. The meaning behind her question was threefold. Before she could answer, she heard the slam of the truck door and the crackle of a satellite phone. "Hi, Betty!"

"Aspen," Betty greeted, stomping with a purpose toward the women. She reached for Mo's pack. "Let me get that in the truck."

"Thanks. Sorry again for the rescue call," Aspen said, moving to take off her own pack.

"No need," Betty said. "How you feeling, sport?"

Aspen knew she was talking to Mo, so she turned to finish removing her pack before depositing it into the back of the vehicle as well.

"My ego might be more bruised than my shoulder," Mo responded, her voice taking on a familiar lilt, something Aspen hadn't heard in days. "But, yeah, I can't really put any weight on it."

"That's concerning," Betty gruffed, stepping toward Mo. "Immaculate sling, Aspen."

"Thanks." Aspen crossed by the women to sit in the truck. She reached forward and unlaced her boots, groaning in pleasure as she kicked them off her feet. "Oh, I needed that."

"I bet," Mo said before reaching down to grab the pair with her good hand, placing them on the floorboard in front of the passenger seat. Her body was so close to Aspen, it made her shiver slightly. "Here."

Before Aspen could reply, Mo had moved away. Betty opened the back door of the truck, ushering Mo inside.

"Let's get on the road. You gonna need a hospital?"

"Uh, I don't think so. Aspen has done enough."

Aspen felt the full sting of that, so she adjusted her body fully inside the truck and slammed the door behind herself. She focused on buckling herself in, the air thick with the awkwardness she had been incubating since before the phone call. Betty climbed in and started the truck, flinging it into reverse in her usual abrupt way.

"Y'all get the wind phone installed?"

The question hung in the air as the truck maneuvered back onto the access road, rumbling down toward the highway.

"Yeah," Mo said. "On a beautiful maple. It was nestled between a few redwoods, right off the bank."

"Coordinates?" Betty directed toward Aspen.

"I have them."

"All right. Well, let's get you super happy people back to civilization."

The rest of the drive was mostly silent, save for the sound of the truck's tires sliding across the gravel road. It didn't take too long before they were back on Route 101, right past Big Lagoon Bridge. Aspen kept her eyes on her hands, mentally going over exactly what her final words would be to Mo.

"The bar for dinner, I assume?" Betty asked, her voice taking on an unusual softness.

"I would—" Mo began.

"No, let's drop Mo off at her car. She's gonna need a shower before she goes into town," Aspen steamrolled, doing her best to keep her voice firm.

Betty seemed to wait for a rebuttal from Mo, which never manifested. "And you?"

"My cabin."

"Affirmative." Betty sighed, the speed of the truck seeming to pick up. "It's up past the trailhead, correct?"

"Yes."

"All right, then you're first, Mo."

The truck zipped through Orick, passing by the bar. Aspen kept her eyes down on her hands, praying that Mo would just get out and go to her Subaru without protest. It would be easier that way. Betty swung the truck onto another gravel road, moving it down and toward the locked ranger gate. When she placed the truck into park and moved to get out, Mo flung her door open and removed her seat belt.

"I'll walk to it."

"I still have to unlock it."

"Aspen." Mo's voice was small but firm. "Can I talk to you?"

Aspen's heart skipped a beat.

"I'll need help with my bag and—"

"Yeah…" Aspen faltered, removing her own belt and stepping into her untied boots before hopping out. "You can unlock the gate and move it, Betty. I'll help her to her car."

Betty nodded, so Aspen moved past Mo, stepping on the rear tire to reach Mo's pack. Once it was hurled over her right shoulder, she began moving down the trail toward the Outback, praying she would trip over her laces. Maybe the fall would knock her out, removing her from having to have this painful conversation.

"Aspen?" Mo asked from behind her. "I'm really confused about what's going on here."

"What do you mean?" Aspen replied as nonchalantly as she could, keeping her focus on the road. "We did it. We hung the phone."

"With all due respect, we did a lot more than hang a phone," Mo said, her voice taking on a tone of frustration.

Aspen quickened her pace.

"And now you're giving me the cold shoulder? I'm sorry if I'm confused, but it's like the branch gave me whiplash."

"Maybe it did." Aspen shrugged, reaching the rear of the car. "Open, please."

"Are you really doing this?" Mo reached her hand into the handle of the back gate, a few beeps emitting from the hatch as it opened autonomously.

"Doing what? Isn't this what we agreed on?" Aspen waited for the door to open fully before tossing in Mo's pack. She then finally met Mo's eyes, seeing discouraged desperation. "You needed closure, I butted in. I dragged you into the woods to hang a phone and almost got you hurt. Twice. I wanted a no-strings-attached fling, you agreed. We did it, on multiple fronts, and I somehow got you out without you dying. You've changed the trajectory of your life and now you can go back to the Bay with your head held high."

Mo's face fell, her mouth opening to speak before closing again.

"I'm happy you got to talk to Annie again, I am. But we..." Aspen pointed between the two of them with emphasis. "We were never gonna work."

"I just thought...with your birthday coming up..." Mo's voice was full of hurt and confusion, her hand bracing herself on her car.

"I will have my birthday like I do every year—in the bar, doing my thing, living my life the way I've always lived it."

Mo swallowed hard before meeting Aspen's eyes. "Okay. If that's what you want."

"It is."

Mo didn't reply, only nodding before pushing the button on the hatch for it to close. She then gave Aspen a small, desolate wave before moving toward the front of the car. Aspen listened as she opened and closed the door, starting the car's engine not long afterward. Aspen felt her chest pull apart as she moved back up the hill, her eyes blurring with tears, trying desperately to focus on Betty's truck.

She climbed in while Mo sped by, the sound of the Outback's tires on the gravel shattering her heart. A sob ripped from her lungs just as she buckled herself in. Betty reached across the car to slam the door.

"There, there, kid."

Aspen didn't respond, instead curling up in the seat to cry.

* * *

The walk from Periwinkle to the bar doors seemed to take an eternity. Aspen's feet dragged along the ground, her knees and back aching from a lack of rest. As she stepped onto the stoop, her hands fluttered into her hair, attempting to tame what she knew was unruly. She reached into the pocket of her jeans, pulling a hair band from the depths. With practiced hands she pulled her hair into a sloppy low pony before rubbing her fingers up and down over her face. Then she reached for the door, letting the sounds of folk music and Sunday football repeats hit her like a sack of bricks.

"Fuck that's loud," Aspen muttered, her head throbbing as she trudged toward the bar.

Her eyes made a quick scan of the place, noticing the only patrons were playing pool in the back. She ignored them, turning toward the edge of the bar. She touched the back of the first barstool she encountered before her brain cruelly reminded her that this was where Mo sat the first night they met. Her chest ached at the memory, but she slid into the seat anyway.

"Wow, you look like shit," Virginia's familiar voice tutted. Aspen placed her hands on the bar before meeting her boss's gaze. "Are you okay?"

"Yeah, just tired. The trip was a success." Aspen tried to play it off, giving Virginia a thumbs-up. "Can I have a whiskey neat?"

"Oh Lord, honey, not the whiskey," Virginia scolded but reached for the glass and a bottle anyway. "What happened?"

"Nothing," Aspen whined, even as she tried to make her voice sound unaffected. Virginia poured a double, causing her to wince at how well the woman knew her. "Thanks."

When Aspen reached for the glass, Virginia's hand moved to cover the top, stopping her from taking it. "If you promise to talk, you can have the drink."

"Not fair." Aspen groaned in frustration.

"And you think you dragging your sorry ass in here all mopey and depressed a good week before your trip was supposed to be up is fair?"

"We finished. The phone was hung, the dead wife was talked to, the butch has gone back to the Bay." Aspen tugged on the glass. "Finito."

"You've spent too much time with me." Virginia sighed, releasing the glass. "God, what have I done?"

Aspen, shocked Virginia had given in so easily, removed her hand from the whiskey and just stared. Virginia turned away, moving down the bar to yell into the kitchen, "Two classics, pronto! Bring 'em out yourself, we are at the end of the bar."

Aspen wrinkled her brow as Virginia made her way back, grabbing another glass and filling it with tequila. "Uh..."

"What? You think you gonna drink alone?"

Aspen shrugged, watching as Virginia made her way from behind the bar to slide in next to her. She then clinked their glasses together before downing the gold liquid in one go.

"Oof," Virginia scoffed, glancing knowingly at the glass. "Still burns."

Aspen looked to her own glass, her fingers barely playing with the edge. "Sorry."

"Now what're you apologizing for?"

"Everything," Aspen breathed out.

"What happened?" Virginia asked calmly, slowly lifting herself up to grab both bottles before pouring herself another tequila.

"I don't know." Aspen took a sip, letting the whiskey numb her tongue before swallowing.

"Well, the last bit you called me about…" Virginia clicked her tongue against her teeth, downing another shot like it was water. "You asked me for help. Saying you couldn't just sleep with her?"

"Yeah."

"Did you sleep with her?"

Aspen downed her glass in response, her face contorting as the liquid passed down her throat and into her stomach.

"Okay, so you slept with her. Was it terrible? Did she do something—"

"No." Aspen turned suddenly, putting up her hand to stop Virginia from finishing her sentence. "Everyone keeps saying stuff like Mo ruined it. And, like, no! Besides being rightfully grumpy for some of it, she didn't do anything wrong. She is the opposite of wrong."

"Alrighty then," Virginia mused, pouring more whiskey into Aspen's glass. "What did you do wrong?"

Aspen blew a raspberry at that question, mulling over whether to lie. But she knew Virginia wouldn't let that fly, so instead she pulled a deep breath into her lungs before answering. "I started to feel something for her and I—I can't do that."

"Why the hell not?" Virginia asked just as the kitchen door swung open, Salvador trotting their way with two heaping plates of burgers and fries. "Over here, you lug!"

Aspen dropped her head, bringing her glass up to sip as Salvador placed the plates and a container of ketchup in front of them.

"It's a new thing of ketchup, Aspen," Salvador explained. "I know how you are."

"Thanks, now go check on Charlie and his crew," Virginia snapped, reaching for the ketchup.

Aspen watched as she squirted a large clump onto her plate before drizzling some over her own fries, snapping closed the lid with as much emphasis. Virginia grabbed a drenched fry and popped it into her mouth, chewing in her usual dour way.

"Eat."

Aspen nodded, grabbing the burger to take a small bite of the edge, her stomach growling at how good it tasted. She followed it up with a larger bite, listening to Virginia's own grunts of approval.

"Nothing like a classic." Virginia beamed. "Now, why can't you love her again?"

"I'm not in love," Aspen protested weakly, her face still in her cheeseburger.

"Bullshit."

"It was just a little fling," Aspen explained, putting her food down before turning toward Virginia. "We both know I shouldn't have been there. I inserted myself into some random woman's problems and I really should have minded my own business. Am I feeling down? Sure. But it's only because I embarrassed myself for a fling."

"Are you dumb? Because that didn't seem like no fling I've ever seen you have."

"Exactly. I took it too far. I did too much." Aspen grabbed a fry, dragging it heavily through the ketchup. "Mo lives in the Bay, I live in Orick. She's stoic, I'm happy-go-lucky. She has a dead wife, I have a dead life. It would never work."

"Aspen, honey, there are cell phones," Virginia said, sounding exasperated. "Besides, you aren't some princess bound to Orick by a witch. You can leave, you know."

"No, no. I'm meant to be here. I'm the happiest here."

Virginia tilted her head in doubt.

"I am happy here."

"Are you trying to convince me, or yourself?"

Aspen pushed her plate away, turning fully toward Virginia. "I'm ready."

"Huh?"

"The bar. I want to take over so you and Sal can retire. Finally enjoy your lives." Aspen looked between Virginia's eyes, pleading. "You've done so much for me, for my entire life, it's the least that I can do for you both. You deserve happiness."

"Honey, I—" Virginia blinked, her mouth slightly slack with confusion.

"Just say yes."

"But Mo—"

"She doesn't matter. I know what my life is about, and it's this bar. This place. The redwoods are my home, not the Bay." Aspen's chest burned.

Virginia studied her face. Aspen did her best to look convincing, even as her heart begged for a voice. Even as her brain told her to stop.

"You've never wanted the bar," Virginia finally quipped, her eyes still glaring hard into her own. "I've got to think about it."

"My birthday is next Wednesday." Aspen held her palms out in an attempt to convince Virginia, doing her best to keep her emotions under control.

"You need to think about it," Virginia said.

"I don't think so."

"Well, your eyes say something totally different."

Aspen blinked at that, turning back to her food. She picked at her fries, shrugging. "I'm not cut out for love, Virginia."

"Keep lying to yourself, Aspen." Virginia laid a hand over Aspen's wrist, softly moving her thumb over the back of her hand. "Once you're done doing all that fibbin', call her. Make it right."

Aspen laughed her words off, even as they tugged tears into her eyes. "I think I'm done talking now."

"Alrighty then." Virginia squeezed her wrist before letting go. "I'll let you know about the bar."

"Thanks."

With that, Aspen listened to Virginia work her way off her stool. Not soon after, the sound of the kitchen doors swinging open and shut reached her ears. The sound echoed in her chest, reminding her she was alone again. Alone was definitely Aspen's lot in life.

CHAPTER TWENTY-ONE

"Is there a way I can meet with you before I start paying for sessions?"

"Of course. We can do a free fifty-minute chemistry meeting. That way you can see my office, check out my vibe, and I can explain to you the kind of therapy I offer. It can help to make sure my style will match your therapy goals."

Mo sighed, sliding to sit upright on the patio chair just outside of Hecate Tattoo. The street was sparsely populated, a side effect of a summer weeknight near Stanford University. She liked the easy quiet, though, especially in comparison to Bud's overbearing nature inside the loft apartment.

"I heard uncertainty in that exhale," the woman pointed out, causing Mo to laugh.

"No, no. I am committed to starting therapy, Kate. I just…I don't know if I'll be around for office visits," Mo explained, her voice lilting. She reached up to rub at her shoulder, the dull ache still reminding her of there. Of her. "I might be commuting back and forth—"

"Oh, really? Did you want to do virtual, then?"

Mo grimaced. Why was her first thought when scheduling therapy about Aspen? It was a fling. Nothing more, nothing less. Yet, here Mo was, considering her while making appointments. Even bringing commuting up. Her head began to spin. "It's complicated?"

"Ah, okay." Kate's voice was firm but comforting. "How about we meet in the middle? Chemistry sessions can be in person, but we play whether or not you want to do virtual by ear? I'm fine with being flexible."

"Sure. I'm sorry."

"No need to be sorry, Mo. I'm a therapist. It's kind of my job to be good at accommodating your needs. What's your schedule look like this week?"

Mo looked across the street, the sun barely showing above the buildings as it made its descent for the day. The slow sunset matched her dim mood, reminding Mo it had been a few long, hard days since she had spoken to Annie. Since Aspen left her at her Outback.

"I'm free tomorrow? And like, every day after that?" Mo shrugged. "I am still trying to figure my life out."

"Let's do it tomorrow, eight in the morning," Kate confirmed, her keyboard strokes evident in the background. "Sound agreeable?"

"Yeah, eight o'clock," Mo said just as the bell above Hecate Tattoo's door rang. She turned to see a beautiful woman exit, her newly tattooed arm shiny from the Saniderm. Mo watched her confidently stroll across the street, looking proudly down at her arm as she went. "Can you email me your office's address?"

"Certainly. I will see you tomorrow, Mo."

"Okay," Mo mumbled, hanging up the phone with a huge exhale.

"Who were you talking to?"

Mo jumped, turning to see Opal slide into the patio chair next to her. "Fuck, you scared me."

"I'm sorry." Opal reached out to lightly rub along Mo's arm. "I finished my appointment early, so I thought I'd come sit with you. Here."

"It was just my new therapist," Mo explained, turning more toward her friend just as she handed over a cold, tall can of hard cider. She graciously took it, nodding in appreciation. "Thank you."

"I know you prefer cider to red wine." Opal smiled, bringing her own wineglass up to her lips for a quick sip. "It's a new brand at the co-op down the street. I'm unsure if it's any good or not."

"I do love cider."

"How's your shoulder?" Opal asked, her voice inquisitive.

"It's fine. I still don't think I needed to go to urgent care," Mo replied, studying the can with so much fervor that she didn't hear Opal's response. It was white with a drawn picture of a man in a black suit, sporting a tall black top hat. *Drysdale* and *Humboldt Cider Co.* were drawn in wooden block letters, printed across the side and bottom. Mo's heart sank.

"Mo?" Opal asked with worry, her hand back on Mo's arm. "Is everything okay?"

"I'm sorry," Mo whispered, setting the unopened can down between her feet. She stayed bent over, wringing her hands. "Did I miss a question?"

Opal didn't answer right away, instead leaning down to take her can of cider. Mo then heard a gentle scrape of the patio chair, causing her to look up. Opal was sliding her chair to look directly at Mo, and she tilted her head in confusion.

"Turn your chair for me," Opal commanded gently. "We need to talk."

Mo did as she was told, sliding her own chair toward Opal until their knees were touching. At first she looked into her friend's eyes, but that proved to be too difficult, so instead she looked over her shoulder at the orange and pink sky. After a long moment, Mo heard the telltale pop of a can being opened.

"Here."

Mo took her drink, staring at the can for a few moments before taking a sip. It tasted exactly like it did a few weeks back when Aspen served it to her. Mo smiled, even as her chest burned at the memory.

"I want to tell you a secret. I usually struggle sharing my thoughts, but you're family, so I want you to know."

That got Mo's full attention. "Of course."

"The past couple of years, when April rolls around, the burnout of just"—Opal clicked her tongue, obviously trying to choose her words carefully—"living feels more catastrophic than the last. Like a bomb has been strapped to me, ticking down, waiting patiently for the springtime lull before exploding inside of my chest and shattering everything that makes me... me. I used to wonder if I was on some sort of depression clock, doomed to feel smaller than an ant every late spring from here to eternity. This year is when it finally hit me. April was when Annie would ask me about our yearly hiking trip."

Mo fully met Opal's soft brown eyes.

"Let me rephrase that." Opal's lips tilted awkwardly as her head moved slightly to the left. "April was just the month when Annie would beg me to hike Redwood Creek with her again. All of my built-up anxiety, creative blocks, daily fatigue...I would leave it along the rocky creek bed with my best friend at my side. And when Annie died, I couldn't see myself going back there. Traversing that place without her sounded inconceivable. It felt like betrayal. But this past April, I did. It was incredible to be there, and while I was obviously alone, I wasn't alone, you know?"

Mo nodded along, unsure of how to respond.

"And I know Bud and I pushed a little too hard. It was difficult enough to lose her that we didn't want to lose you too. I just thought about the peace it brought me and maybe, just maybe, it could do something for you too. So when I saw the light in your eyes again when you returned..." Opal hesitated, leaning forward to catch Mo's gaze again. "What happened in the redwoods?"

"I don't really know," Mo responded, her hand instinctively rubbing at her shoulder.

"I know you're a private woman," Opal continued, still staring intently. "So I'm going to just tell you what I see and you can decide whether or not you are ready to talk, okay?"

"All right."

"You've not had this kind of light in your eyes since before Annie passed away. Bud told me this morning that you did in fact get the phone installed. The one the woman you met suggested?"

"Yes." Mo shifted uncomfortably, her mind picturing Aspen. "Aspen."

"Aspen," Opal repeated back. After a few moments, a knowing smile widened on her face. "Did you talk to Annie?"

"I did." Mo nodded. "I wished I had done it sooner, honestly. But I didn't really know that was an option. Aspen helped a lot with that. Uh, the phone and stuff."

"Aspen," Opal said again, leaning even closer. "I see."

"You see what?" Mo playfully complained, stopping herself from squirming under Opal's stare.

"The light comes from the journey to Annie, but it also comes from Aspen."

"Uh…"

"But there is disappointment too." Opal leaned back, crossing her arms in confidence. "In you, I mean. When you got back. I doubt Annie would disappoint you, right?"

Anxiety welled up inside of Mo, so she took a long chug of her cider instead of answering right away. She weighed her options in her head, mulling over how to work this. Opal wasn't wrong—all of those perceptions were there. As obnoxious and loud as a roadside billboard.

It was high time Mo leaned into them.

"Am I that easy to read?"

"Always." Opal nodded, grinning nostalgically. "It was one of Annie's favorite things about you, I'll have you know."

"I bet." Mo smiled. "I kind of surface-level talked about it with Bud, but uh, yeah. Aspen and I were kind of a no-strings thing? Probably why I seem happy. It has been a while."

"Explain."

"I don't know…it was just a fling? More than anything I think she helped me ground myself. Find adventure in a pit of despair. Her ideas and backpacking knowledge helped me reconnect with Annie. She gave me all the tools but none of the judgment. It was nice to work through some of my grief, for sure." Mo was trying to explain, but her mind was all over the place. "Aspen is a gorgeous person. Inside and out."

"I believe Bud did mention the fling, though he referred to it as a one-night stand," Opal replied, looking up toward her loft apartment with a roll of her eyes. "He tries."

"He does," Mo agreed, taking another long gulp of cider. "You two were too close to it. To her, I mean. I think I needed the space away from you both. From Palo Alto. I don't think I was gonna find any answers here."

"Right." Opal's face fell a tad as she began to absentmindedly trace one of the tattoos on her left wrist.

"I say all that to say thank you, Opal. Thank you for pushing, even if I was a pain in the ass about it. Which I'm sorry for, by the way."

"No need to apologize. We were just as pushy," Opal said. "But I want to talk about the Aspen part some more."

"Oh no," Mo joked. "My pretherapy therapy."

"Mo," Opal warned playfully before continuing, "While I am overjoyed you're going to therapy again, the disappointment in your eyes comes back when you talk about the fling. So I don't want you to skip over it. Why?"

"Well…" Mo weighed her options.

"It wasn't a fling, was it?" Opal finished for her.

Mo shook her head, then shrugged. With a deep breath, she finally broke. "Not to me…but that's, like, my fault."

Opal slid forward at that comment, her eyebrows tilting in confusion. "How is that your fault? I think you are allowed to feel things for her."

"Yeah, but she made it very clear—multiple times, in fact—that it was no-strings fun." Mo shrugged again, finishing the last bit of her cider off. She crushed the can in her hand, tilting to set it against the wall of the building. "I just took it too far."

"How's that?" Opal probed further, squinting at Mo with interest.

It was a simple question. One that, when run through Mo's mind, was even more unclear.

"Umm…" Mo took in a deep breath before finally giving in. "I fell in love with her. Or am I falling in love with her? Unsure, to be honest. This stuff is all so foreign to me."

Mo kept her eyes averted, not looking forward to seeing pity in Opal's. But it was only a few quick moments before she felt Opal slide her arms under her own, pulling her in for a tight hug.

"That's incredible," Opal squealed in her ear, releasing a smile from her face. "I'm so happy for you, Mo."

Mo pulled back, meeting a thrilled Opal grinning from ear to ear. "It's something, I guess."

"Why do you say that?"

"It's too early to know." Mo shrugged and swallowed. "The only thing I do know is that she doesn't feel the same."

Opal leaned back into her chair, her face falling to something more pensive than elated. Her bottom lip pulled between her teeth, and she reached into her shorts to pull up her phone and began tapping away.

"She was very clear. Even if I—" Mo began rubbing her palms together. "Even if I wanted her to feel differently."

"But you're in love with her?" Opal repeated, her eyes still on her phone.

"I don't know?" Mo tilted her head back and forth, her body alight with conflicting emotions. "It's the only word I can think of to encapsulate how I feel. But it's a big word."

Opal slid her phone into her pocket, placing her now smug gaze on Mo. "You like her."

"I adore her."

"Then you've got to tell her."

"I don't know about that." Mo felt uneasy at that thought, leaning back into her chair and crossing her legs. "That sounds…"

"Scary?" Opal offered.

"Insane?" Mo ran her fingers through her hair. "What if she doesn't feel that way about me?"

"What if she does?" Opal's eyes glinted like she knew something Mo did not. "What if she pushed you away because she is just as scared as you?"

A flicker of hope lit inside Mo's chest, catching fire to her nervous system as those words sank in. "How would you know that?"

Opal laughed. "She's a single lesbian living in the rural redwoods. She is one hundred percent afraid of commitment."

"Oh." Mo searched her memory, trying to find anything to support that notion. "She was married."

"Really?" Opal replied. "To who?"

"A man. And from her stories, he was a traditional man who wanted to claim her more as a trophy than a partner," Mo gruffed. "Wait, how did you know she was a lesbian?"

"Bud." Opal shrugged. "The man tells me everything."

"As he should, honestly." Mo smiled. "I don't know. I'm too old and too broken to know if I have a shot with Aspen. And I said something to Annie about it—"

"Annie would want you to try," Opal interrupted, reaching forward to lightly touch Mo's leg. "You deserve to be happy, Mo. Sure, you might be a broken pile of popsicle sticks now. But you're getting a therapist, you know where you need to improve. You've got the glue in front of you, just put yourself back together again."

"I was not the nicest person to her," Mo said, anxiety building.

"How so?"

Mo didn't know if she wanted to fully broach that topic, so she changed it. "What if I'm not what she needs?"

"You won't know until you try." Opal turned to glance toward the door to the shop before meeting Mo's eyes again. "I told Bud that we couldn't push you like we did again, but—you obviously still need just a little convincing. Why don't you go to your therapy tomorrow, then leave for Orick?"

"Just like that?" Mo was overwhelmed, her mind running a million miles a minute.

"Life is just like that." Opal shrugged, leaning forward still sporting that smug smile. "I texted Bud. He's upstairs packing your stuff, just like we did before you left the first time. There are some things in this world that you can overthink, and right now, Aspen is that."

"I—"

"What happens when you think about Aspen?" Opal cut her off.

"My body kind of…lights on fire," Mo replied instantly. "Like an anxious, infectious warmth."

"What happened when you last saw her?" Opal asked, her focus steely.

"I asked her why the sudden change, and she brushed me off. I asked about her birthday." Mo flinched, remembering how cold Aspen was. "She didn't want me around. I should respect that."

"When is her birthday?"

"Uh…" Mo checked her phone. "Day after tomorrow."

"That's your chance, Mo." Opal leaned in, her voice determined. "The worst she can say is no again. But you'll always know you tried. And that is far more fulfilling than sitting here wondering, isn't it?"

Opal's words bounced around her mind like it was a pinball machine, keeping Mo in a perpetual state of what-if. "I don't know."

"And that's okay," Opal said. "Use that to go find out."

Mo could only blink. Opal stood, sliding her chair back into its usual position. The sun had already set, dusk finally urging the streetlights to come on. Opal gestured Mo to stand, so she did, watching as her friend put her chair back and grabbed her discarded can.

"Are we going inside?" Mo finally asked.

"Yep." Opal nodded. "When do you have therapy?"

"The chemistry meeting is tomorrow morning."

"Good," Opal replied, pulling open her shop's door and gesturing for Mo to go inside. "Gives you plenty of time to get back to Aspen."

Mo could only laugh, even as she felt hope rise inside of her.

* * *

Mo rubbed her shoulder for what felt like the millionth time, her mind everywhere but here in the room with her new—maybe—therapist. Opal's pep talk from the day before had unleashed a flurry of hope, all of which was pushing her north, even as her anxiety was attempting to keep her here, in Palo Alto. She tried to focus on the woman in front of her. Kate was about her age, dressed very comfortably in tan hiking pants and a light-blue short-sleeved button-up. Her long, black hair was braided into long braids, framing her bright lime-green glasses that popped against her golden-brown skin. Kate was quietly observing her, so she focused on the wall behind her, taking in the many diplomas and licenses.

"Kate Mehta. Licensed Marriage and Family Therapist in the State of California," Mo read aloud, coughing slightly. "Cool."

"It is. I am very proud of my accomplishments." Kate smiled warmly, switching which leg was over which. "I feel we've touched on quite a few areas of struggle in this session. All of which I would be very happy to unpack with you in future sessions."

Mo nodded, watching as Kate gently looked at her watch. She leaned forward slightly, readying herself to get up and leave. She wanted to go back to Bud and Opal's, figure out her next move from underneath the blanket of her impromptu bed above Hecate Tattoo, and alleviate this ever-present anxiety. But Kate must've noticed, putting up a gentle palm for her to sit back. She complied, nervously scratching her arm again.

"We still have twenty-five minutes left," Kate said, clicking her pen once. "There seems to be something urgent on your mind. Do you want to talk about it?"

Mo was taken aback by Kate's sudden observation. "You're a therapist."

"I am," Kate said, smiling a cute lopsided smile.

"Fuck it." Mo blew out breath before unloading. "I told you my wife died and how it made me kinda suicidal, but not suicidal enough for you to write anything in that book that might give me a grippy-sock vacation. But what I didn't tell you was that I was pushed by my friends to go to the redwoods, where I met this adorable, funny woman—her name is Aspen, by the way. And I just felt everything and nothing at all. But pretty soon she was everything and I began feeling things in general. Like a light switch had been flicked, you know? But I had started out treating her badly, like an asshole. And I apologized and she helped me and she made me feel wanted. And, like, needed? Not once did she judge me or treat me like a crazy widow who couldn't get over her dead wife and, like, I thought something was there. But she said it was a fling. It didn't feel like a fling. But I agreed for it to be a fling and she kinda pushed me away and I came back here and I can't stop thinking about her and Opal says I should fight for her. Should I fight for her?"

Kate's smile grew larger. "I think—"

"She doesn't want me there and I should respect that right?" Mo interrupted, her mouth and mind on overdrive. "She is someone I can see myself being with. Someone who understands me, my love for Annie, but I'm—I'm not in a condition to love someone, right? I mean, I am here. Therapy is a waypoint on the journey to a relationship—"

"Hold on." Kate put up her palm again. "Let's focus on that little bit there, first. What makes you think you aren't in a condition to love someone?"

"I'm in therapy. I lost everything. I—"

"The fact that you are here is proof you can love," Kate explained. "Real, healthy love isn't built overnight. It's conditioned through actual care. Being here, working on bettering yourself, that shows that you care."

"Oh." Mo mulled it over. "I guess it kind of does, huh?"

"You said she pushed you away." Kate changed the focus, writing as she talked. "Did you get to tell her how you feel?"

"Kind of."

"Not in the way you wanted, maybe?"

"No."

"Okay." Kate scribbled some more, before looking up at Mo. "Then why not try starting there."

"I—" Mo protested on instinct.

"No." Kate stopped her. "You came here to me to help you put your life back on track, right?"

"Yeah." Mo nodded. "I just don't want to break any rules."

"There is no rule book for this process, Mo. You can try to speak with Aspen, and if she says no, she says no." Kate stood. "And by the gigantic thought-vomit that just happened, I think you are ready to go tell her."

Mo followed suit. "You really think so?"

"It's always worth a try." Kate smiled sweetly. "Would you like to set up a virtual appointment for next week? Same time?"

"Yes." Mo nodded.

"Then get moving, Mo. It's quite a drive to the redwoods. We will speak next week."

Mo raced out the door, barely hearing Kate's wish of good luck as she flew down the hallway.

CHAPTER TWENTY-TWO

"Why does it have to be a Wednesday?"

Aspen's bemoaning fell on inattentive ears. Salvador and the kitchen staff were too busy trying to whip each other with aprons than listen to her whining. She shifted her weight, crossing her arms as she watched the three of them run and yell in the kitchen, not a care in the world. It was selfish to be jealous, but it was her birthday. Why couldn't she share in that joy?

"Hey, kiddo," Salvador yelled, darting out of Ben's grasp. "Throw me the tongs!"

Aspen looked over at the utensil but found herself unable to reach for it. Her mind instead drifted to Mo, wondering what she was doing right now. What they would both be doing if Aspen hadn't told her to leave? Guilt washed over her again, so she pushed through, grabbing the tongs and sliding them down the long prep counter toward Salvador.

"Aspen!" Virginia's curt yell echoed from out in the bar.

She turned and, excited for a distraction, quickly darted through the swinging door to scan the bar. Still no patrons in sight, just the dying light of sunset filtering through the dated bar shades. Aspen turned toward Virginia, who was standing near one of the main bar stations, wiping down a pint glass. "What's up?"

"Been thinking," Virginia replied lazily, continuing to wipe the glass like she was an extra on *Cheers*. "Wanna think with me?"

"Bar is dead," Aspen mused, moving next to Virginia before reaching into the small dishwasher near Virginia's legs. She grabbed a piping-hot rocks glass with her bare hand before snatching a spare rag off Virginia's apron. "Don't mind if I do."

Virginia only grumbled nonsensically in return. Aspen's body was abuzz with tension. Was this the time? Was she acquiring the bar? A part of her yearned for the responsibility, even as the rest of her wanted to see Mo. To be back on the trail, answering random questions, picking little fights, and lighting another fire. The memories were so consuming that she almost didn't hear Virginia's question.

"Do you remember how we met?"

Aspen nearly dropped the glass she was wiping. "Uh, yeah, when I was a kid. I always went to Janice—your mom's house— when my parents were away. You kinda took over after she passed."

"I am sure you know this, but my momma was really fond of you. She hated seeing you locked in that tiny-ass RV for days at a time, wailing for your parents to come home." Virginia turned to look at Aspen, her eyes serious. "Watching them same movies on repeat. Eating ramen. Talking to no one but your stuffies."

"I owe her a lot," Aspen said, slightly uncomfortable with this conversation. "She saved my life."

"No, no. She told me the story. You saved your life by reaching out to her. Sure, she was an adult and she was willing, but you always knew when to get yourself the help you needed. When I took care of you after she died, I never forgot her words." Virginia swallowed harshly. "'Kid's got more than just a will to survive. She wants to live.'"

Aspen didn't respond, instead twisting to rack the glass she was holding before gingerly grabbing another. Her skin was prickling with energy, her heart yearned to see Janice again. To introduce Janice to Mo. Watch Janice glare at Mo and click her teeth, always a tad more judgmental than a situation called for. Her stomach did a flip at the thought.

"So, with that in mind, my answer is no," Virginia stated with gusto, turning to rack her glass and cross her arms. "I'm gonna sell the bar. Just not to you."

Aspen's face fell, but she very quickly noticed it was the only part of her body that responded. "What?"

A small smile curved at the edge of Virginia's lips. "I ain't selling this bar to you, Aspen Anderson."

"Why?"

"Because this isn't what you want. You want to live. To actually live. And for once, I want you to acknowledge that being here…this ain't the living you want." Virginia pointed toward the back of the bar. "Living in the redwoods, sure, I'd believe that. But Orick? This bar? This life? No, this ain't your calling. This is where you've run to, but it ain't where you're gonna live."

Aspen couldn't do anything but laugh, blinking rapidly as she tried to digest Virginia's words.

"Am I wrong?"

"No," was all Aspen could get out before she moved to lean against the bar. "I just—I don't know what to do."

"It's your damn birthday, for Christ's sake." Virginia scoffed, pointing toward the parking lot. "Get in your car and drive down to the Bay. I am sure if you scream 'Butch' a few times on the street corner, some nice lesbian will save you."

"If I did that…" Aspen turned to glare at Virginia, feeling no animosity toward the statement. "I wouldn't find the butch I want—"

Virginia shot forward, gripping Aspen in her arms tightly. "Finally, you admitted it! I thought I was gonna have to resort to putting an ad in a paper. Or maybe calling the feds. Do they help find lost lesbians?"

"I don't think the FBI finds people just because you were shitty to them." Aspen giggled, pulling her arms out so she could return the hug. "I'm sorry, how did you not selling the bar to me turn into me being happy?"

"Because it wasn't about the damn bar, you peanut." Virginia squeezed her harder. "It's about you finally acknowledging you fucked it up with Mo."

"You remembered her name," Aspen uttered softly, leaning back to look into her eyes.

"I do know it, contrary to popular belief." Virginia hummed, shifting her weight. "Look, I ain't saying Mo is the end-all be-all of your problems. But if I didn't push you to try, what kind of mom would I be?"

Aspen's heart skipped a beat. "Aww, Virginia. I don't know—"

"Don't you say a word." Virginia sniffed, holding up a shaky finger. "You'll make an old woman cry."

"I just..." Aspen turned to look at the door. "I think I really messed this one up."

"Naw, just made it a little more difficult. Besides, you don't really need to find anything to do just yet. You still have a job here, and you've got a few backpacking trips lined up. There is still time."

"Time, huh?"

"Remember what you said when you got back?"

Aspen shook her head, her eyes still on the front door. Just as she was about to turn back to Virginia, some movement in the small window of the door drew her attention. She focused in on a familiar brown tuft that was barely visible. Aspen's heart began to race. She held her breath as she waited for the door to swing open. Standing in front of her was a nervous-looking Mo, decked out in one of the hiking outfits she had picked out for her.

"Mo?" Aspen whispered, her mind unable to process the whirlwind that was the past ten minutes.

"Happy birthday!" Mo announced loudly, lifting her arms up slightly to show a pair of coffees and what looked like tin-foil-wrapped sandwiches. "I believe it goes...Hi! I'm not a stalker or serial killer, but instead a very sorry woman with delicious coffee."

Aspen could only stare, her mouth hanging open slightly as a slight chuckle escaped her lips.

"You said, 'I'm not cut out for love.'" Virginia's lowered voice scared her, and she turned to meet the woman's knowing gaze. Before Aspen could react, Virginia leaned forward and undid her apron. "Prove that was just a fib and get out of here."

"All right," Aspen breathed, quickly removing the apron before darting to escape from behind the bar. Just as she made it halfway across the room, she stopped abruptly. "I gotta clock out."

"Don't worry about it," Virginia chastised.

Aspen nodded, shuffling quickly until she was right in front of an extremely anxious-looking Mo. "Hi."

"Hi." Mo shrugged, the lopsided smile seemingly stuck to her face. She suddenly pushed a coffee cup toward her. "For you. Happy birthday."

"Thank you." Aspen took it, studying the cup. "Wait, did you get this—"

"From the gas station. I, uh, asked next door. Odessa was very kind to me."

"How did you—"

"Sorry. I'll explain. I meant to be here this morning, but I didn't start driving until like ten. It took a lot of convincing to get Joe to open up and make these just for me. Especially with it not being breakfast and all. Anyway, uh, here." Mo handed her a toasty sandwich. "Bacon, egg, and cheese. All I had to do was drop your name. Both Odessa and Joe bent over backward to make this pretty meager birthday celebration happen. Sorry it's not more, I just…I had to come back. And if I thought too much about it, I was gonna chicken out."

Aspen searched Mo's eyes, sincerity and affection written plainly on them. Guilt built up from her stomach, and she flicked her eyes toward the door. "Wanna get out of here?"

"Yeah, if you want to." Mo shifted again. "You can just take these and have a happy—"

"Shh, let's go." Aspen put the sandwich in the crook of her palm next to her coffee, then grabbed Mo's free hand, dragging her toward the door.

* * *

Aspen had no idea where to take them, so she just told Mo to follow her back to her cabin. The drive felt more like teleportation, and she soon found herself gripping her coffee and sandwich on her porch, watching as Mo backed her Outback into the spare spot by her shed. It felt awkward to stand and wait, so she quickly looked around, remembering she still hadn't bought any furniture for her deck.

"Shit," Aspen grumbled.

"We can just sit on the steps," Mo offered, suddenly standing in her pathway, still smiling that adorable smile. "Though it is getting a bit dark."

And like her cabin knew she needed it, the porch light popped on, illuminating the space beautifully. Mo laughed deeply, like she was releasing built-up anxiety, so Aspen just shrugged and moved to sit on the steps. She gingerly placed her coffee and sandwich down to her right before patting the place next to her with her left hand.

"Sit."

"Thanks," Mo replied, sitting next to Aspen.

Aspen could feel warmth radiating off Mo and had to resist leaning into it. Instead, she took a quick sip of her coffee, tickled that Mo somehow got the ratio of sugar and milk correct without knowing it. Turning to look at her companion, she watched as Mo nervously unwrapped her sandwich, taking a tentative bite. Aspen swallowed, opening her mouth to say something but deciding against it. She followed Mo's lead and dug into her own sandwich. It was lukewarm now but still salty and well balanced, causing her to let out an approving moan.

"This is totally worth embarrassing myself," Mo stated with approval. "I'd wake that man up at two in the morning if these were my reward."

"He'd make you pay a pretty penny, though," Aspen warned, her heart screaming for her to move on from the small talk. She wrapped up the rest of her sandwich, dropping it on the step between her legs. "Mo, I gotta—"

"No, nope, notta," Mo interrupted, placing her right hand onto Aspen's leg. "Let me talk first."

The motion reminded Aspen of her injury, so she swiveled toward her, reaching out to touch Mo's arm. "Oh Jesus, I am terrible. I forgot about your shoulder. How are you doing?"

"I'm fine." Mo pulled away but still turned so their gazes would catch. "I came up here to tell you something, and if I don't get it out, I'm scared I never will."

Aspen nodded, wringing her hands under Mo's determined gaze.

"When I came up to the redwoods," Mo began. "I didn't have an actual goal. My friends begged me, and I half-ass agreed. They said it was to get over her, to move forward with my life. It was an idea I cannot fathom even to this day ever accomplishing. I just…I didn't know who I was anymore, or where I fit in. And then I met you, Aspen."

Aspen's mouth dropped open slightly, her entire body buzzing with affection. Mo reached forward and grabbed her hands, lightly folding them back and forth between her own.

"You, a total stranger, somehow made and executed a plan that pushed me forward. Never once thinking of your own personal cost or if I was even worth helping. Which, with how my attitude was, I am still surprised you didn't leave my ass on that trail. And you did it all without making Annie seem less than." Mo closed her eyes momentarily before continuing, "That meant more to me than anything. And no matter how hard I try, I don't think I could ever repay that kindness. A kindness that you offered almost effortlessly."

Aspen's heart swelled at Mo's words. She didn't know how to reply, so she just nodded and hoped it would suffice.

"I say all that to say, if you want our relationship to end at that, it would be okay. You've done more than enough for me. But you didn't just help me on that journey. I also started to fall in love with you." Mo's voice wavered, and she squeezed Aspen's hands. "You're gorgeous, funny, and every moment with you feels special. Falling asleep next to you in that tent was so easy for me because I knew I'd be waking up next to you in the morning. You occupy all of my thoughts, and even when I don't realize it, I find myself planning my schedule with you in mind. I didn't want to be some little fling. A side of enjoyment."

"I—" Aspen began, but Mo squeezed her hands, shaking her head.

"Let me finish. This isn't some romance movie where I show up in the end and we say we are in love and drive off into the sunset. We are real people." Mo slid in closer, her eyes entrapping Aspen's attention. "We have real fears, real lives, and we make real choices. And I know what you said. But when I was on the phone with Annie, I told her about how I felt about you. How I was going to shoot my shot. But I let you leave."

Mo blew air through her nose, and Aspen let her take her time with this, even as everything in her begged her to return her affection.

"I went back to Palo Alto. A place I thought was my home, but it just doesn't feel like that anymore. I got a therapist. I've looked into some remote work. I am going to get my life back on track." Mo leaned in closer. "But my life doesn't feel like it's on track without you in it."

"Mo," Aspen breathed, pulling out one of her hands to cup Mo's face. "I'm sorry."

Mo's face fell, and Aspen immediately pulled her in for a soft kiss, hoping to quell any doubt. "I didn't mean 'I'm sorry, I don't feel that way,' I meant more like, 'I'm sorry I told you to leave.'"

Mo let out a relieved cough, clearing her throat fully of the emotion before sneaking another kiss. Then with a sigh, she leaned back to search Aspen's eyes. "Good, I was ready to ugly-cry all the way back to Palo Alto tonight."

Aspen smiled affectionately, her chest feeling fuller but also lighter. "I was just so scared."

"It took a bit, but I figured that out," Mo said, tilting her head back and forth for emphasis.

"I—I am still not sure what I feel, but I do…" Aspen took in a deep breath. "I do feel so much for you. I want to try. I want to see if we can make this work."

"Really?"

"Yeah." Aspen nodded. "I'm sorry I pushed you away. Helping you with Annie was second nature and I thought I had a hold on everything, but you turned out to be a whole ton more than I initially bargained for."

"I have that effect on people."

"I don't have experience with this," Aspen explained. "But I do want to try. If you want to try?"

Mo looked around theatrically before shrugging. "No idea. Not like I just did a full-on monologue or anything."

"You are so obnox—" Aspen started, but Mo cut her off with a hard kiss, pulling her in close.

Aspen melted into her, slowing the pace and enjoying every second she could of this kiss. But, her body must have betrayed her, as Mo gently pulled away and gave her an inquisitive look.

"Talk to me," Mo whispered, searching her eyes.

"When I told you what we had was just a fling…I didn't mean it. I feel bad that I said that instead of communicating with you. But—" Aspen drew in a thick breath. "I still don't know. My life has been stagnant for far longer than I care to admit. And you, Mo, you are going places. Seeing your renewal has brought me so much joy, but it also reminded me of how much nothing my life really is."

Mo didn't respond right away, instead using her good arm to push herself up. Aspen watched as Mo maneuvered herself behind Aspen, gently placing each of her feet on either side of her. "Do you wanna lean back?"

"Sure." Aspen laughed, leaning back into Mo and allowing her to wrap her arms around her. Mo then began to gently rock, causing Aspen's eyes to close as she leaned into the embrace.

"I know I can't change that perspective with words," Mo said slowly, continuing to softly rock. "And while it's nice to know that you feel something for me, I don't want to be an added stress in your life. But I do want you to know, there isn't a thing that I've seen that is stagnant about you."

"I appreciate that, but I'm a thirty-something-year-old woman who lives in a run-down cabin and works at a slow-ass rural bar," Aspen said, allowing Mo's motion to relax her. "I'm not really 'dating' material."

"I don't care about all that," Mo replied. "And if you feel like you want to change anything about your life, I would support you. In any way possible."

"Really?"

"Of course," Mo said, kissing the side of her head.

"I just...I guess I can try?" Aspen finally gave in, her mind still jumbled. "I'm so glad you came back, even after how I acted."

"Me too."

"I want to try, but I can't promise everything will work out." Aspen opened her eyes and craned her neck to look at Mo. "Is that enough?"

Mo kissed her lightly. "It's enough. We will take this one day at a time, and before you know it, you may be surprised where you end up."

CHAPTER TWENTY-THREE

"Wait up!"

"No," Aspen yelled back, giggling.

"How are you so quick?" Mo whined, stopping to lean against a tree. Her back was burning under the weight of her pack, and she was now wishing she had asked to just hike out from the access road. "I need a break, dammit."

"Our campsite isn't far," Aspen called from up ahead.

Mo looked up, unable to see any trace of the woman. She scanned the creek, watching as the water quickly flowed over the rocks and down around the bend. Her eyes flicked upward at the few redwoods ahead, and she smiled. She'd recognize those trees anywhere.

Aspen suddenly appeared around the corner, the wood structure tied to her pack peeking out over her head. Mo couldn't help but notice how beautiful she was, grinning from ear to ear with her hair pulled into two messy buns. It melted away any annoyance her running ahead had brought up inside of her.

"Come on, slowpoke," Aspen shouted, waving her hands erratically. "We've got things to do."

Mo groaned in mock annoyance but pushed herself off the tree anyway, her hands going to the straps of her pack. She willed her legs forward, keeping her eyes on the rocky bank as she pushed. Once she arrived in front of Aspen, she looked down and shot her the best faux angry look she could muster.

"No grumpy girlfriends allowed," Aspen warned playfully, putting up a singular finger of warning.

"That's not a real rule—" Mo began, but Aspen placed the finger firmly over her lips.

"It is," Aspen announced proudly. "Annie and I already talked. No grumpy girlfriends allowed on the phone."

"Okay," Mo groaned but couldn't keep herself from grinning stupidly at her. She looked over Aspen's shoulder, recognizing the bank that led to the trees. "Glad we didn't have to swim this time."

"Yeah, coming in July helps." Aspen turned to look toward the trees. "Can you believe it's been over a year?"

Mo sighed happily, reaching down to grab Aspen's hand and squeeze it. "A whole year of torture." Aspen poked her lightly in her ribs. "Ow!"

"You deserved that," Aspen said before stepping forward, pulling their joined hands with her. "Come on, we are gonna put our stuff on that bank over there. We need to set up camp, but I am just too excited. I wanna go see Annie's phone now."

"Sounds good to me." Mo's heart swelled.

Aspen pulled her quickly to the sandy bank, Mo watching as she expertly removed her pack. Attached to the rear was a prebuilt wooden cover for the phone, and Aspen took care to remove it from the bungees holding it on. "Put your pack against the rock over there, then you can grab the tools from inside my pack. We can go install it now."

Aspen's excitement was contagious. Mo used it to get straight to work, pulling her compact day pack from her own bag. She then moved to Aspen's bag, taking care to grab all the tools and supplies Aspen so diligently packed.

"Got it?" Aspen asked excitedly, the wooden structure now perched on her shoulders.

"I love how excited you are." Mo smiled up at her, zipping the bag closed. "All right, I'm ready."

"Awesome! Let's go check on that phone," Aspen squealed, trotting quickly up the bank and into the thick of the tree line.

Mo waited a few seconds to pull in a deep breath before whispering, "We're coming, Annie."

Then she followed Aspen, her knees happy to have only the weight of the tools. It wasn't much of a climb, and she kept her eyes on the terrain, not wanting to see the phone until she was all the way up at the maple. The ground leveled out, and as she noticed the roots of the tree, a hand was softly laid on her shoulder.

"Hey," Aspen whispered reverently, her hand slowly moving back and forth across her shoulder blades.

"Hey." Mo glanced over at Aspen, giving her a quick grin. Then she turned her eyes to the tree and, more importantly, Annie's phone. "We're back."

The phone was filthy. Moss, dirt, and grime clung to random nooks and crannies, allowing only a bit of the blaze orange to show through. But for a phone hung in the woods for over a year, it didn't look much worse for wear. Mo slowly removed her backpack and grabbed the bottle of cleaner and microfiber towel out of the main pocket. She sprayed a bit of cleaner onto the rag then began wiping away, taking extra care to clean every inch. As she worked, Aspen started setting up the items she was going to use to mount the cover.

"She is going to love these new digs," Aspen said, moving behind the tree to set up the ratchet straps she brought along for the cover. "I'm super excited to make this a place that everyone can enjoy."

"Me too." Mo sighed, working the edge of her rag into the thin edges of the receiver. "I kind of half expected the phone to be gone."

"Actually, I didn't," Aspen replied wistfully. "I just felt like it was still here, you know?"

"Yeah." Mo laughed, moving to clean around the hanger and dials. "You think the cover will hold?"

"On my honor as a Girl Scout."

"I don't remember…were you a Girl Scout?" Mo asked, finishing the final touches.

"Hell no." Aspen pulled the ratchet straps tight against the tree. "But I tested this on a big-leaf maple near the cabin with great results. It will help the nails stay strong and keep us from having to screw into the tree itself."

"I trust you," Mo said with pride, backing away to admire her handiwork. "Phone is clean."

"Awesome. The straps are installed. I'll get the cover situated on them, then install the nails." Aspen came around the tree, moving to stand in front of Mo. "I want you to turn around for this part, please."

Mo rolled her eyes but did as she was told, receiving a quick kiss as payment. "You drive a hard bargain, Aspen."

"I aim to please. Just give me a few moments, it shouldn't take that long."

Mo took in a deep breath, crossing her arms as she looked out over the creek. She didn't believe she would ever get tired of the tall, tall trees. Their thick green expanse was a beautiful contrast to the lazy blue of the California sky. Redwood Creek's winding banks, clear water, and bountiful stones worn from years of tumbling down. It was euphoric. Especially with Aspen by her side.

"I got the business license, by the way," Aspen suddenly said, her voice nonchalant but curious. "We can start getting the permits. Maybe lead some snowshoe hikes come winter?"

"Really?"

"Yeah, and if that goes well, we can book some good-sized backpacking trips next summer."

Mo smiled warmly, resisting the urge to turn around. "It's cruel to tell me our business is almost up and running and I can't even kiss you congratulations."

"That's why I did it. So you wouldn't embarrass me."

"In front of who? The squirrels?" Mo said with mock indignation.

"Annie, duh!"

"Oh, well. I doubt she cares. She's probably just as excited."

"Just a few final touches left." Aspen moved on, the sound of a hammer hitting nails confirming her words. "And then it'll be ready for you to make your call."

"Our call," Mo corrected.

Aspen didn't reply, but Mo swore she could hear a tiny gasp of approval. A few more moments of hammering passed before she finally felt Aspen's hands on both of her shoulders.

"You ready?"

Mo nodded and turned just as Aspen squeezed. The wooden cover looked like it jumped right out of a fairy tale, almost majestic in its details. The bright orange tin roof contrasted beautifully with the redwood used to make the awning and side boards. That's when Mo noticed something different. A tiny matching redwood sign she didn't recognize was now hung below the phone, its orange, painted lettering barely recognizable from where she stood. Mo stepped forward, squinting to read it in its entirety.

Annie's Telephone of the Wind
For anyone and everyone who has lost someone they've loved, but not lost their love for the someone they lost.

"Oh my God," Mo uttered, tears welling in her eyes. She turned slowly to meet the gaze of an already crying Aspen. "You didn't have to…"

"I did," Aspen assured, stepping closer to Mo. "Annie's telephone of the wind."

"It's so nice," Mo mumbled, overwhelmed. She turned to the phone, taking in its newfound beauty. "No, it's perfect. Thank you."

"Don't mention it."

Mo slid her hand into her pocket, slowly fingering the small, cold object she found inside. After a few moments, she removed it, using her other hand to absentmindedly play with the strand of paracord she had added to it. After a few moments, she reached forward and set the fire starter right on top of the phone, watching as the paracord dangled off the side.

"Annie's treasure?" Aspen asked, sniffling.

"Yeah." Mo looked over at Aspen. "I think it'll make a great first gift from Annie. I think she'd want to give it, you know, to a traveler who may need it."

"Totally." Aspen reached to squeeze Mo's hand. "I love you."

Mo, surprised, turned fully to meet Aspen's eyes. "Did my ears deceive me or—"

"I love you," Aspen repeated, her eyes solidifying this precious moment as a warm smile crept out from the corners of her mouth.

"I love you, too," Mo returned, her heart swelling. "Are you ready to talk to her?"

"Yeah."

Mo reached for the receiver and began dialing the numbers, Aspen's hand warm on the crook of her elbow. After she finished, she put the receiver between her and Aspen before speaking.

"Ring, ring." Mo laughed. "Annie?"

Bella Books, Inc.

Happy Endings Live Here

P.O. Box 10543

Tallahassee, FL 32302

Phone: (850) 576-2370

www.BellaBooks.com

More Titles from Bella Books

Hunter's Revenge – Gerri Hill
978-1-64247-447-3 | 276 pgs | paperback: $18.95 | eBook: $9.99
Tori Hunter is back! Don't miss this final chapter in the acclaimed Tori Hunter series.

Integrity – E. J. Noyes
978-1-64247-465-7 | 228 pgs | paperback: $19.95 | eBook: $9.99
It was supposed to be an ordinary workday...

The Order – TJ O'Shea
978-1-64247-378-0 | 396 pgs | paperback: $19.95 | eBook: $9.99
For two women the battle between new love and old loyalty may prove more dangerous than the war they're trying to survive.

Under the Stars with You – Jaime Clevenger
978-1-64247-439-8 | 302 pgs | paperback: $19.95 | eBook: $9.99
Sometimes believing in love is the first step. And sometimes it's all about trusting the stars.

The Missing Piece – Kat Jackson
978-1-64247-445-9 | 250 pgs | paperback: $18.95 | eBook: $9.99
Renee's world collides with possibility and the past, setting off a tidal wave of changes she could have never predicted.

An Acquired Taste – Cheri Ritz
978-1-64247-462-6 | 206 pgs | paperback: $17.95 | eBook: $9.99
Can Elle and Ashley stand the heat in the *Celebrity Cook Off* kitchen?